FOGBOUND

also by joseph t. klempner

Irreparable Damage
Flat Lake
Shoot the Moon
Change of Course
Felony Murder

FOGBOUND

joseph t. klempner

THOMAS DUNNE BOOKS
ST. MARTIN'S MINOTAUR
NEW YORK

THOMAS DUNNE BOOKS.
An imprint of St. Martin's Press.

FOGBOUND. Copyright © 2003 by Joseph T. Klempner. All rights reserved.
Printed in the United States of America. No part of this book may be used
or reproduced in any manner whatsoever without written permission except
in the case of brief quotations embodied in critical articles or reviews. For
information, address St. Martin's Press, 175 Fifth Avenue, New York, N.Y.
10010.

www.minotaurbooks.com

Library of Congress Cataloging-in-Publication Data

Klempner, Joseph T.
    Fogbound / Joseph T. Klempner. — 1st ed.
       p. cm.
    ISBN 0-312-31067-6
    1. Reality television programs—Fiction. 2. Capital punishment—
Fiction. 3. New Jersey—Fiction. 4. Retirees—Fiction. 5. Judges—
Fiction. I. Title.

PS3561.L3866F64 2003
813'.54—dc21

                                                        2003046821

First Edition: November 2003

10 9 8 7 6 5 4 3 2 1

According to my particular faith, one isn't supposed to name a child after a living relative; to do so is thought to invite bad luck. It seems my parents must not have been aware of the rule, or chose to ignore it, naming me as they did after my uncle Joe.

While I can't say whether it's been any help to him, it's certainly done wonders for me. I trace my love of the sea directly to him, as well as what little knowledge I have of sailing. On my very best days, I hope I share his insatiable curiosity and fundamental sense of decency. And in spite of the break with tradition, my life continues to be filled with nothing but good luck.

So I belatedly forgive my parents for their ignorance or obstinacy, and I remain forever indebted to Joe Teller for allowing me to share his good name.

FOGBOUND

ONE

The Lincoln Navigator snaked its way through the tall grass of the salt flats. It was too much car for the narrow dirt road, but the rental agent at the airport had talked them into it when he'd heard where they were headed.

"You'd be better off with four-wheel drive," he'd told them. "Those roads get washed out every time it rains, and before you know it you're knee-deep in sand."

They'd taken his advice, not so much because they were really afraid of getting stuck, but because Trial TV was picking up the tab. So what if it cost an extra thirty dollars? They were working with a six-figure budget here, right? In fact, the top suits at Trial TV were betting on this case to eventually draw them even with Court TV in terms of market shares, or even pass them. Which wasn't too shabby, considering that Ricki and her friends over there had enjoyed a monopoly for nearly ten years before any competition came along.

Gradually, the color of the road began to change, from the reddish clay they'd seen so much of to a lighter sandy shade, telling them they were finally getting close to the ocean.

At one point the road narrowed to a single lane, and the driver slowed to cross over a rickety wooden bridge. A small sign told them they'd left the mainland and were now on a protected barrier island, and would be prosecuted to the full extent of the law if they were to disturb bird nesting areas or discard trash of any sort.

"Think they give you the death penalty here for littering?" the woman asked.

"Wouldn't be surprised," said the driver. "You weren't kidding when you said the old guy lives like a hermit, were you?"

"No," she said, "I wasn't kidding."

"You sure he's our man?" asked the other man, from the back seat.

"Oh, he's our man, all right." She smiled, a very pretty, made-for-TV smile. "Just wait till you see him."

When they drove up, he was out back, mending shrimp nets. Even though they couldn't see him at first, they pretty much knew they'd find him there. His old red pickup truck was parked right there in the driveway, after all, and his little sailboat bobbed at its mooring, not a hundred feet offshore. And a curl of smoke rose from the chimney—or at least from the top of the lighthouse, where there must have been a chimney of some sort. Besides which, according to what they'd been told in town, he was just about always there; he no longer went anywhere else, it seemed.

Not that it had always been like that. In his day, he'd been one of the most famous judges in the country, except maybe for those who made it to the United States Supreme Court. And he'd even been considered for that at one time, until his fierce opposition to the death penalty and outspoken support for abortion rights caught up with him and killed off any chance he might have had.

But all that had been long ago. Now he was an old man, his tall frame bent over, perhaps by the winds that constantly swept the barrier islands, or perhaps to better withstand them. His face was lined and leathery, and sorely in need of a shave. And his hair—his magnificent shock of snow-white hair—looked as though it hadn't met up with a comb or brush in days.

His hearing, which had never been much to brag about, had

by now pretty much quit on him altogether, and he might not have noticed their arrival at all, had it not been for Jake. The old Labrador, his coat as black as his master's was white, barked twice—his way of letting it be known that they had visitors. And a moment later, they were joined by three strangers, two men and a woman. City folk, from the look of them.

"Judge Jorgensen?"

It was the woman who spoke, stepping forward from the men. She was pretty and poised, he noticed. In her thirties, he guessed, and doing a pretty fair job of fighting off forty. A woman of business, no doubt. A lawyer, perhaps, or—even worse—a politician. And to top it off, a Northerner, a Northerner who'd been practicing her drawl the whole way from the airport.

"I'm Jorgensen," he said.

"And I'm Jessica Woodruff," she said, offering a hand for him to shake. It felt soft and small in his own, but that was to be expected: His were oversized, gnarled from age and arthritis, and rough from sea salt and rope burns. "This is Tim Harkin, and this is Ray Gilbert." He shook their extended hands, found them not too much different from hers.

"Forgive us for barging in like this," she said, "but your phone's unlisted, and—"

"It's not unlisted," he said. "It doesn't exist." He'd given up the damn thing years ago, shortly after his wife had died. The only calls had been from people wanting to sell him things, and he didn't need anything. Or at least, what he needed he could find at the general store, over in town.

"Perhaps you read our letter." It was one of the men who spoke up now, though August Jorgensen had already forgotten his name.

"Perhaps," said Jorgensen, though it was more likely that he hadn't. He read books and a local newspaper. Mail held little interest for him. Anything that arrived with less than first-class postage went into the fireplace unopened; envelopes with his address typed in or affixed with a preprinted label he considered highly suspect; in the end, only those that were hand-lettered tended to make the cut. "Perhaps," he repeated.

"Do you think we might have fifteen minutes of your time?" It was the woman, back in charge of things.

Jorgensen looked the three strangers up and down. Wherever they'd started out from, they'd come a long way to see him. The wind was beginning to kick up, and though he hadn't been aware of the cold while he'd been busy with the shrimp nets, he felt it now. And he could see from the way they arched their backs and shifted from one foot to another that they did, too. "Why not?" he said. "Come on in, I'll make us a pot of tea."

They followed him and Jake inside, single file. Lighthouses were generally built with small doors, almost always set on the lee side, away from the weather. They ducked their heads as they entered, following Jorgensen's cue, even though he was the only one tall enough to have hit the crossbeam. Once inside, they gawked around like tourists, as though grasping for the first time that it was truly a lighthouse that he lived in, and not some modern structure with a faux façade.

They climbed the circular staircase to the second level, where he put a match to the old woodstove and lit it with a *whooshing* sound that startled them. He filled the kettle with bottled water, knowing that the slightly brackish taste of his tap water—something he himself had long ago become accustomed to—would be a problem for his guests.

"Sit," he said, motioning to the four mismatched chairs that ringed a table, the top of which had once been the transom of a wooden boat, and still read—if you squinted hard enough from just the right angle—RACHEL III, ST. MARYS, GEORGIA.

They sat.

"So," he said, once they were sipping tea that was no doubt too strong for them, and nibbling toast that was too stale, "refresh my recollection, if you would. Tell me again what was in the letter, the business that brings you out here."

This time it was the second man who spoke, the one who hadn't said a single word up to that moment. He slowly put down his cup and fixed August Jorgensen with a stare that was direct without being impolite. "What we want to know," he said, "is if you might be willing to handle a case."

TWO

Jorgensen chuckled. Years of solitude had eroded much of his social skills, but not all, and he knew better than to laugh out loud. Still . . .

"Let me see if I heard you correctly," he said. "You all," waving at the three of them, "want to know if I want to *handle a case*."

"That's right." The woman was back in charge.

"Handle a case," he repeated, the words making no more sense than they had the first time he'd heard them. "As a . . ."

"As a lawyer."

"You realize," he said, "that I haven't practiced in, what, *thirty years*?"

"Thirty-three, actually. *State versus Tomlinson.* Aggravated arson. Davis County. Acquitted on all counts." Evidently, she'd done her homework.

"But why should you feel the need to *exhume me*, after all this time? Have I missed something else in the mail? Have all the lawyers in the state suddenly decided to stop practicing and run for governor, or gone off to start up computer businesses?"

It was their turn to chuckle at his attempt at humor, and they did, without overdoing it. But they said nothing to let him off the hook.

"Besides which," he said, "I'd bet my dinner that I've got a lawyer or two sitting right here at this table."

"And you'd go to bed a full man," the quiet one conceded.

"Though none of us practices much. Jessica's an anchor and director for Trial TV. Tim here heads up the Southern States' Court Monitoring Program. And I do a little teaching down at Tulane Law School."

"I can promise you," said Jorgensen, "that my answer to your proposal will be no. But since you've come all this way—not to mention that you took the trouble to look up my last trial before they put me on the bench, where they figured I'd be able to cause less trouble—you may as well tell me what this case is, which no one else seems willing to take."

"Oh, there are plenty of others willing to take it," said the one formerly quiet. "In fact, all told, the defendant's had, what, half a dozen lawyers?"

"Eleven, actually," said Jessica, the Trial TV anchor. "Eleven lawyers in sixteen years." Jorgensen guessed that back in law school, she'd been the goody-good who sat in the first row and came to class having read all the cases three times over, looking to show up the rest of the students.

"Eleven lawyers in sixteen years," Jorgensen repeated. "Let me take a wild guess. Our man is a murderer. He's on death row. He's pretty much exhausted his appeals. He has no viable claim of actual innocence, and all of his legal issues have been shot down."

No one disagreed.

"So now, with nothing else to go on, you figure it might be worth a shot dusting me off and winding me up, and holding a sort of Judicial Old-Timer's Day, to see if I could appeal to some kangaroo court on geriatric grounds."

"It's not exactly some kangaroo court," said Gilbert, the law professor.

"The state supreme court?" Jorgensen asked.

"Higher."

"The Fourth Circuit?" It had been August Jorgensen's last assignment, the federal court that sat in Richmond and had appellate jurisdiction over all the district courts of Virginia, West Virginia, North and South Carolina, and Maryland.

"Keep going."

Jorgensen smiled. There was only one place to keep going. "The Supremes."

Professor Gilbert nodded. "Not your everyday kangaroo court, you have to admit."

Jorgensen shrugged. "Bigger kangaroos," he said. "Anyone want more tea?"

No one did.

"So who's the defendant?"

This time it was Tim Harkin who spoke. "Man by the name of Wesley Boyd Davies."

"Black." Jorgensen had meant to say "African-American," but "black" had come out. He was so old that "negro" had once been correct, and before that, "colored." He tried keeping up on these things, but it wasn't easy.

"Black," said Gilbert.

"What a surprise," said Jorgensen. "And the victim—or victims—were white."

"There was only one," said Gilbert. "And, yes, she was white."

"And before he killed her," guessed Jorgensen, "he raped her."

"Actually, the coroner couldn't say if it was before or after, or for that matter if it was an actual rape, as opposed to—"

"Lovely," said Jorgensen. He didn't need to hear the details. The scenario was familiar enough. It was cases like this that had driven August Jorgensen from the bench. Not the horror of them—by that time he'd seen enough of the terrible things human beings could do to each other that he'd become all but immune to the shock. No, it hadn't been the horror; it had been the sadness of the cases, the incredible sadness about them. Sadness for the victims, their lives cut short, their fates undeserved. Sadness for their families, left behind to struggle with loss and anger and a never-satisfied need for "closure." Sadness for the defendants—always black, it seemed, always poor, often illiterate, invariably "slow" or "troubled" or "challenged," or some other nice euphemism for retarded, and almost always victims themselves of some sort of horrible abuse when they'd been growing up.

It was enough to destroy you.

And in Jorgensen's case, it almost had. At first, he'd tried his best to approach the cases analytically, to see them as purely legal problems. If the proof had been sufficient and the trial fair, he went along with his colleagues and reluctantly voted to affirm the conviction. But the more he looked into the cases, the more he had to look into the defendants, and after a time it became impossible to see them merely as cases, or crimes, or trials. They were *people*. And with the ascendancy of the Rehnquist Court and its increasing willingness to overlook trial errors as "harmless," there came a point for Jorgensen when he could no longer tell himself that by affirming a conviction they were simply engaging in a legal exercise. The thing was, each time they affirmed a conviction, sooner or later a man died. How long could he keep on telling himself there was anything harmless about that?

Not that long, it turned out.

His first heart attack had been a "minor" one, a warning, his doctor told him. But there was every reason to believe his second one would kill him.

"Exercise," his doctor told him, "exercise and a proper diet. And above all, you must avoid stressful situations."

Jorgensen had laughed. He'd have laughed now, too, but the sadness got in the way. That, and he didn't want to be rude to his guests. They'd taken the trouble to come out here, after all. The Trial TV anchor, the law school professor, and the other guy, whatever he did. He admired their willingness to do battle for this defendant, to go up against the forces who meant to kill him. He envied their ability to do it, he really did. Of course, they were a lot younger than he was. Looking at them, he wondered what it would take to burn them out, to drain the fight from them, to send them off to their own lighthouses. Five executions? Ten? Twenty? Himself, he'd lost count, finally. But it had reached the point where he'd had to drink himself to sleep, he knew that much. And even then, he used to see their faces in his dreams.

Above all, you must avoid stressful situations.

"I'm afraid I'm not your man," said August Jorgensen.

The three people sitting around his table smiled politely. If they'd done their homework—and it seemed they had—they hadn't come out here thinking it would be an easy sell.

"Don't you at least want to hear what the issue is?" asked Jessica Woodruff.

"No," said Jorgensen, as firmly as he could. He closed his eyes, willing his guests to vanish from his kitchen. But even in the darkness, they were there. The faces. Not the faces of Jessica Woodruff, Tim Harkin, and Ray Gilbert. No, the faces he saw were the faces of Dwayne Luther Crawford, of Joseph Edward Hollis, of Felix Angel Rodriguez, of Willie Lee Williams. Eyes still shut, he began speaking in a weary monotone. "Blacks were systematically excluded from the panel. The prosecution withheld exculpatory evidence. A key witness had a secret deal with the police that was never revealed to the jury. The defendant is severely retarded. He was denied access to expert witnesses. His lawyer was inexperienced, underpaid, and slept through significant portions of the trial." Jorgensen could have gone on and on; there were too many issues to list, too many faces to remember.

Jessica Woodruff reached for her purse. Jorgensen had a momentary vision of his wife doing that, pulling out her cigarettes, lighting up. When he first met Marge, he'd loved the way she did it, loved the ritual of it, loved how sophisticated it made her look, loved the smell the burning match made, even liked the smell of the first puff of smoke. "I was born in Durham," Marge had told him, when he'd asked her about her smoking. "My daddy farmed tobacco, his daddy farmed tobacco, and his daddy's daddy farmed tobacco. Of course I smoke." Later, when her coughing became a part of the ritual, he liked it far less. And finally, by the time they'd both realized it was going to literally be the death of her, he'd learned to hate it, to hate it with a passion he reserved for little else.

Death.

Passion.

Death and passion.

If one was going to be passionate about something, it might as well be something worth being passionate about.

But he needn't have worried, not about Jessica Woodruff, anyway. What she took from her purse was not a pack of cigarettes, but a manila envelope, which now she extended in his direction, as though it were some sort of peace offering, presented in ceremonial fashion.

"We've taken quite enough of your time," she said—rather formally, he thought. "Is it all right if we leave this with you?"

He didn't take it from her, but he didn't say no, either. Again, that would have been rude. She smoothed out the crease in it and placed it on the table. He could see his name typed on the outside of it, THE HONORABLE AUGUST L. JORGENSEN. Still he said nothing.

"May we call again in a week or so?" Ray Gilbert asked. "Once you've had a chance . . ."

"I have no phone," Jorgensen reminded them.

They nodded in unison, as if to say they already knew that.

"So how do you think it went?" Jessica Woodruff asked her companions.

"You were right about his looks," said Harkin. "Reminds me of that famous photo of Judge Learned Hand."

"And that *voice*," said Gilbert.

There was a pregnant silence in the car, which the anchorwoman in Jessica Woodruff felt compelled to break after a couple of beats. "What I mean is," she asked, "do you think he's up to it?"

"He'll be okay," said Harkin. "But I still wish you'd consider doing it yourself. In my book, blonde and beautiful beats old and craggy every time."

"Well, I appreciate the blonde and beautiful part, but no thanks."

"Why not? As I recall, you had a pretty good batting average as a prosecutor."

That much was true. Jessica Woodruff had been an assistant district attorney in New York County, where Bob Morgenthau ran as good an office as any in the country. She'd cut her teeth trying sex cases, but soon realized there was room for only one leading lady there, and it was going to be Linda Fairstein. She'd transferred over to one of the regular trial bureaus, where she'd specialized in homicides.

"I had the best murder conviction rate in the office," she said now, "but only because I was smart enough to pick and choose which cases I wanted to try."

"I always thought," said Harkin, "that it was the defendant who decided whether or not to go to trial. Or at least the defendant and his lawyer."

"Shows how much you know," said Jessica. "Oh, the defendant *thinks* he's deciding, you're right about that. But what really used to happen was this: I'd take a good look at the case and size up my chances of winning or losing. If I figured it was a lock, a case I couldn't lose, I wouldn't offer them any kind of a lesser plea. The defendant would figure, 'Why should I cop out to the top count?' In other words, he'd be forced to go to trial. On the other hand, if I saw I was going to have problems, I'd offer them a manslaughter plea, something they could live with.

"Then, after a couple of years, I had enough seniority that they used to let me take cases from other assistants—you know, to trade. So I made it my business to follow the Rule of Three."

"Okay, I'll bite," said Harkin. "What's the Rule of Three?"

Jessica smiled. She was clearly enjoying her little discourse.

It was one of the things that made her such a compelling anchorwoman to her fans. "Most homicides are either shootings or stabbings, right?"

Both men nodded in agreement.

"Say you get a case with a single gunshot or a single stab wound. Right away, you're going to have a problem proving intent to kill. One shot, or one slash, just isn't enough. At the other end of the extreme, you've got the defendant who empties all fourteen rounds from his automatic into the victim, or stabs him seventy-five times. The jury—at least a Manhattan jury—is going to find he acted under the influence of extreme emotional disturbance. Either way, I'm going to end up with nothing better than a Man One.

"But give me a case with three gunshots or three stab wounds, and I'll get a murder conviction every time out. Just enough to show intent to kill, but at the same time not so much to suggest extreme emotional disturbance."

"The Rule of Three," said Harkin.

Jessica smiled again.

Gilbert leaned forward from the back seat. "But nobody would expect you to win Wesley Boyd Davies' case," he told her. "You'd be like David going up against Goliath. And the American public just loves underdogs."

"The American public may love underdogs," Jessica conceded, "but they have no patience for losers. When's the last time you heard anything about Marcia Clark, or Chris Darden?"

"Who?"

"My point exactly. This case isn't a career-maker, it's a career-*breaker*. I'm thirty-one years old," she lied, "and not quite ready to have my career broken, thank you."

"But August Jorgensen?"

"August Jorgensen," said Jessica, "has no career to be broken."

THREE

He busied himself for three full days. He stacked wood, split more wood, stacked it, cut wood, split it, and stacked it. It was mid-October, and winter wouldn't come to the Outer Banks for another two months, but when it came, it tended to come with a vengeance. It wasn't just the cold—he was far enough south that it rarely dropped much below freezing. No, it was the dampness, the dampness and the wind when it came from the east, off the ocean. And when there was no wind, there'd be fog, thick shrouds of fog that would rise from the ocean and envelop the lighthouse for days at a time. So no matter how much wood he cut and split and stacked, he could never have too much.

On the morning of the fourth day, a fresh breeze picked up from the south, and he said to Jake, "Hey, fella, want to go for a sail?" And the old Lab, who knew exactly what that meant, rose from his spot by the wall—it would have been his corner, but lighthouses tend to be notoriously short of corners—barked once, and wagged his tail.

They rowed the little dinghy out to the catboat, where he tied it fast to the mooring. Jake jumped onto the bigger boat and made a quick inspection of it while Jorgensen climbed aboard. There was half a foot of water above the floorboards, but ten minutes at the hand pump took care of that. Jorgensen untied the halyards and shook them free. He loosened the sheets, so that when the sail was raised it would swing free, keeping the boat from tugging at the mooring line. Then, pulling hand over hand on the main halyard, he began to raise the sail.

The catboat was gaff-rigged, with a single large sail held to the mast by a series of wooden hoops. With the sail dropped, the hoops piled up lifelessly on top of each other around the base of the mast. But as Jorgensen hoisted the sail now, each hoop rose in turn and danced skyward, until the topmost reached the very tip of the mast. As the last of the hoops cleared the deck, the long boom came free and swung back and forth in a lazy arc. He repeated the process with the peak halyard, which lifted a small spar near the top of the mast, stretching the sail to its full height.

Next he checked the sail for damage, and saw none. Once bright red, it had faded over the years to a dull rust color, which Jorgensen much preferred. And it was canvas, real old-fashioned canvas. No plastic, no Dacron, no Mylar, no space-age miracle fibers. The boat itself was unpainted wood, as was the tiller, the rudder, the gunwales, the chocks, the mast, and the boom.

Canvas and wood.

Up at the bow, Jorgensen uncleated the line, leaving it running once through the eye of the mooring. He gave the bitter end to Jake, who took it and held it tight in his retriever's vise of a mouth. Once, when they'd been trying to reef the sail in the middle of a sudden squall, the dog had slipped overboard with a line in his mouth. He'd never once loosened his grip on it, so much so that Jorgensen had been able to reel him back in and pull him aboard with it.

Back at the stern now, Jorgensen took up the slack in the lee sheet with one hand, and wrapped his other around the tiller. Then, as the breeze stiffened the sail and swung them away from the dinghy, he whistled once and shouted, "Cast her off, mate," and Jake obliged by dropping the line from his mouth. The bitter end quickly slipped through the mooring eye, and they were free.

With the breeze coming up out of the south, Jorgensen knew it would be safe to head out into the open ocean. The same gusts that would be on their starboard heading out would be on the portside carrying them back in. And the old catboat, whose one-sail design made her ill-fit to point close to the wind, was at her best on broad reaches such as this.

Marge had never been much of a sailor. She'd loved the sea, and it was for her that they'd bought the old lighthouse once it had been decommissioned and came up at auction. But she'd loved the sea as a landlubber loves the sea, as something to gaze upon from the beach, to listen to at night, to take long walks beside, and—at the end—to take comfort from, as she lay dying.

So it had been to Jorgensen's delight to discover that, like he himself, Jake was a born sailor. His Labrador genes gave him a head start, instilling in him a love of everything to do with water—whether swimming, splashing, drinking, running in circles beneath a waterfall or sprinkler, diving off a dock or into a pool, or tirelessly attacking the stream of a hose. But it went beyond that. When they were sailing, he seemed to love the very waves and swells themselves—not only the splashing and spraying, but the rhythmic rising and falling of the boat, the heeling to one side or the other, the rolling, the yawing, the pounding. His ears never rested, taking in every sound— the beating of the canvas, the slapping of the fixed lines, the groaning of the boards, the smacking of the waves against the hull, the whistling of the wind through the fittings. He drank in every smell—the salt spray of the sea, the oiled wood baking in the sunlight, the fishiness of the seaweed as they skimmed across the flats. And, standing surefooted and openmouthed at the bow, his long nose pointing their heading like a compass needle, he was the quintessential lookout, ready to bark out at the first sign of lurking danger or unexpected delight.

His love for sailing, in other words, was a perfect match for that of August Jorgensen.

They sailed out a good five miles—out beyond the sandbars,

beyond the banks, out to where the swells were a good eight feet from tip to trough, out to where they could no longer make out the lighthouse—before coming about. On the way back in, Jorgensen tried to fool Jake by setting a course a good fifteen degrees north of their intended landfall, but the old dog would have none of it, pointing to the exact spot where the lighthouse would come into view, and barking until Jorgensen made the correction.

And when finally the faded tower appeared in the distance, dead ahead of them, Jake looked back over his shoulder and shot the old man his best "I-told-you-so" look.

"Good boy," said the captain.

There'd be time for hugs and treats later. For the moment, there was still work to be done.

Although it was growing dark, no beacon shone from the top of the old lighthouse, only a faint light from a porthole halfway up. The Coast Guard had been decommissioning lighthouses up and down the coast for years, finding that computers turned out to be better light-keepers than humans. But in the case of the Fog Point Light—the official name of Jorgensen's, as it appeared on nautical charts—they'd simply discontinued it altogether, advising mariners to look for the newer Sand Harbor Light to the north, or Tallman's Tower to the south. The problem was, the barrier islands were shifting over time. With each new storm, tons of sand were washed away from the ocean side, to be redeposited on the backside of the next island in the chain. The net result was that the islands themselves were literally moving westward, toward the mainland. And the Fog Point Light, which had once stood more than a quarter of a mile inland, now found itself less than a hundred yards from the breakers. In another six or seven years, the water would be lapping at Jorgensen's door; once that happened, it would make short shrift of the lighthouse. Concrete reinforced with half-inch rebar made for strong stuff, but it was nothing before the sea.

All of which suited August Jorgensen just fine. In six or

seven years, Jake would be dead, and if he himself were still alive he'd be nearing ninety, too old by far for this world. Let the sea come and get him; there surely were worse ways to go.

He reheated yesterday's soup for dinner, and awarded Jake the bone. It had been a good sail and a good day, and it galled him to ruin it. But ruin it he must; he knew that. For four days now he'd put it off, and with each day it loomed larger. He put another log into the wood-burning stove, found a jelly glass, and poured himself an inch and a half of blackberry brandy. It was all he allowed himself any more, and only in the evening, to keep the chill from his bones. Then he walked around to the other side of the kitchen table, to where it had sat, untouched, for all of these four days.

The manila envelope.

The present they'd left behind for him.

"Is it all right if we leave this with you?"

Bastards. Sneaky bastards. They'd known what they were doing. They'd known he wouldn't be able to leave it there forever, wouldn't put it out of sight, wouldn't throw it away unread. They'd known that sooner or later, he'd have to get around to it.

But beyond that, they'd miscalculated; they'd underestimated him. Oh, he'd open it up, and he'd read whatever was inside—he was only human, after all, and humans are by nature curious animals. But he hadn't spent the past four days in idleness; each day, he'd forced himself to imagine what he'd find inside, envisioning all sorts of heart-rending handicaps and sickening injustices. A defendant born to an alcoholic mother and an abusive father, abandoned in his early teens to a life on the street, driven to commit some petty crime that went inexplicably, horribly wrong. A court-appointed lawyer who'd never handled anything more serious than a speeding ticket, reimbursed by the state at a rate of fifteen dollars an hour. A no-nonsense trial judge elected on a law-and-order platform. A politically ambitious prosecutor determined to win a verdict—and a death sentence—whatever the cost. A jury suckered into believing they were only making a "recommendation" that the defendant die, a recommendation that the judge was free to reject.

Though he'd never rejected one yet.

Not that they were told that.

A state appellate court that, when forced to concede that there might have been a shortcoming or two to the trial, smugly proclaimed that, "While the law says the accused is entitled to a fair trial, nowhere does it say he's entitled to a perfect trial."

And in imagining it all, in distilling it down to the single most horrendous scenario he could conceive, befalling the most pathetic defendant ever, Jorgensen had been able over time to desensitize himself, to steel himself against whatever it was that lay inside the manila envelope.

In fact, earlier that very day, out on the ocean, out of sight of home—out of sight of land itself—it had suddenly come to him that something else would be in there, too. It might be right on top, the very first thing he'd see upon opening the envelope. Then again, it might be buried somewhere in the middle, ready to jump out at him when he least expected it. Or they might have saved it for the bottom of the deck, the joker, the wild card revealed at the last moment, just in case he hadn't been won over yet.

And that something else?

That something else would be a photograph, a photograph of the defendant. The face, the human being. The human being who'd be put to death if August Jorgensen refused to help them.

And just as he'd steeled himself against the facts, so had he steeled himself against the face. He'd pictured a frightened black young man, a malnourished boy, a crying baby abandoned in a dumpster. He'd pictured dull, uncomprehending eyes, a nose broken in infancy, a mouth horribly misshapen by some genetic disorder. He'd pictured pain—pain and poverty and privation.

Until at last, he'd felt prepared to open the envelope.

Sitting in the back of a New York City cab creeping along West Thirty-fourth Street, Jessica Woodruff answered her cell phone on the second ring. Even before she spoke, she knew from her Caller-ID feature that it was Brandon Davidson, Trial TV's president.

"Hello, Brandon," she said.

"Hello, Jess. How are you?"

"Other than stuck in midtown traffic, fine. What's up?"

"I was just wondering if you're going to pay another visit to the hermit, and try to firm things up with him."

"I will if you like," she said. "Though personally, I'd like to give him some more time to think it over. The old fart fancies himself a moralist. Hell, he thinks he's the last moral being on the face of the earth. He'll come around, Brandon, but not if he feels pressured. He's one of those idealists who needs to think he's doing it for all the right reasons."

"And what are the right reasons, Jess?"

"You know. Truth, Justice, the American Way. That kind of crap."

"Are you sure he's the one we want?"

"Yes, I'm sure. He's even craggier looking than his photos."

"You don't think a bla—an African-American might be better?"

"Who are you going to get, Johnnie Cochran? I told you, Brandon, there are no African-American appellate lawyers. They're all too busy trying cases."

"Or making guest appearances on your show."

"That, too," she said. Then, more quietly, "I miss you."

"Careful," he said. "You're on a cell phone."

FOUR

If August Jorgensen thought he'd figured out what he'd find inside the manila envelope, and was prepared to deal with whatever irresistible emotional impact it was designed to have upon him, he couldn't have been more mistaken. Slitting it open at one end—he had no patience for those little metal clips, or those annoying red strings wrapped around cardboard circles in whichever direction you hadn't counted on—he emptied the contents onto the table in front of him.

And in the process, surprised himself.

No haunting photograph of Wesley Boyd Davies stared back at him. No background study of his childhood years presented itself, no I.Q. test score revealing him as "borderline retarded." No letters slipped out, attesting to his having become a born-again Christian in prison, or having taught himself to read or write. No recantations of witnesses, no regretful affidavits from jurors who would have voted differently if only they'd known this or that, no apologies from lawyers who hadn't been up to the task.

None of that.

What slipped out of the envelope instead were four sheets of paper, nothing else. Each was a Xerox copy—Jorgensen could tell they were copies, the originals having been made on notebook paper, the kind they make you use in school. In the copying process, the ruled lines had faded some, grown wavy here and there, or disappeared altogether. No words adorned the sheets, except at the bottom right-hand corner, where the single letter "B" appeared.

What they were, were drawings. Drawings of trees, of pastures, of a meadow, of a clearing in the woods. Drawings made in pencil, or perhaps, as Jorgensen looked more closely and studied the details, pen and ink.

Extraordinary drawings.

Exquisite drawings.

And in that instant, as he sat immobilized and transfixed at his kitchen table, he knew that all his imagining, all his steeling, all his desensitizing, all his preparation had come to naught. August Jorgensen might not be sucked in yet, but in spite of everything, he found himself nibbling at the bait.

They came back a week later, as promised. As he let them in the door, Jorgensen thought he noticed just a hint of a smirk on Jessica Woodruff's face, her way of letting him know that she'd been the culprit, that leaving the drawings had been her idea.

Even then, he tried to say no. But the drawings had done their work on him; he knew that, and they knew it, too; they must have been able to see it in his eyes.

The fog had rolled in, and even though it wasn't actually raining, you got wet after a while if you stayed outside. And although Jorgensen was used to it and dressed for it and wouldn't have minded, his guests had their city clothes on. So they went inside, pulled up chairs and gathered around his kitchen table once again, the four of them, and Jake went off to one side of the room, circled a small area a couple of times, and lay down. And they began to tell him the story of Wesley Boyd Davies.

FIVE

The year 1964 was a strange one in the black South, a year of confusion and contradiction. The sudden death of a young Northern president, who'd spoken of hope and justice and opportunity for all, was still fresh in the minds of many. A Texan slept in the White House now, a Texan with the sleepy-eyed look and lazy drawl of a Southern plantation owner, but whose speeches were full of notions about civil rights and a Great Society. Meanwhile, half a world away, a white man's war was being fought against yellow men, but it seemed to be mostly black men who were coming home in body bags. And a nation that was too short of money to feed its hungry children and repair their dilapidated schoolhouses was eagerly spending billions of dollars to strap a man into a spaceship and send him to the moon to gather rocks.

Just about halfway through the year, in the early afternoon of the twenty-sixth day of June, four miles outside of the little, town of Sweetwater, South Carolina, a child was born to Hattie McDaniel. Although it was her sixth child—and she would go on to bear two more thereafter—it would be her only son. The boy was given a form of his father's first name as his last, but little else from the man, a migrant farm worker who'd caught a truck north several months before the birth, never to return. Thus, right from the beginning, Wesley Boyd Davies stood apart from his siblings in three distinct ways: he was a boy; he was the only one in the family to carry the Davies name; and his sisters would make a contest of seeing who could spoil him the most.

But there were other, more ominous differences.

Because Boyd—as everyone called him, except the youngest of his sisters, who to this day refers to him as "Boy"—was born at home, attended by an unlicensed midwife, there are no medical records associated with his birth. Hattie has been dead ten years now. Asked once about prenatal care, she'd replied to an investigator that she went for "reglar checkups," but was unable to say where or by whom they were administered. Boyd's early pediatric history is almost as elusive. The only record of his first three years is to be found in a six-line entry subpoenaed years later from the Defiance, South Carolina, Children's Hospital.

> The boy appears to be healthy and well-nourished, and suffers from no obvious deformities. He makes poor eye contact, however, and displays little or no speech. In addition, his head seems to be a bit large for the rest of his body.

Developmental disabilities often go largely unrecognized in preschool years, all the more so in poor (and poorly educated) families. In Boyd Davies' case, there were additional reasons for this to have been the case. Hattie had to have been preoccupied with the business of trying to feed, clothe, and nourish a houseful of children on a welfare check. The task of tending to the young ones often fell to older siblings, who were themselves still children. Their response was to do their best to satisfy the baby's needs, and to even anticipate those needs in order to head off crises. Thus, when they figured Boyd might be getting hungry soon, they fed him; when they thought his diaper might be wet or soiled, they checked it; if they saw him fidgeting, they picked him up, handed him the nearest toy to distract him, or rocked him. Rocking seemed to work best of all.

Given such immediate attention to his perceived needs, an infant has little motivation to develop speech (which, early on, is pretty much a matter of asking for things). So if Boyd was literally speechless for the first three or four years of his life—and by all accounts that appears to have been the case—nobody worried about it too much. After all, he seemed to be getting whatever it was he wanted, without ever having to fashion his wishes into words.

All that changed with the beginning of school. By the age of six, children are expected to be verbal, noisy, and downright rambunctious. Boyd Davies was none of those things. Not that he was mute; that much was clear. But his utterances seemed to come in the form of single words, often monosyllables, or short phrases repeated over and over. And what he said often seemed to have no connection to what was going on around him at the particular moment. Thus, if his teacher were trying to interest the class in learning the names of various geometric shapes, Boyd might be heard to mutter, "No dogs, no dogs, no dogs."

It was assumed that he was retarded, and at some point in second grade he was pulled out of class one day and administered a battery of tests. This was 1971 now, and developmental psychology had already advanced to the point of recognizing that, particularly in impoverished rural areas, intelligence testing was of little value if it was overly skewed toward either verbal skills or accumulated knowledge.

No written record exists of how Boyd Davies performed on the tests he was given. But one of his teachers, a woman by the name of Lavender Washington, who is today in her eighties, says she remembers.

"Boyd did terrible in vocabulary," she told an interviewer. "And when they asked him word relationships—like, 'Cow is to milk as hen is to what?'—he had no clue what they were talking about. He couldn't say who was the president of the United States, or what day of the week it happened to be, or anything like that. But when they showed him pictures of blocks—you know, big stacks of blocks where you can see some of them, but others are hiding behind them and you have to figure out how many there are altogether—he got a perfect score on that, he did. And in the next part of the test, where they'd show him something, like a book or a pencil or something more complicated, say a radio? And then they'd take it away after a minute, and ask him to draw it, from memory? Well, let me tell you. That boy drew like a regular grownup artist, he did. It's a crying shame they didn't save some of those drawings he made, it really is."

As for the individual who'd administered the test, he (or perhaps she) had been understandably confounded, concluding that Boyd was of normal, or possibly even exceptional, intelligence, but suffered from some sort of mysterious learning disability that prevented him from reading and properly developing language skills.

Today, remedial classes and special instruction might offer some hope to such a child. One-on-one tutoring has proved successful in certain cases. But again, this was the early '70s, and such things were unheard of in rural black schools in the South. Instead of receiving help, Boyd Davies was simply held back in second grade for another year, and another after that. He never did learn to read or write, and his speech improved only slightly over the years. And, simply by not moving forward with his age group, he naturally became the biggest and strongest in each of his classes. That fact, when added to his strange behavior and virtually nonexistent social skills, soon branded him as a target for the name-calling, petty insults, and sadistic pranks of crueler and cleverer children. And despite Boyd's generally passive nature and his tendency to be withdrawn and even isolated, on rare occasions he reacted by emerging from his shell and lashing out at his tormentors.

For that, he earned the reputation of a bully.

As for his uncanny drawing ability, little encouragement was given. Instead, his talent was viewed as so completely out of character as to be unnatural and even freakish—something to be discouraged, if not forbidden altogether.

"The thing was," says Lavender Washington, "Boyd didn't draw like you or I might draw. You handed him a crayon or a pencil and a piece of paper, and told him to draw something he'd seen, and he'd just start off doing it like some kinda machine you'd a wound up, and he'd keep at it until he was finished. It didn't seem a part of him, it really didn't. And back in those days, there was folks who believed in spirits and devils, and stuff like that. And there was some who even whispered that the boy might be *possessed,* if you know what I mean."

In late June of 1976, when Boyd had just turned twelve and the rest of the nation was preparing to celebrate the Bicentennial, the family was burned out of its home. The fire was termed "suspicious" by the local volunteer rescue company, and there were some who thought it might have been a race-motivated case of arson. Around that time, there had been a dozen or so such instances, with bands of black youths breaking into and looting white-owned stores in town, and older whites retaliating by firebombing homes in "Niggertown," as they called it.

There was a second theory that made the rounds. Boyd Davies was known to play with matches. Not that he liked to set fires, at least not so far as anyone can say with certainty. But several of his sisters recall that he could spend an hour with a box of matches, striking one after the other, watching intently as the flame burned down toward his fingers. By one account, his fingertips were often blackened and burned, though to watch him, he never seemed to notice the pain. This phenomenon contrasted sharply to the way he reacted to other stimuli. Bright lights, for example, could cause him acute distress, and certain common household odors he found so intolerable that they'd cause him to run from a room in anguish.

In any event, while it's possible that one of Boyd's matches caused the fire that destroyed the family home, no one knows for sure. But even if it did, it's highly unlikely that Boyd intended the result.

Hattie McDaniel had a sister living outside of Pittsville, Virginia, about halfway between Lynchburg and Danville and not much else. Her sister had come down with polio in the mid-fifties, had been left badly crippled, and had recently lost her husband. For two years she'd been trying to find someone to help her take care of her house. Now, no doubt out of need as much as devotion, Hattie answered the call. She piled six of her children (one had died, two had found husbands and moved out) and all of her worldly belongings into the back of a truck belonging to a farmer she'd paid fifty dollars cash. The truck broke down five times, the farmer spent almost as much time underneath it as he did behind the wheel, and the 300-mile journey ended up taking them the better part of four days. But when it was done, Boyd Davies was a Virginian.

Which, for some, might conjure up visions of early colonists, country gentlemen, and Confederate soldiers. For August Jorgensen, all that came to mind was that in the thirty-four years since the U.S. Supreme Court had reopened the door to capital punishment, Virginia had established herself as the execution capital of the Fourth Circuit, ranking second nationwide only to Texas in the number of men she'd put to death.

The local school board, at that time centered in Leesville, had a no-exceptions, "all-pass" policy, meaning that students moved ahead one grade—and only one grade—each September, no matter how poorly (or, for that matter, how exceptionally) they might have done during the previous school year. This policy they not only applied to Boyd Davies, but applied retroactively. For Boyd, it meant that his three holdbacks (in addition to spending three years in second grade, he'd also been required to repeat third grade once) were summarily overruled, and when he showed up for classes that fall he found himself not in fourth grade, but in seventh.

Junior high school.

To someone like Boyd, who'd struggled unsuccessfully to keep up with children half his age (but presumably had been able to take at least some measure of comfort from surroundings that were familiar and teachers who knew him), one can only imagine how disorienting the change must have been.

Records have a way of disappearing over time, and today there remains virtually no paper trail to chronicle Boyd's adjustment to his new school surroundings. From the accounts of his sisters and other anecdotal evidence, however, it seems to have been marginal at best. By seventh grade, students are expected to have mastered reading and writing to the point that it's second nature to them, to be proficient in math and science, to be on their way to learning a second language and in some cases a third, and to have developed the social skills they'll need as adults. Boyd, of course, mastered none of these things. He was given failing marks in just about everything, and after a while, no marks at all. Again he was tested, and although no record of the tests can be found, one of his sisters reports that again he was found to possess certain aptitudes that prevented the school from classifying him as "retarded."

Among his classmates, Boyd was a complete outcast. But there exists some evidence that younger students occasionally sought him out as a playmate; and if so, this wouldn't be an altogether surprising phenomenon. After all, Boyd had grown accustomed to being around children much younger than he was. What he lacked in skills and socialization, he made up for in size and strength.

It was an uneasy alliance, however, and one that would ultimately figure in Boyd's undoing.

Boyd was promoted to eighth grade along with his classmates in 1977, and the following September he entered high school. There, for the first time, he ran into teachers who openly questioned whether it made any sense for him to be in school at all. Although he'd shown no signs of violence, he tended to speak out in class inappropriately, his out-of-context remarks (and sometimes they were not so much remarks at all, but mere sounds) producing distractions for his teachers and those of his classmates who were more intent on learning than being entertained. Several teachers complained to the principal, who promised to look into the matter.

In December of 1978, a determination was made that for the good of both Boyd and his fellow students, he would be reassigned to a special school in Roanoke. But Pittsville was nearly fifty miles from Roanoke, and well outside the school bus routes. The president of the school board informed Hattie McDaniel that he was willing to reimburse her at the rate of five cents a mile if she would drive her son to and from classes; but without a car, Hattie was in no position to take him up on his offer.

So in the end, Boyd simply stopped going to school. His last day was January 31, 1979. He was fourteen years old.

If idleness is indeed the Devil's workshop, Boyd Davies was being offered an open invitation to hell. With no school to fill his hours, and his mother busier than ever caring for two younger siblings and a crippled sister of her own, Boyd found himself left alone for long stretches of time. And if there was one thing he was good at, it was being alone. Not that he ever seemed to do anything, according to most accounts. Instead, he'd sit around the house or take up a spot on the front steps, or wander off into the surrounding fields. He'd find some object—it could be a rock, a pine cone, an old license plate, an empty plastic bottle—and spend hours holding it up to the light, examining it from all angles, touching it to his tongue, even muttering to it. The things he muttered never made any sense (at least not to anyone but Boyd himself); yet he repeated them over and over, his voice never changing in volume, pitch, or inflection. His family was content to leave him be, grateful that at least he wasn't getting into trouble.

But trouble can be a funny thing, and sometimes it has a way of seeking out its victims. Boyd Davies' strange remoteness, which confounded his own family and repelled his age peers, for some reason attracted younger children to him. Not always, and not a lot of them, but a discernable pattern was beginning to develop. At fourteen or fifteen Boyd's only friends—and the term friends may be something of an overassessment here—were youngsters of seven or eight. They tended to be outcasts themselves, unwanted at home and for a variety of reasons ignored or ridiculed by their own classmates. Perhaps they found Boyd no more than uncritical of them; given Boyd's limited ability (or willingness) to interact with anyone, it's doubtful they could have found much more. But for whatever reason, they were drawn to him—if for no other reason than to sit with him, play in the dirt alongside him, and on some level share the strange, silent world he inhabited.

If it was a pattern that seemed harmless enough, and one that even suggested a bit of a symbiosis for the older child and the younger, in time it would come to have the very gravest of consequences.

SIX

As August Jorgensen sat listening to his visitors, the afternoon wore on. From time to time he would excuse himself, rise from his chair, and add a log or two to the stove, to keep ahead of the chill. One of the problems of the old lighthouse was that it was extremely difficult to heat. Poorly insulated when built, it had developed cracks and chinks in the masonry over the years, and the fittings around the portholes had chipped away badly. A spiral metal staircase wound itself from ground level all the way up to the light chamber, a full seventy-two feet above, and there was simply no effective way to trap the heat in the lower rooms. Interior walls and doors had been added in the mid-fifties, but they were anything but airtight. The result was that—along with its other virtues, faults, and idiosyncrasies—the structure provided indisputable laboratory proof of the old proposition that heat rises.

That said, it was still October, and had it not been for his guests, Jorgensen might not have had a fire going in the stove at all. He'd long ago learned the value of long johns and wool sweaters, and was accustomed to fifty-five degrees or so as a tolerable indoor temperature for the fall months. His Scandinavian upbringing, he attributed it to.

But it wasn't the indoor conditions that concerned Jorgensen at the moment, so much as what was going on outside. The cooler, drier air that had settled in was thirsty for moisture. And though summer was long over, the ocean was still warmed by the Gulf Stream, as it flowed north from the Caribbean, hugging the seaboard up the length of Florida and the Carolinas, where it would be shoved out a bit at Cape Hatteras, only to find the coast again and follow it all the way up to Cape Cod, before running into Maine and Nova Scotia and being turned out to sea for good.

And as the cooler, drier air sucked the moisture up and out of the warm sea spray, fog was born. The same fog that a hundred and fifty years ago had prompted men to fashion a tower at the land's edge and place a light atop it, to warn off mariners. The same fog that had been rolling across the barrier islands, settling in, and enveloping them for centuries, for millennia, for as long as there had been land and water.

Now, as Jorgensen squinted out through the porthole, seeing nothing, he could tell it was socked in pretty good. And with the breeze already dropping as the evening neared, he knew it'd be around for a spell.

"We won't take much more of your time," said one of his guests. The law school professor, if memory served him.

"Not to worry," said Jorgensen. "I'm afraid you won't be going anywhere till morning. And I trust you'll put up with fish stew."

For a time, Boyd Davies was put to work in the fields, cutting grass, piling up stones to make a fence, or pulling weeds out of the vegetable patch. But it didn't work out too well.

"The boy would get like real innerested in a stone or somethin' like that," recalls one of his sisters, "or stop to stare at the root of some turnip, like he'd never seen nuthin' in the world like it. Only then he'd go and do the same ezzack thing all over again, an hour later. It wasn't that he was *bad* or anythin' like that. It was jest that in the end, you couldn' get no work outa him. Thassall."

So for Boyd, it was back to idleness—idleness broken only by the occasional companionship (or at least the company) of children half his age.

Which might have been fine, but for one thing. If Boyd's verbal and social skills showed virtually no signs of developing with his years, outwardly his body was growing up on schedule. By the time he was fifteen, the boy was taller than his mother, and Hattie stood an even five-six. Over the next three years, Boyd would grow another half a foot, ending up just a shade over six feet tall. And although he never seemed particularly interested in food (other than to poke it around on his plate and stare at it), he must have been eating something, because subsequent records attest to his having reached 205 pounds by adulthood.

But Boyd's size wasn't the only thing that was changing. Where before his face had been smooth and soft, now the beginnings of a mustache and beard appeared. Round, boyish features gave way to the longer, more angular ones of an adult. And although he still spoke little, on the occasions that he did, his voice was noticeably deeper.

Inside his body, other changes were taking place—changes in glands and hormones, changes that awakened stirrings and itches, leading in turn to urges and cravings and needs—all part of God's great design for propagating the human race.

But hardly the thing for a little boy walking around in the body of a grown man.

"It wasn't Boyd's fault," one of his sisters would explain later. "The little boys would come around, 'cause even though he was big like a grownup, they could play with him like he was one of them. They'd climb on his back, rassle with him, punch him with their little fists—he never seemed to object. And the little girls, they'd pull up their skirts to tease him, like little girls do, or try to tickle him, to see if they could get a reaction out of him. For the most part, he'd pay them no mind, pretend he didn't notice what they were up to. But every now and then, he'd sneak a look, you know, or maybe tickle one of them back. He was different from other people, Boyd was. But he was still human."

The local police were a bit less charitable in their assessment of the situation.

According to Juvenile Hall records (at the time, a boy was considered a juvenile in Virginia until his sixteenth birthday, at which time he was deemed a youth and could even be treated as an adult, if the offense happened to be serious enough), Boyd was arrested three times. On each occasion, a complaint was signed by the parent of a considerably younger child. Two of the arrests were for "public lewdness," the equivalent of indecent exposure, a relatively minor infraction, particularly in the case of a youngster. The third arrest was more troubling. The official charge was sodomy in the third degree, and although the complaint has long since been destroyed or lost, there is some suggestion that Boyd was accused of inserting a finger, or fingers, into the vagina of a seven-year-old.

Because of his status as a juvenile—and more likely because he was widely viewed as a "retard"—Boyd was permitted to plead guilty to a lesser offense and avoid incarceration. But he was ordered placed on "court supervision" (presumably a strict variety of probation) until his twenty-first birthday.

Hattie McDaniel was determined to see that her son got into no further trouble with the law, and she put him on the shortest of leashes. She confined him to the house; she made a habit of taking him with her whenever she went out; and she "deputized" his sisters, requiring them to immediately report to her any transgressions committed by Boyd that they might become aware of.

Hattie's vigilance seems to have paid dividends for a while, because from the time he was placed on supervision until shortly after his seventeenth birthday—a period of a year and a half—there appear to have been no further instances of Boyd's getting into trouble, and his name doesn't appear on any of the Pittsylvania County arrest blotters.

All that ended one August evening in 1981.

One of Boyd's sisters recalled later that the family was sitting around the dinner table when they heard a car drive up. That fact itself was unusual. Neither Hattie, her sister, or just about any of their friends owned a car. Folks who came calling would take the Greyhound bus to Gretna, over on Route 29, and walk the two miles to the house.

One of the little children—for by this time Hattie had become a grandmother several times over, and the house was now home to three generations—ran to the window, looked out, and reported breathlessly, "It's the po-lice, Nana!" And indeed it was. They were there for "Boyd Davis," they explained, and for a moment the family took hope from their mispronunciation of his last name. But their hope was short-lived. The warrant one of them held in his hand had the correct spelling. And shortly beneath it, the words "RAPE IN THE FIRST DEGREE."

The officers were decent enough. They allowed Boyd time to get dressed—he'd been shirtless and shoeless when they'd arrived—and say his good-byes, which were characteristically brief. Then they put handcuffs on him, walked him out to their car, put him in the back seat, and drove off.

Three years would pass before he'd come home.

It seems that Hattie's vigilance had been less than perfect. According to court documents, two weeks earlier Boyd had been down by the railroad trestle bridge, about half a mile behind the house. There he'd been playing with two girls, one ten, the other eight. The ten-year-old had taken off some of her clothes, saying she wanted to wade in the creek, and had dared the others to join her. At that point the eight-year-old had left and run home, "to tell." She returned forty minutes later, with her father. When they got there, her sister and Boyd Davies were lying on the bank of the creek. Both of them were naked. When the ten-year-old's father threatened to beat her, she cried out that Boyd had made her take her clothes off and had "done things" to her.

The girl was taken to a doctor, who upon examining her

found a slight enlargement of her vaginal opening, which he characterized as "consistent with penetration." When asked by the doctor, in the presence of her father and two detectives, if the young man had "put his thing in there," she hesitated for a moment, then nodded her head up and down once.

Boyd was given a court-appointed lawyer named Owen Hubbard, a black man now in his seventies. One can imagine Hubbard trying his best to explain to his client that he was looking at thirty years in prison if he were to stand trial and be convicted. And one can hardly fault him for prevailing upon Boyd to accept a reduced plea that carried a maximum of seven years, but would have him out in two or three.

"And he was mighty lucky at that," Hubbard said afterwards. "Had that been a little white girl who'd a cried rape, they'd a thrown away the key. You can bet the farm on that."

Following his sentencing, Boyd was sent to the processing center in Lynchburg, where he was classified as an adult, rather than a youthful offender. One would be hard-pressed to imagine what criteria the authorities relied upon to make such a determination, other than the seriousness of the original charge and the physical size of the defendant, but make it they did. From Lynchburg, Boyd was transferred to the Brushy Mountain State Prison, near Bluefield, in the western tip of the state. The prison is Virginia's maximum-security adult facility, housing the system's most hardened and dangerous murderers, robbers, and rapists. Almost all are recidivists serving double-digit sentences; many are in for natural life.

When he arrived at Brushy Mountain, Boyd Davies was all of seventeen years old.

"I'm an old man," said August Jorgensen, rising from his chair at the table. "My wife, God rest her, used to complain I like to eat with the chickens. But I can't help it, habits are habits. When it starts getting dark outside, I start fixing supper. So as we used to say in Richmond, we'll be in recess for a while."

"Why don't we come back and finish tomorrow?" suggested Jessica Woodruff.

"Take a look outside," Jorgensen told her. "When the fog gets socked in like this, only an idiot would try crossing the narrows back to the mainland. I know these roads like the back of my hand, and even I'd be hard-pressed to make it. Miss one turn, and you're in the drink."

The three of them moved to the porthole and went through the motions of peering out into the distance. Jorgensen might have saved them the trouble by telling them what they'd see. The answer would have been simple: nothing, absolutely nothing. But they did their peering anyway. After a moment, their protests diminished to apologies, and from there to thanks.

It had been a good summer for shrimping. Not like years ago, when he and Marge could wade into the shallows, stretch the long, weighted net between them, its cork floats bobbing on the surface, drag it to shore and come up with hundreds—no, thousands—of shrimp, squirming and wriggling and sparkling in the sunshine.

It had taken him only half a day to train Jake to work one end of the net. He'd grasp it in his mouth, swim out parallel to Jorgensen until the water was too deep for him to stand, and paddle around in circles (dogs are good at many things, but treading water in one spot didn't seem to be one of them), waiting for his cue. Then, with a whistle from Jorgensen, he'd head back in, the net still firmly in his mouth. As they neared the shore, the weight of their catch would become considerable. Jorgensen, wading, would struggle to drag his end of the net, sometimes slipping in the sand or stubbing a toe on a rock, on occasion even letting the net slip from his hands.

Jake never let go.

And the irony was, he wouldn't eat the shrimp. Not live, not shelled, not cooked, not disguised and buried in any of his favorites. He'd wrinkle his nose, snort once or twice, step back, and shoot the old man a look, as if to say, "You expect me to eat *cat* food?"

Now Jorgensen pulled a small bag from his freezer, and another, and another after that. Setting them into water to thaw, he began chopping up onions and peppers and tomatoes and okra and potatoes, and anything else he could find. But no garlic; he hated garlic. He remembered how, for one of his birthdays, Marge had presented him with a custom-made charm on a thin silver chain. He'd had to look closely to see that it was a tiny figure of a vampire. "Wear that around your neck," she'd told him, "and it'll ward off garlic." He smiled now at the thought of it.

In a little oil, he began sautéing the onions, adding the rest of the vegetables depending on the amount of cooking time they'd need. When they were good and brown and beginning to stick to the iron skillet, he poured in some fish stock, some tomato juice, and a little white wine, then added a couple of bay leaves. He gave the mixture a stir, put a lid on the skillet, and turned down the flame to let it simmer.

"Take a walk upstairs," he told his guests, "and pick out rooms to sleep in. Then make sure you leave the doors open, so they'll warm up a bit."

He watched them file up the staircase, grasping the rail tightly and watching their feet. It took some getting used to, it did. The first morning they'd brought him home from the pound, Jake had balked at the sight of the steps, whining and cowering in terror that he'd slip through the openings. But by evening he'd gotten hungry enough to give it a try, and by now it was second nature to him, just as it was to Jorgensen.

He set the table, using mismatched bowls and silverware and glasses, and jelly jars when he ran out of glasses. He wasn't used to company, and didn't much care for it. But fog was fog, and he'd been speaking the truth when he'd told them there was no way they could make it to the mainland until morning. Besides which, the story of Boyd Davies had already gotten to him. Not because it was out of the ordinary; it wasn't. Oh, the details were different; they always were. But if the defendant hadn't been born brain-damaged, then he'd been horribly abused as a youngster. If he wasn't severely retarded, then he'd developed schizophrenia as a teenager. In Boyd's case, it had been his total lack of verbal and social skills. It was almost as if there was a rhythm to the stories, a predictable cadence that was—in some strange and unfathomable way—familiar and comforting, even as it was haunting and disturbing.

He lifted the bags from the water they'd been standing in, and spilled the contents onto a chopping block that was nothing more than a cross-section of a pecan tree that had grown too big for its own good. He added the fish first, stirring the pieces into the stew. There was redfish and mullet, monkfish and sheepshead—whatever had been unlucky enough to be in the way when Jorgensen and Jake had dragged the shrimp net up onto the beach.

He found a loaf of bread in the freezer and put it into the warming oven of the stove. Marge had lobbied hard for a microwave, but he'd always hated gadgets, and had explained that it might make trouble for his pacemaker.

"You don't have a pacemaker," she'd said.

"I might get me one," he told her.

His guests were descending the stairs gingerly, complimenting him on the rest of his home and thanking him again for his hospitality. He stirred the stew, adding some sea salt and hot pepper, and poked a fork into a piece of fish. It resisted for just a second before flaking. He added the crab and shrimp, and put the cover back on.

"Smells divine," said Jessica Woodruff, and indeed it did. "What is it you call it again?"

August Jorgensen shrugged. "I call it the sea," he said.

With Boyd Davies' communication skills virtually nonexistent, little is known of his three years at Brushy Mountain. Prison records suggest he was an average inmate, being "written up" for minor infractions of the rules on four occasions, and placed in solitary confinement once, for a period of five days.

Though one can hardly imagine a confinement more solitary than Boyd's to begin with.

His mother and two of his sisters visited him, but only on the rarest of occasions. From Pittsville to Bluefield is only a hundred miles as the crow flies, but by bus it took nearly five hours, and cost thirty-eight dollars. And it wasn't as if Boyd had anything to tell them once they got there, anyway.

This much is known: By the time Boyd came home three years later, his body was covered with old bruises, and scarred in half a dozen places. He could no longer bend the middle three fingers of his left hand, or raise his right arm above his head. His left eye was half shut, leaving him forever after with an appearance that, if you didn't know him, you'd think was slightly sinister.

In all other respects, he seemed the same—at twenty, a little bit older, but just as quiet, just as withdrawn, just as unreachable, and just as totally absorbed in absurd little things that couldn't possibly have interested another human being for more than a second or two.

There was one other thing. Since Boyd had been released after serving only three years of a seven-year sentence, he still "owed" the state four years. The way the state went about securing this debt was to place Boyd on parole for the balance of his sentence. As a parolee, he was informed that any arrest, for however trivial an offense, would land him back in Brushy Mountain for the next four years. He could be strip-searched at any time, compelled to submit to random urine tests to detect the presence of alcohol or illegal drugs, and subjected to unannounced searches of his home (which, in Boyd's case, meant his family's home, and all their belongings). But most onerously, he was required to report every two weeks to a parole officer in Lynchburg, fifty miles to the north.

His parole officer, a man by the name of Sean Kenny, remembered Boyd's first visit years later. "He shows up the first time with his mama. Can you believe that? A twenty-year-old man, and he's got to bring mama along, to hold his hand. I knew right away he was never going to make it, not with an attitude like that. But that wasn't all. He'd never once give me a straight answer to my questions, or pay attention to something I was trying to tell him, even when it was for his own good. And he had this nasty way of never making eye contact, of always sneaking me a glance out of the corner of one eye, like he was mocking me, trying to get over on me. He was some piece of work, that one was."

Hattie McDaniel recalled the meeting somewhat differently. "There was no way I was going to put him on a bus and let him go by hisself. So I took him. And they gave him a white man, Irish fella. And I said to him, 'Sir, my son is different. You gots to understand, to make some allowances.' And you know what the man says to me? He says, 'Miss Davis'—he never could understand that my name wasn't the same as my son's, and that even Boyd's name wasn't Davis—'Miss Davis,' he says, 'this here is America you're living in, and under our constitution, it's your son's right to be treated ezzackly the same way as everyone else.'"

According to Sean Kenny's records, Boyd Davies reported to him three of the first five times he was supposed to, each time accompanied by his mother or one of his sisters. After that, he simply stopped coming altogether. Eventually, Kenny cited Boyd for being in violation of his parole, and got a judge to issue a warrant for his arrest, describing him as an "armed and dangerous fugitive from justice." But the warrant squad was understaffed and badly backed up at the time, and none of them ever did get around to driving down to Pittsville to look for Boyd Davies. Had they done so, no doubt they would have found him sitting out back of the family home, staring intently at some twig or leaf or rock, as though it held the very secret of the universe.

That armed and dangerous fugitive from justice.

With the fog as thick as it was, there was no way to tell when afternoon turned to evening, or evening to night. Once the dinner dishes were done, and his guests had outdone one another in serving up compliments to the chef, Jorgensen suggested they adjourn to the study, where they might be more comfortable.

The study was one level above the kitchen, and therefore a bit smaller and cozier. That was the way things worked in the lighthouse: since it was slightly tapered, everything got smaller as you climbed upward—the study, the three bedrooms, and finally the observation room. The observation room was tiny, barely eight feet in diameter, though it opened up onto a platform, a deck of sorts that wrapped around it a full 360 degrees. Atop that stood the light chamber, the glass-enclosed housing at the center of which was the light itself, around which swung a highly polished mirror, in order to create the perfect illusion of a flashing beacon for a ship feeling her way up or down the coast.

But no more.

They settled into more comfortable chairs in the study, and though there were electric lights, Jorgensen lit an old oil lamp instead. He offered them brandy, which one accepted but two declined. And as he listened, they told him the rest of the story that had brought them there.

About a mile from the house where Boyd Davies lived with his mother, aunt, sisters, nephews and nieces, was a small tobacco farm. There are no small tobacco farms to speak of anymore, and this was one of the very last. The big tobacco companies (which actually today are even bigger food companies) have bought up all the family farms, to better control costs and insure uniformity of product. But back in 1985, there were still a few in private hands, and this was one of them.

The family that owned and worked the farm was named Meisner. They were white people, Lutherans, with ancestors that had come over from Holland or Germany, or perhaps both, when coming over meant making the trip by boat. Kurt Meisner was a hardworking, God-fearing man who—despite the fact that he'd been injured in an accident with a wood-

chipper—rose with the sun, worked all day, and had no toler-
ance for those who didn't. His wife Anja never seemed to
stray beyond the walls of her kitchen, except for Sunday services or special occasions. She baked her own bread, churned
her own butter, pickled and canned fruits and vegetables, took
care of the house, and saw to the needs of four children—
Kurt, Jr., sixteen, Katrinka, fifteen, Peter, thirteen, and Ilsa,
eleven.

Other than the fact that tobacco prices were falling and
expenses rising, things seemed to be going tolerably well for
the Meisners. All four of the children helped out on the farm
and in the home. There was food on the table and a couple of
dollars in the cookie jar, and young Kurt was even talking
about being the first in the family to attend college.

Then, one afternoon in mid-September, Ilsa, the youngest,
who by rule always arrived home from school by four o'clock
at the very latest, failed to show up. A call to the school confirmed that she'd been in class, had left when school let out at
2:40, and had been seen in the company of two other girls,
setting out for the two-mile walk home. The two classmates
were soon identified and contacted; they lived closer to the
schoolhouse, and each had arrived safely at her respective
home. Ilsa had continued on alone, as she did each day.

The local authorities—which in this case meant the county
sheriff's office, since Pittsville was too small to afford its own
police department—were promptly notified, and they in turn
contacted the state troopers. Bulletins were broadcast, a
description of the missing child was circulated, and officers
drove up and down the two-mile stretch Ilsa had last been seen
on, knocking on doors and asking if anyone had seen her or
noticed anyone suspicious in the area.

No one had.

A call was placed to the nearest field office of the FBI, over
in Charlottesville. The special agent in charge (for some reason, all FBI agents are called "special") explained that in the

absence of evidence of foul play, they couldn't become officially involved in the case for twenty-four hours; after that it could be presumed to be a kidnapping, with sufficient time for the victim to have been transported across state lines, giving them a jurisdictional basis to enter the investigation. In the meantime, however, the special agent agreed to "monitor developments" and offer advice as requested.

Around 10:00 that night, a deputy sheriff found Ilsa's book bag beneath a tree, about a quarter of a mile off the road she'd been walking, and an equal distance past the point where the second of her girlfriends had waved good-bye to her. By midnight, a search party had been formed, and dozens of local residents were combing the woods and fields, stopping every so often to shout the girl's name.

No one answered.

Although it was a moonless night and there was a shortage of flashlights among the searchers, they kept at it until dawn, crisscrossing the countryside, calling out, and listening in vain.

Among the searchers were Ilsa's father and two brothers. Her mother and sister sat in the kitchen, crying, waiting for news. They were accompanied by a state trooper and a deputy sheriff. Although the family had little in the way of money that would make their daughter a likely target for a kidnapping for ransom, a recording device had been hooked up to the phone, just in case someone called with a demand and instructions to be followed.

No one did.

Shortly after noon, two bloodhounds were brought in by the K-9 unit of the Richmond Police Department and given the scent of the little girl's book bag. One of the dogs promptly led its handler back to the road and all the way to the schoolhouse, proving that its nose was up to the task, even if its intellect wasn't.

The other dog had more luck. Pulling its handler behind it, it made a beeline further into the woods, stopping only when it reached a creek bed that, given the time of year, was almost dry. Its handler coaxed it across, but the hound failed to pick up the trail on the far side. Brought back to the spot where it had lost the scent, the dog circled around for a minute, before beginning to follow the creek upstream. After a hundred yards or so, it stopped, retraced its steps a bit, climbed up the far side of the bank, and stopped just beyond a big sweet gum tree, at a spot where the dirt was noticeably darker than the surrounding area, and softer to the touch.

According to the coroner, Ilsa Meisner had been manually strangled to death. There were several additional minor injuries to her hands and arms, which he described as "defensive," suggesting that she'd tried to fight off her attacker. There was also a fairly deep gash in the back of her head and an underlying depressed skull fracture, but given the minimal amount of bleeding associated with it, the coroner was of the opinion that the wound had most likely been inflicted postmortem, perhaps during the burial process. "Whoever did this to her might have dropped her head onto a sharp rock afterwards," he theorized, "or accidentally hit it with a pick or a shovel."

It wasn't until he was conducting the autopsy two days later that he discovered that she'd been raped or sodomized, as well. While there was no evidence of ejaculation, the little girl's vagina had been badly torn, "suggesting forcible penetration by an adult penis or a similarly sized object," wrote the coroner. The small amount of dried blood (which upon DNA analysis turned out to be her own) made it impossible for him to determine if she'd been alive at the time of the act, although he added that he hoped it was otherwise.

It didn't take long for suspicion to focus on Boyd Davies. He lived less than three miles from the spot where Ilsa Meisner's body had been buried. He was known to have been seen from time to time in the company of young children (though no one could say with certainty that any of them had been white). He was widely regarded as "different," "strange," and "downright peculiar." And, worst of all, he'd recently been released from prison after serving three years for the rape of a ten-year-old girl.

When the sheriff and three of his deputies came knocking at the door and asked to speak with her son, Hattie McDaniel wished them luck. It's hard to believe that she hadn't heard about the disappearance of the Meisner girl and the subsequent discovery of her body. Perhaps she'd never connected those events in her mind to Boyd; perhaps she had, and already feared the worst. Then again, maybe she simply couldn't bring herself to imagine that her son was capable of committing such a horrible crime.

It turned out the officers didn't want to speak with Boyd, so much as they wanted to have a look at him. And when they had that look, they saw that he was big and scary-looking, what with his bad eye and his habit of staring any way but at them. They noticed that he had cuts and bruises on both of his hands, some of them quite fresh, and dirt beneath his fingernails.

"Does the boy work?" the sheriff asked Hattie.

"No, sir, he don't work," she said.

"Is he in school?"

"No, sir."

"Do you know where he was yesterday afternoon, about three o'clock?"

"Out, I guess."

That was all they needed to hear. Firmly, but politely, they explained that they were going have to ask Boyd to accompany them to their headquarters for a couple of hours, "for investigation." Then they walked him outside, placed him in the back of one of their patrol cars, and drove off. For Hattie, it must have been like déjà vu. Only this time, things would not be the same as last. They would be worse, far worse than Hattie could ever have dreamed.

Long on suspicion but short of evidence, the sheriff's department deserves some credit for the way they went about their investigation. They took color photographs of Boyd's hands, and had a doctor examine him to verify the recentness of the cuts. They took scrapings from beneath his fingernails, saving material for microscopic comparison with soil samples removed from Ilsa Meisner's grave. They confiscated his boots, not only to collect soil samples, but to make plaster impressions from them. From the impressions they made casts, to compare with footprints found at the grave site.

In time, the cuts on Boyd's hands would be shown to be only a day or two old; the fingernail and boot scrapings would prove identical to the soil at the grave; and two partial footprints left nearby would perfectly match Boyd's boots.

Fifty years earlier, that might have been as far as the police felt compelled to go, and their next order of business might have been to find a rope and look for a suitable tree. But this was 1985, not 1935, and—as some sociologists have tried to explain—Southern law enforcement pretty much spent the second half of the Twentieth Century undoing the damage it had done during the first half. So not only did the sheriff and his men refrain from succumbing to the mentality of a lynch mob, they went further in their investigation.

What they did was to interview Boyd Davies.

The man chosen for the job was an investigator, a rank roughly the equivalent of a detective. His name was Daniel Wyatt, and he was a veteran of seventeen years with the department. Physically, he was tall and slender, with narrow shoulders, and he tended to slouch a lot. He had a full mustache, bright blue eyes, and a good head of dark hair that was beginning to gray. But perhaps the most striking thing about him was his voice, which was deep to the point of being gravelly. It was the voice of John Wayne, of Gregory Peck, of Clint Eastwood, all wrapped up into one.

It didn't take Daniel Wyatt very long to realize that he wasn't going to able to interview Boyd Davies in the usual sense of the term. With Wyatt's death in 1993—his gravelly voice apparently a precursor of throat cancer—no record exists as to how he happened upon a successful method of conversing with a suspect who, for all intents and purposes, was not only mute but illiterate. But happen upon it he did.

What Wyatt did was to take advantage of the only communication skill Boyd Davies possessed: his ability to draw. Having once made the discovery (and again, there is no suggestion as to how he made it), Wyatt provided Boyd with paper and pencil, and asked him to draw three pictures for him. We have Wyatt's notes to tell us the requested subject matters:

1. The place where you buried the little girl.

2. The thing you used to dig the hole.

3. The place where you put the thing you used to dig the hole.

And we have Boyd's three drawings, preserved as evidence from his trial. They are faded some, having been made in pencil, on pages torn from a spiral notebook. But they are exquisite in their detail, perspective, and sense of place. The first is of a large sweet gum tree, surrounded by ferns, with a narrow stream in the background. The second depicts a shovel, the handle of which appears to be taped about halfway up. The last shows a group of large rocks or boulders, with the early morning or late afternoon sun (it is impossible to tell which) casting long shadows from right to left.

The investigator pointed to the first drawing. "I want you to take me to this place," he told Boyd Davies. And Boyd took him. That is to say, once Wyatt and two deputies had driven him to the spot on the road closest to where Ilsa Meisner's book bag was found, Boyd led them across a field, into the woods, and over the creek-bed to the grave site, by then cordoned off with yellow crime-scene ribbon.

"Is this where you buried her?" Wyatt asked.

By all accounts, Boyd nodded affirmatively.

Pulling out the third picture, the one Boyd had drawn in response to the final question, Wyatt asked Boyd if he could show him the place he'd drawn. Boyd nodded again, and began to walk further into the woods. After about a quarter of a mile, they came to a gentle rise, followed by a steeper climb. Without ever hesitating, Boyd picked his way over and around rocks of increasing size, until they arrived at a grouping of small boulders not far from a summit. There Boyd stopped and pointed between two of the boulders. One of the deputies moved forward, crouched, and reached down. When he straightened up, he was holding a shovel with black duct tape wrapped around the handle, about halfway up.

The "guilt phase" of the trial lasted four days. The prosecution had no eyewitness, but they had Boyd's drawings, and the way he'd led the investigators directly to the grave site and the shovel. Together, they provided overwhelming circumstantial evidence of Boyd's guilt. His lawyer, a woman from the Midwest named Andrea Katz, who'd been brought down by some national death penalty defense organization to represent him, did her best. But when it came time for her to call witnesses, she simply had none to call.

"There was no way I could put Boyd himself on the stand," she explained afterward. "For one thing, his prior conviction would have come out, and that would have been the end of things right there. But even without that, he simply had nothing to tell the jury. It's not like he ever came right out and told me he'd done it, in as many words, but he never once denied it, either. But that happens sometimes, and when it does, you pretty much know what it means, and after a while you learn not to press your client too hard. There are some things that are just too difficult for people to admit."

Without an alibi or character witnesses (whose testimony again would have opened the door to Boyd's past record), and with her own scientific experts in agreement with the prosecution's, Katz rested. To her credit, she gave an inspired summation, arguing that that the state's case was purely circumstantial, and that without a single eyewitness, the proof couldn't possibly convince them of anything beyond a reasonable doubt.

But the jury didn't buy it; it took them less than two hours of deliberation to return a verdict of guilty.

There followed a "penalty phase," in which the same jurors who had convicted Boyd were presented with aggravating and mitigating evidence, before being asked to decide if he should live or die. Here, for the first time, the prosecution was permitted to tell them about Boyd's prior record—the public lewdness arrests and the rape of the 10-year-old, to which Boyd had been permitted to plead guilty to a lesser charge. They heard that he was a parole violator and a "fugitive from justice" at the time of his arrest. They learned that he wasn't working, and in fact had never held a job in his entire life.

Andrea Katz offered a wealth of mitigating evidence. She introduced school records, test scores, and psychological profiles of her client; and a psychiatrist flew down from Harvard and testified that in his opinion Boyd Davies suffered from a form of autism. But the prosecutor had done his homework, and he was able to get the doctor to concede that in spite of whatever limitations Boyd might have, or whatever syndrome he suffered from, he wasn't retarded, knew the difference between right and wrong, and was fully responsible for his own acts.

Finally, Katz called Hattie McDaniel to the stand, and Hattie described how difficult things had been for her son growing up with no father, no schooling to speak of, no real friends, and no ability to communicate on any meaningful level. And when it was her turn to sum up, Katz spoke passionately for two full hours, telling the jurors that the choice they were about to make was "truly a matter of life of death," that "nothing less than the fate of one of God's own children" rested in their hands, and imploring them to "choose life."

The jurors chose death.

A series of appeals had followed, a series so familiar to August Jorgensen that he could have recited it himself. Up and down

the state courts the case traveled, with a battery of lawyers raising every argument they could come up with. Boyd's mental
condition had never been properly taken into account; the officers who came to his home lacked probable cause to seize him;
they'd failed to properly advise him of his *Miranda* rights; he'd
been denied the effective assistance of counsel; individuals
opposed to the death penalty had been systematically excluded
from the jury pool, as had blacks and other minorities; the evidence adduced at the guilt phase of the trial had been insuffi-
cient; the prosecution had unfairly appealed to the jurors'
sympathy during the penalty phase; and on and on.

It took the lawyers nine years and two evidentiary hearings
before they'd exhausted Boyd Davies' state court appellate
rights. After that, they brought a writ of *habeas corpus* in federal district court, contending that Boyd had been denied
rights due him under the United States Constitution. Losing
there, they began their way up the federal appellate ladder, reit-
erating their arguments at the Fourth Circuit. Twice they'd
made it all the way up to the Supreme Court, only to lose
twice. Now they were headed back there for one final try, one
last-ditch effort to win a new penalty-phase trial, in the hope
that they might persuade a new jury to spare Boyd's life and let
him live out his days in prison.

"And what's the issue?" Jorgensen asked.

"Because of his autism," Jessica Woodruff replied, "Boyd
can't grasp the notion that they actually mean to kill him, or
why."

"Eighth Amendment?"

"Exactly," she said with a smile.

"So under the unique circumstances of this case," said Jorgensen, "executing Boyd Davies would amount to cruel and
unusual punishment."

"Bingo," said the law professor.

"They'll never go for it," said Jorgensen, "not in a million
years. They know it would throw open the floodgates for
every poor slob on death row."

"Which is why the stakes are so high," said Woodruff.

"Don't you see what they're doing?" Jorgensen asked his guests. "They've granted *cert* on the perfect case. A heinous crime, a repeat offender who's demonstrably guilty, and a record showing he not only had effective trial counsel, he actually had *excellent* counsel. They've taken the Eighth Amendment issue in order to knock it down, once and for all."

"Maybe," Jessica Woodruff admitted.

"But we don't know that, do we?" It was the third one, the one from the monitoring program, who chimed in with that remark.

Jorgensen didn't take the bait. Maybe they didn't know what a hopeless long shot it was, but he did. He'd seen too many of these cases, and he knew only too well how the Rehnquist death-majority operated. But that still left him with one question.

"Why me?" he asked. "Why not Tribe or Dershowitz or Boise, or any one of half a dozen others? They know this stuff backwards and forwards."

"Exactly the point," said the professor. "We feel it's time for some new blood."

Jorgensen didn't much care for the metaphor, but he let it go. Jessica Woodruff leaned forward in her chair. "We want you," she said, "because you'll bring something special. People remember how you left the bench out of principle, how you went into—" and here she waved her hand around, "—exile. The following year, you were voted one of America's ten most-admired men. When your name comes up, people associate it with courage, with dignity, with a sense of integrity."

"And the court cares about such things?"

"They will," said Jessica Woodruff, "by the time Trial TV profiles you."

"Ahhh," said Jorgensen, allowing himself a smile. "I'm to become a media star."

"Don't kid yourself," said the monitoring guy. "That TV set of yours is more powerful than you think . . ."

Jorgensen didn't bother correcting him. He hadn't owned a television for close to a decade.

". . . and besides, the time is right. Polls show that support for the death penalty is eroding, at least where life without the possibility of parole is an option. Why, in Illinois, the governor has declared a moratorium on executions, and he's a Republican. And—"

Jorgensen held up a hand. "What about the drawings?" he asked. "The bait you lured me with?"

"We'll run those as a teaser," Woodruff explained. "They'll captivate our viewers, just like they captivated you."

Jorgensen didn't much like the sound of that, but he understood that there was such a thing as the Court of Public Opinion. Trouble was, men like Scalia and Thomas never seemed swayed by it. "If I do decide to get involved with this—and I'm not saying for a moment that I'm going to—what is it you'll want of me?"

"Very little," said the law professor, "at least in terms of your time. The scheduling order hasn't come down yet. Most likely the case won't be heard until late spring. We've already got a team working on the brief, and they'll prepare you for the oral argument. All you'll have to do is be the point man."

"The figurehead," mused Jorgensen.

"If that's what you want to call it, go ahead. But a man's life is at stake here, and—if our thinking is correct—so are the lives of hundreds, maybe even thousands, of other men. Besides which," he added, "we're prepared to pay you. An honorarium, they call it."

Jorgensen knew what an honorarium was. In the year or two following his retirement, he'd been offered a number of them to give speeches at conventions or lectures at law schools. He'd turned them all down. He received a decent pension that, along with his Social Security checks, provided him with more money than he could ever spend. Childless, he had no family to provide for. And he had little desire to make speeches, and even less to give lectures.

He pushed himself up from his stuffed chair with some difficulty; it was why he favored the kitchen. He walked over to the porthole and pressed his face up close to it, cupping his hands around his eyes to block out the glare of the room.

It was full dark now; that much he could tell. But there was no moon visible, no stars, no crests of waves catching the reflection. There had to be ships out there, he knew, great ships making their way up or down the coast. But he couldn't see them, or their running lights.

All he could see was fog.

SEVEN

By morning, the fog had lifted. Over coffee that was evidently stronger than his guests were accustomed to, Jorgensen posed a question. "Would it be all right," he asked, "if, before I give you my decision, I were to pay Mr. Davies a visit?"

"Uh, I'm afraid we're not funded for that," said the law professor. "Right now our budgetary constraints are somewhat—"

"Not to worry," said Jorgensen. "I can drive, and I'll pay my own way."

The three of them exchanged glances. They had to have noticed his truck sitting right there in the driveway, thought Jorgensen. They must have taken him for too old, or too feeble to mix it up with off-island drivers.

"I can take you," said the one from the court monitoring program. "There's no need for you to make such a long trip alone."

"No, no," said Jorgensen, "I'd rather prefer it. Besides which," he added, reaching down to give Jake a pat on the head, "I won't be alone."

There was an awkward moment of silence, and Jorgensen was about to assure them that he wouldn't let the dog do too much of the driving, when Jessica Woodruff spoke up. "I suppose that'll be all right," she said. "I'll have my staff see to it that there's a visitor's pass waiting for you when you get there."

———

They left him the file, or at least the summary they'd brought, a three-inch thick manila folder. Though he'd never handled a death case as a litigant, Jorgensen had sat on enough of them as a judge to know that by the time one of them was in its sixteenth year, the word *file* had become obsolete; *room full of cartons* was more apt to be the case.

He spent the rest of the day with the summary, rereading documents, cross-checking reports, and studying appellate opinions. But he kept coming back to the drawings. They were every bit as striking as the first three Jessica Woodruff had used to bait him. The lines were exquisite; the details real to the point where you wanted to reach out and try to touch the objects. The angles, proportions, perspectives and shadowing were all flawless—less the work of a twenty-one-year-old unpracticed amateur than an accomplished adult artist. He could almost feel the heft of the shovel; the stickiness of the tape wrapped around its handle. He could see the grave site as though he were standing at it sixteen years ago, with Boyd Davies by his side. What had happened that September day, he wondered. What had gone so wrong that it had ended up bringing nothing but tragedy to two families?

He left the following morning, just after sunup. Jake settled his butt into the passenger seat, at the same time managing to stick his nose out the side window that Jorgensen had cracked open for him, knowing that he'd hear nothing but whining if he didn't. Anyone who might have noticed the two of them heading west over the flats and salt marshes toward the bridge that would take them to the mainland would have figured they were off to pick up a sack of groceries and the weekly paper, and maybe a tin of bait while they were at it. But then, they'd have had no way of seeing the small overnight bag wedged behind the driver's seat, or the road atlas resting on the floor, or the three-inch-thick manila folder lying next to it. They would have noticed only an old, white-haired man and his

dog, chugging along in a red Chevy pickup truck, the kind
with bug-eye headlights, a split windshield, and running
boards that looked to be fashioned from pure rust.

The kinda truck you couldn't hardly get no more.

The trip would take them two full days. The truck, which
had either 270,000 or 370,000 miles (Jorgensen could no
longer remember which) could do sixty, so long as it was
downhill with a good tailwind and the windows were rolled
up, but under normal conditions fifty or fifty-five was more
like it. It got about twelve miles to the gallon, only you didn't
want to fill the tank more than halfway, because if you did it
tended to leak. Which was just as well, because both the driver
and the passenger were getting on in years, too, and the same
could be said of them. The combination made for frequent pit
stops, some at filling stations or diners, but just as many by
trees or bushes. *Men's bushes,* as Jorgensen liked to think of
them. He didn't know what Jake thought of them as, but
whatever it was, the arrangement seemed to work.

They picked up I-77 outside of Columbia, and headed north,
crossing over the state line sometime in the late afternoon. By
6:00, Jorgensen's back was feeling it, and he pulled off the interstate a ways past Charlotte, at a little town called Cornelius. Cornelius had been the name of the wise old elephant in the *Babar*
stories, if Jorgensen remembered correctly. He liked children's
stories: Things were simpler in them, more straightforward.

If the meatloaf and redeye gravy at the local diner were
good, the mashed potatoes were a bit on the lumpy side, but
nothing compared to the mattress at the Sleepy-Time Motel.
Jake solved the problem by finding a spot on the floor that
suited him. Jorgensen, his bones weary from the drive, slept
fitfully, dreaming at one point that he was lying helpless on his
back on a plate, while someone ladled gravy over him. Only
when he looked closer, he could see that it wasn't a ladle at all
they were using, but a shovel—a shovel with duct tape
wrapped around the handle, halfway up its length.

EIGHT

Brushy Mountain State Prison looms as a giant wall, set atop a hill and visible for miles from whatever direction one approaches. The bricks that were used to fashion the wall a century ago were molded from the red-brown clay of the surrounding Allegheny Mountains. The result is that the wall takes on the color of the ground from which it rises. It is the color of iron, of soil, of the earth itself.

But August Jorgensen lived by the sea, and to him it looked less like a wall and more like one of those giant ocean-going tankers you saw riding high and dry at anchor, its rusted hull risen up from the depths.

He identified himself and was permitted to drive through the gateway, where he was directed to park his truck in a visitor's spot and leave his dog.

"Unless he's one of those seeing-eye ones," said a guard.

"No, no," said Jorgensen, "I'm afraid he's not." But the thought of a guide dog navigating for a blind driver caused him to chuckle and smile at the guard, in appreciation of the man's little joke.

The guard didn't smile back.

There was an inner wall, smaller and less imposing than the first, but it had gun towers at each corner and was topped with big loops of razor wire. Razor wire is exactly what it sounds like: It is barbed wire (or *bob*-wire, as they say in the South), only instead of sprouting pointed barbs every four inches or so, it sprouts razor blades.

Jorgensen took the manila folder, a pen, a legal pad to take notes on, and his reading glasses. Everything else he left in the truck. He knew from having been a defense lawyer years ago that he'd be going through metal detectors inside, and that any loose change, keys, or paperclips in his pockets would only set buzzers off and be taken from him.

He was ushered into a sign-in room, where he was required to produce identification and fill out a handful of forms. They wanted his full name, address, nationality, date of birth, year of admission to the bar, and about twenty other particulars. He was required to promise in writing that he was a member in good standing of the bar, that he was unarmed, and that he wasn't smuggling drugs or other contraband into the prison. He was made to wait while a lieutenant confirmed that arrangements had been made for him to visit Wesley Boyd Davies. Then he was made to wait some more while someone contacted someone else on the unit where Davies was housed, and an officer could be dispatched to escort the inmate to the attorney visit room.

Finally, after almost an hour, Jorgensen was told they were ready for him. He was directed through a series of steel doors, each of them electronically opened by a guard housed behind thick glass. The last of the doors opened into a large room containing small tables bolted to the floor. At each of the tables were two or three flimsy plastic chairs, the kind you could hit someone with, Jorgensen figured, and not hurt him too badly.

Except for a guard who sat behind a desk on a raised platform, overseeing everything, there was only one other person besides Jorgensen in the room. He was a black man, seated at one of the tables. He was dressed in a prison-issue blue jumpsuit. And he looked to be about thirty-five years old.

Jorgensen walked over to where he sat. "Are you Boyd Davies?" he asked the man.

The man said nothing, and didn't look at Jorgensen. But he nodded up and down once. Jorgensen sat down opposite him. "My name is Jorgensen," he said, "August Jorgensen. Some people have asked me to help you with your case. I'm here to find out if that's okay."

"That's okay," said Boyd Davies.

Well, that was certainly easy, thought Jorgensen. "Good," he said. "Before I ask you a few questions, is there anything you want to ask me?"

"Ask me."

"Any questions you have?"

"Questions you have."

And it dawned on Jorgensen that Boyd Davies wasn't so much answering him as he was repeating the last few words of everything he heard. *Echolalia,* they called it, a behavior characteristic of autism.

"What is your name?" asked Jorgensen, pointing his finger at Davies' chest on the word *your.*

It took a moment, but Davies replied, "Boyd."

"Hello, Boyd. I'm August."

"Hello."

"Hello."

If it was a less ambitious start, at least it seemed to get them acquainted. "How are you, Boyd?" Jorgensen tried next.

Nothing.

"Are you okay?"

"Okay."

Hard to tell from that.

Jorgensen was stumped. Here he'd driven for the better part of two days, waded through a small mountain of bureaucratic red tape, and waited for an hour, only to find out he hadn't the vaguest idea of how to communicate with his client. His would-be client.

Then an idea hit him. He took the legal pad he'd brought, and slid it across the table in front of Boyd. Then he handed him the pen. "Draw something for me," he said.

Boyd looked down at the objects as though unable to make the connection between them, or between them and what Jorgensen had just said.

"Can you draw a face?" Jorgensen asked him.

"A face," Boyd repeated. But he gave no sign of comprehension.

"A happy face?" Jorgensen suggested, forming his mouth into an exaggerated grin. "Or a sad face?" inverting it into a pout.

No reaction.

"How about Boyd?" he tried. "Can you draw Boyd?"

Still nothing.

"Can you draw anything at all?"

Apparently not. Apparently whatever gift, whatever talent the young man had once possessed, had died at some point, somewhere within these walls. In a last-ditch effort, Jorgensen picked up the pen himself, reached for the pad, and began drawing himself. He wasn't much of an artist, and he ended up with a crude stick figure, standing next to a lollypop tree. He rotated the pad 180 degrees, so that it faced Boyd, and offered him the pen.

But wherever Boyd Davies was at that particular moment—if indeed he was anywhere at all—it wasn't at a place where he could take pen and paper and make things come to life.

It was dark by the time Jorgensen got back outside to his truck. He found a motel south of a town called Rocky Gap. It wasn't until he was feeding Jake that he realized he himself hadn't eaten since breakfast. But he was tired, far too tired to go looking for food. He stretched out on the bed and, within minutes, fell asleep with his clothes on, even his shoes. He felt old and exhausted, and very far from home.

———————

"So do you think he'll do it?"

The voice was Brandon Davidson's, checking in with Jessica Woodruff by cell phone, fifteen minutes before Jessica was to take over as anchor for Trial TV's afternoon segment of "You Be the Jury."

"Oh, he'll do it," she said. "That's not what worries me."

"Okay," said Davidson, "what worries you?"

"I don't know. He insisted on going up to the prison, and meeting with the defendant."

"What's wrong with that?"

"Nothing," said Jessica. "Only I don't like working with people who need to control everything. Why couldn't he just say yes or no, and then, if he's going to do it, just go with the program?"

"He's from the old school," said Davidson.

"What's that supposed to mean?"

"Well, when he was on the bench and used to find himself in the minority—which was most of the time, naturally—he was never satisfied just saying he disagreed with the majority. He always insisted on writing something. And his dissenting opinions were usually so well written that more often than not, he'd drag another judge or two with him. The majority always prevailed, because they had the votes. But if you were to sit down and read the full opinions, you'd see he was almost always on the right side of the issue."

"Well," said Jessica, who hadn't sat down and read a full opinion since law school, "I just wish he wasn't such a weirdo. I don't like working with people who like to make waves. It makes me nervous."

"He'll be okay," said Davidson. "What are you covering this afternoon?"

"Some trial from Florida. Nine-year-old kid brings a loaded revolver to school for 'Show and Tell.' Prosecutor wants him tried as an adult, so they can lock him up for fifteen years."

"And the audience?"

"Pretty evenly divided."

"Ratings?"

"Eighteen-five. I've been on the phone with the defense lawyer, trying to talk him into putting the kid on the stand. I figure we could break twenty if he does. The kid's cute."

"Good," said Davidson. "What's Court TV doing?"

"The usual. Timothy McVeigh, the World Trade terrorists, Al Sharpton."

"Jerkoffs."

"I've got to go, Brandon. Makeup wants me."

"Okay, babe. Break a leg."

"Thanks."

Mercifully, the drive home from Brushy Mountain didn't take nearly as long as the drive up. At least it seemed that way to Jorgensen. It always seemed that way, in fact. There was something about heading home, some mysterious gravitational force that exerted itself on you, and drew you in as you got closer and closer. He decided to drive straight through, even though Marge would have told him not to trust his eyes after dark. But the thought of another night lying on a bad mattress in a cheap motel made him shudder, and he tightened his arthritic hands around the steering wheel and pushed on.

"To the lighthouse!" he shouted. "To the lighthouse!" And if he aimed the words at his dog, who responded with a concurring wag of his tail, August Jorgensen knew full well that the rallying cry was meant for himself.

NINE

For two days it blew hard, huge sheets of rain driving relentlessly against the weather side of the old lighthouse. Jorgensen used every towel he owned to mop up around the portholes, and when he ran out of towels he used old shirts. He ventured out only once, to have a look at how the catboat was riding at its mooring. He knew the lines were good and the mooring itself would hold—he'd salvaged a huge mushroom anchor from an old PT boat and sunk it deep in the mud. Still, he was worried the sheer volume of rain might swamp the open boat.

But it looked to be okay, as far as he could tell. Jake was all for rowing out to it and bailing it out, but Jorgensen told him no, not in this weather.

Back inside, he changed out of his soaking oilskins and climbed the spiral staircase all the way up to the light chamber. There he stood and watched as long, jagged streaks of lightning lit up the horizon and illuminated the surf directly beneath him. The glass surrounding him was thick, he knew, hurricane thick, and the lighthouse was topped with a lightning rod. He felt a safeness here he couldn't possibly have described. The more the sky lit up, the louder the thunder crashed, the harder the rain drove—the safer he felt.

Beyond that, there was a majesty to it, an incredible majesty. He had lived right here for a dozen years, in fair weather and foul, and right here he would die, when it was his time. It was a shame about Boyd Davies, behind the Wall at Brushy Mountain, and it would have been something to get to argue a case before the Supremes. But this was his home; he belonged here. He would leave the courtroom battles to younger men and women. Right here he had all the battle he needed. What a trivial, insignificant contest *Davies v. Virginia* was, when compared to the likes of *Man v. Nature,* or *The Sea v. The Land!*

Toward the evening of the third day it cleared, and Jorgensen surveyed the damage, as he always did after a storm. A few new chinks and cracks had appeared in the outer wall of the lighthouse, but nothing too serious. It was definitely time to do some major recaulking around the portholes. And as soon as the sea calmed a bit, he and Jake would row out to the catboat and bail her out. But the biggest impact the storm had had wasn't on the lighthouse or the boat, but on the beach. A good twenty feet of sand had been washed away, leaving Jorgensen's home that much closer to the advancing ocean.

"We better hurry up and die," he told Jake, "before old Neptune comes and gets us."

On the fourth day there was a letter for him when he called at the post office. It had no return address, but a postmark told him it was from some place called Falls Mills, Virginia. Back at the lighthouse, Jorgensen slit it open. There was a handwritten note, which he read first.

Dear Mr. Jorgensen:

My name is Homer and I am a C.O. at Brushy Mountain State Prison. I got your name and mail address off the sign-in sheet in Reception. I thought you might like to have this. You left it behind in the Counsel Room after your visit Monday.

There was no closing, no signature, no last name (or perhaps no first name) to go with "Homer." All of that made Jorgensen wonder if the man had maybe been aware that he was violating some administrative rule by sending whatever it was that was inside. Nor could Jorgensen remember leaving anything behind: He'd remembered to take his folder, his legal pad, his pen, and his reading glasses. Everything else, he'd made a point of leaving back in the truck.

He checked the envelope. All that remained in it was a single piece of paper, which he removed. It was folded in thirds, but even though the outside of it was blank, he recognized it as one of the sheets from his legal pad. He couldn't remember having taken any notes at the visit; there'd been nothing to take notes about. Then he remembered the stick figure he'd drawn for Boyd in an attempt to get Boyd to draw something of his own. Nice of Homer to return it, but hardly necessary. He unfolded it.

No doubt it was the combination of what he saw, measured against the low level of his expectations, that caused Jorgensen to react as he did. Imagine an unsuspecting visitor walking into the Sistine Chapel and looking up, fully expecting to find a dropped ceiling, courtesy of Home Depot.

It was astounding. No, it was more than astounding. It was absolutely incredible, so incredible that it was almost frightening.

What August Jorgensen was looking at was a portrait of a man, rising from the slope of his shoulders and the base of his neck to a three-quarter view of his face, on up to an unruly shock of hair. A cinderblock wall in the background identified the setting as the counsel visit room at Brushy Mountain. Jorgensen could tell from the ruled lines on the paper, and from one or two places where the folds of the paper had smudged the pencil marks, that it was a drawing he was staring at. But had it not been for those clues, he would have bet everything he owned in the world that what he was holding in his hands was a professionally taken, studio-quality photograph of himself.

Suddenly aware that his knees were shaking, Jorgensen lowered himself onto one of his kitchen chairs, his eyes never leaving the portrait. Vanity had never been one of his vices, and surely it wasn't vanity that riveted his gaze now to the likeness in front of him. Indeed, had it been about vanity, Jorgensen might have found much to dislike in the face. Deep creases gave the flesh a texture that was nothing short of leathery; hollow cheeks accentuated the facial bones and suggested the outlines of the skull hovering just beneath the skin; eyes set so deep as to hint at blindness; hair so unruly as to defy even a passing acquaintance with brush or comb.

But it was more than that. Looking hard, Jorgensen was struck by how very tired the man looked. Not just tired, but worn out, weary. And weary not just from lack of a night's sleep or long hours behind the wheel, but from something far more draining—as though there was some terrible, terrible sadness deep inside the man's heart.

His heart.

Had Boyd Davies merely been committing to paper what was in front of him? Or had he seen something beneath the surface, something that Jorgensen himself hadn't been aware of? What was it that had prompted Boyd to put pencil to paper as soon as Jorgensen had walked out the door? And how on earth had he been able to create a likeness of someone he'd seen for less than an hour, and even then had barely seemed to take notice of?

If August Jorgensen had a head full of questions, he had no answers. But he'd picked up a lesson or two in his eighty-plus years on the planet, and one of them was this: *When the fish are biting, don't switch your bait.* Well, evidently he wasn't the only one who knew that rule. Each time, someone had dangled it in front of him, and each time it had been the same: a young man's strange, uncanny ability to capture the world and re-create it on a piece of paper. First it had been a TV woman named Jessica Woodruff; then a long-dead detective named Daniel Wyatt; and finally a corrections officer wanting to be known only as Homer. Each time, he'd taken the bait. Twice he'd felt the prick of the hook and managed to spit it out. But they say the third time's the charm, and as is the case with most of those old sayings, there must be some truth to it, or they wouldn't keep saying it.

So when Jessica Woodruff stopped by a few days later to get his final answer, her driver waiting in a car with its engine running, Jorgensen hemmed and hawed a bit. But once he'd used up his quota of hems and haws, he told her yes, they could count him in.

In plain and simple terms, he'd been caught.

TEN

The Eighth Amendment to the United States Constitution decrees, among other things, that the government may not inflict "cruel and unusual punishments" upon any person. Just what a cruel and unusual punishment might be, the authors of the amendment never got around to specifying. So, as with most words and phrases in the document, the task of answering that question fell to the courts, specifically the justices of the Supreme Court. And over the years, there has been no shortage of interpretation on the subject.

Torture, it would seem, is definitely cruel and unusual; so, too, are maiming and dismemberment. But surprisingly enough, death—most people would consider its infliction the ultimate punishment—is not, in and of itself, cruel and unusual. The basis for such a seeming paradox is entirely historical: Centuries ago, back when the Eighth Amendment was drafted and adopted, executions were relatively commonplace. In Seventeenth-Century England, for example, pickpockets were hanged in the public square, even as their competitors worked the crowd. Hence, no matter how cruel executions might have been, one would have been hard-pressed to say that, at least to the authors of the Eighth Amendment, there was anything unusual about them.

To be sure, some limitations have been put in place over the years; and today, while states are free to impose and carry out death sentences, they may not do so indiscriminately. Limits exist in terms of eligibility, proportionality, and methodology. For example, it would be cruel and unusual (and therefore prohibited) for a state to impose death upon a child of ten, say; or as a penalty for shoplifting or stealing a car; or by stoning, burning at the stake, or some other method likely to entail protracted and agonizing suffering.

Some states, furthermore, have adopted death penalty statutes more restrictive than required by the Eighth Amendment (just as some have declined to get into the business of death altogether). In terms of methodology, the guillotine, the hangman's noose, the firing squad, the gas chamber, and the electric chair have all but given way to the syringe—the thinking being that lethal injection is more "humane," and accordingly less subject to constitutional challenge as cruel and unusual. And yet, electric chairs still exist in one or two states, and to this day, Utah allows a condemned man to choose death by a firing squad. Nothing cruel and unusual about that, says the Supreme Court.

Age limits vary from state to state, too, with some reserving capital punishment for those over twenty-one or eighteen, while others have displayed a willingness to execute offenders as young as sixteen. But no state authorizes death for the truly young; a law that did so in this day and age would no doubt be rejected as cruel and unusual.

Nowhere in the debate, however, has there been more disagreement than in the area of the mental capacity of the accused. Some states have expressly exempted the mentally retarded; others have left the matter up to juries, allowing them to consider a defendant's retardation a "mitigating factor" in their deliberations. For a long time, the Supreme Court pretty much managed to avoid the issue. For the majority of the justices, it seemed that sufficient protection was afforded by the natural screening process that takes place before and during trial. In other words, a defendant who's so feeble-minded as to be incapable of understanding the charges against him will usually be found unfit to stand trial in the first place. And one who's so mentally ill as to be unable to conform his conduct to the law will presumably be adjudged insane by the jury. Conversely, a defendant competent enough to stand trial, and sane enough to be found guilty at that trial, is fully qualified to die.

But after years of stonewalling, the justices had recently agreed to consider an appeal of a retarded man, whose lawyers were asserting that killing him would be cruel and unusual. Unfortunately for Boyd Davies, "retarded" was a club he didn't belong to. No showing had ever been made that Boyd was retarded. Illiterate, yes; uneducated, surely. But going back to his childhood, every time he'd been tested by someone using a nonverbal protocol (in other words, having him figure out how many blocks were hidden behind the visible ones), he'd done well. So retardation was out of the question, and however the Supreme Court happened to come down on that particular case, it wouldn't save Boyd. And there was no spillover, no "interest-of-justice" doctrine that would prompt the justices to use common sense and say, "Well, if you can't execute a retarded person, you can't execute one with a serious developmental disorder, either." No, for the Supremes, the rule was that you decided cases on the narrowest possible grounds, if indeed you were forced to decide them at all.

Of course, it was precisely that sort of thinking that had driven August Jorgensen from the bench years earlier. Now here he was, stepping back into the fray, taking up the cause of a man who wasn't retarded, had been found competent prior to trial, and sane during it.

So just where did Boyd's autism fit into the equation? The Supreme Court, in granting his lawyers one final writ of *certiorari,* had said it would limit its analysis to a very narrow question: Could a competent, sane, non-retarded individual, who was nonetheless incapable of understanding the connection between his criminal act and his execution, be put to death without violating the Eighth Amendment?

At a hearing some months earlier, defense experts had testified that Boyd showed no evidence of being able to make that link in his mind; prosecution experts had, with equal certainty, assured the court that he could. It was a state of affairs that no longer surprised Jorgensen so much as nauseated him. As a judge, he'd seen too many times how easy it was for each side to line up teams of experts with long and impressive résumés to come into court and swear to one thing or another. They were mercenaries, willing to sell their opinions to the highest bidder. And the law, priding itself on its adversary system, not only put up with them, but embraced them as a substitute for real science.

But a funny thing had happened at Boyd Davies' hearing. After all the experts were done testifying, the hearing judge had surprised everyone. Instead of deciding that Boyd did or didn't understand why he was to be killed, the judge had ruled that it didn't matter—that the Commonwealth of Virginia was free to execute him either way.

Had the hearing judge simply chosen to say he believed the prosecution's experts, that would have been the end of it. The Fourth Circuit would have ruled that the judge hadn't abused the wide discretion accorded him; the Supreme Court would have declined to review that ruling; and Boyd Davies would likely have been a dead man by now.

Instead, by ducking the factual issue, the judge had created a legal one. When his ruling went up to the Fourth Circuit, they'd quite predictably affirmed it. (Hell, Jorgensen remembered enough about his old colleagues in Richmond to know they'd affirm a lynching, if given half a chance.) But the *certiorari* application to the Supreme Court had been granted, meaning that at least four of the justices—and Jorgensen had no trouble guessing that meant Souter, Ginsberg, Stevens, and probably Breyer—had voted to hear the case. Of course, that still left a majority of five, and the odds of winning over Rehnquist, Scalia, Thomas, O'Connor, or Kennedy on a death case were right up there with being able to walk on water.

And the funny thing about it was that even if the defense

were to win, their victory would be limited, and no doubt short-lived. For if the Supreme Court agreed with them, and said you couldn't execute someone who didn't understand why you were doing it, they'd send the case back to the Fourth Circuit, which in turn would remand it to the hearing judge, with instructions to make a decision one way or the other. And as soon as he said, "Okay, I find that Davies understands why he's going to be killed," that would trigger a final appeal, but one limited to the question of whether there'd been a sufficient factual basis for his finding. "Yes," the Fourth Circuit would be sure to rule, and the Supremes would quickly pass with two words: "*Cert* denied." Their quaint way of saying, "Strap him down and hook him up." At best, Boyd Davies would have won a few more months among the living.

But Jorgensen knew enough to understand that in the business of death, "a few more months among the living" was often as good as it got. Nowhere esle did the old saying, "Where there's life, there's hope," take on as much significance as it did in the world of capital punishment. The governor of Virginia wasn't likely to declare a moratorium on executions. But then again, the same thing could have been said about the governor of Illinois, and *he* had. Or maybe some long-lost blood or semen sample would surface, some jailhouse informer would admit he lied at the trial, some detective would acknowledge that he coerced the confession out of the defendant.

When Death comes knocking at the door, even a two-minute delay in answering it amounts to a reprieve of sorts.

So what was Jorgensen to do? They'd pretty much admitted they only wanted him on the defense team as a figurehead, someone to lend his white-haired presence to the cause. They had their own people doing legal research; they had a team writing the brief; they even had somebody who was going to prepare him for the oral argument. No doubt they had a slew of experts on autism, too. All Jorgensen knew about it was what he'd learned from the movie *Rain Man*—ninety minutes of the Gospel According to Hollywood.

And if he'd read the reactions of his visitors correctly, they hadn't even much liked the idea of his going to visit Davies at Brushy Mountain.

But having agreed to help, he couldn't very well do nothing, could he? He wasn't going to sit around for the next six months, and then let them carry him into the courtroom like some *windup doll,* ready to spout their words for them. It was bad enough that the American people had been made to suffer through eight years under an actor-president; the last thing they needed now was an actor-lawyer.

And while here Jorgensen—who'd never heard of *Ally McBeal* or *L.A. Law* or *Judging Amy* or *The Practice* or dozens of other lawyer shows before them—had made the mistake of seriously underestimating the needs of his countrymen, his deficient thinking only goes to show how very out of touch one can get when one lives in an old lighthouse on a barrier island, deprived of so much as a single television set.

As he sat with his brandy that evening, Jorgensen tried to imagine what it would be like to argue Boyd Davies' case before the Supreme Court. The trouble with appellate arguments was that they were so impersonal, so sterile, so bloodless. They were always about issues instead of people. Sure, they bore people's names—*Miranda v. Arizona, Terry v. Ohio, Furman v. Georgia*—but only as captions. The defendants were never there, nor the victims they'd hurt, nor the families on either side, whose lives would never again be the same. There were no vindictive or reluctant witnesses, no smug arresting officers, no earnest jurors struggling to reach a verdict.

There were only the lawyers.

For all the years Jorgensen had sat on the Fourth Circuit, listening to appellate argument after appellate argument, he'd hungered for the human story behind the case. Who was this man, referred to before the court only as "petitioner" or "appellant?" Wasn't he a real living person, complete with parents and children, hopes and dreams, fears and foibles? What kind of a child had he been? What did he look like? Jorgensen had always tried to imagine what could have gone so terribly wrong to take a man and turn him into a name, a number, a caption, a citation.

A footnote.

He drained the last of his brandy, feeling its pleasant heat spread out from his throat and across his chest. If he could do nothing else, August Jorgensen told himself, he was determined to make another effort to get through to Boyd Davies, to find the person locked up inside the body. And the first step, he knew, was to get himself ready. That meant moving beyond *Rain Man,* learning something about the mysterious affliction known as autism.

Eight hundred miles to the north, Jessica Woodruff lay on her double bed in her designer-decorated apartment on Manhattan's Upper East Side. Alone. She hated being alone. But it seemed to come with the territory, at least when you were dwelling in the territory of seeing a married man.

"Give me time," Brandon kept telling her. He was working on a plan. As best as she could figure it out, his plan was trying to manipulate his wife into being the one to ask for a separation. That way there'd be less anger, less guilt, less alimony, and less child support. Furthermore—and he kept stressing to Jessica how important this was for everyone concerned, far more important than the anger and the guilt and the money, which he assured her he had plenty of and could care less about—there'd be no suspicion that the two of them had been carrying on behind his wife's back.

Then, after a month or two of separation, it would be the most natural thing in the world for him to start seeing someone else. Especially someone bright and young and single and attractive, someone he already knew from Trial TV. "Be patient," he kept saying. "It's going to work, you'll see."

But time and patience were two things Jessica had never had an overabundance of, and was rapidly running out of.

The other thing she was beginning to run out of was her certainty that August Jorgensen was in fact the right person to argue Boyd Davies' case before the Supreme Court. What had ever made her think he was up to it? The man was in his eighties, for God's sake. He had no telephone, no beeper, no computer, no E-mail, no fax machine. He was half deaf, didn't see well, and had hair sprouting out of his ears and nose. And he lived like some sort of recluse, in that, that *lighthouse* of his.

She opened her bedside table drawer and rummaged around until she found half a joint and a monogrammed silver lighter. The joint she'd been given by a cameraman at the studio; the lighter had been a gift from Brandon. She lit the joint and inhaled deeply, holding the smoke in her lungs until she began to feel lightheaded. She repeated the process until the joint was nothing but a roach, and was too small to hold without burning her fingers.

He sure did look the part, though. And his voice—God, his voice was great. When the oral argument got close, she'd set up a long interview with him, let them pick up his baritone and zoom in on that face of his. The camera would absolutely love him. Later on, when the case was over and the book was out and the movie rights sold, they could have Max von Sydow read for the role. He'd be perfect. He was almost a double for the old guy.

Come to think of it, maybe they ought to bypass Jorgensen altogether, and ask Max to argue the case before the Supreme Court. Now there was an idea. She giggled at the thought of it. She'd have to remember to run it by Brandon first thing in the morning. He'd get a kick out of it, Brandon would.

The ringing of the telephone startled her, actually made her jump slightly, even as she lay on the bed. Realizing she was too stoned to carry on a business conversation, she waited for the caller-identification screen to tell her who it was. Only when she saw it was Timothy Harkin, calling from the Southern States' Court Monitoring Program in Atlanta, did she pick up.

She didn't work for Harkin.

"Hi, Tim," she said, trying hard not to slur her words.

"Hello, Jessica."

"What's up? It's nighttime up here."

"Here, too."

There was a pause. Jessica hated pauses. On the air, they made for uneven interviews. Off the air, they usually signified trouble. And trouble wasn't something she needed right now, straight or stoned.

"What's the matter?" she asked.

"I've been thinking," said Harkin.

She almost said, "That's bad," but managed to restrain herself. Settled instead on, "What about?"

"You know. The whole thing."

"Don't go getting cold feet on me, Tim. You yourself agreed that there are times the end justifies—"

"I know, I know. But how can you be so sure we're doing the right thing? I mean—"

"You're damn right I'm sure," said Jessica, in as firm a voice as she could muster. "Listen, Tim. We've been over thish a hundred times." *Thish* was bad, but Jessica let it slide. Correcting it would have only served to highlight it. In television, they trained you early on to ignore your mistakes, leave them behind you. Just plunge ahead, focusing on the prompters or winging it, as though it had never happened.

"Tell me it's worth it," Harkin was saying.

"It's more than worth it," said Jessica. "It's worth it a thousand times over. You know that as well as I do, don't you, Tim?"

"Yeah," said Harkin. "I guess I do. Look, I'm sorry to have bothered you, Jessica."

"That's all right. Remember, though, it's definitely worth it."

Shut up, she told herself. It was the grass, she realized.

Whenever she smoked, she developed a tendency to repeat herself over and over.

After exchanging good-byes and hanging up the phone, Jessica made a mental note to call Brandon Davidson the following day, and tell him about Harkin's second thoughts. But whether it was the joint she'd smoked or the late hour, come morning she'd have more pressing things on her mind, and she'd completely forget about her conversation with Tim Harkin.

ELEVEN

August Jorgensen owned no telephone, no television, no VCR, no microwave oven, no dishwasher, no garbage disposal, no fax machine, and no electronic kitchen gadgets. He'd once had some of these things, but over the past dozen years, he'd been simplifying, or "paring down," as he liked to call the process. A less-charitable friend of his once suggested to him that what Jorgensen was really doing was getting ready to die. "We're all getting ready to die," Jorgensen had observed, "one way or another."

Books Jorgensen had by the hundreds—probably the thousands, if you wanted to count those that lurked in the bottoms of closets or bided their time huddled together in cardboard cartons. But of all the books he had, at least so far as he could ascertain, not one of them had anything to say about the subject of autism, save a well-worn Random House dictionary, vintage 1966, which provided him with this nugget of wisdom:

> **au•tism** (ô'tiz em), *n. Psychol.* the tendency to
> view life in terms of one's own needs and
> deires, as by daydreams or fantasies, unmindful
> of objective reality. [AUT- + -ISM] —**au'tist**,
> *n.* —**au•tis•tic** (ô tis' tik), *adj*.

It didn't take him long to decide that if the editors were incapable of spelling the word *desires,* perhaps he shouldn't put too much stock in the rest of their information, either.

But what to do?

The local library was utterly worthless, he'd long ago found out, unless you were looking for books on Confederate heritage or Bible study, or a complete set of the Hardy Boys' adventures; the nearest one that might have anything on the subject was a good hour and a half's drive. Same for the university, over in Charleston. He wondered if there might not be some national association or foundation concerned with the disease, the way there was with diabetes and cancer and heart disease. He could look them up and send them a letter, or call them on one of those 800 numbers they all had now, and ask them to send him pamphlets and stuff like that. The process might take some time, but time was certainly something he had.

So the following morning, when he'd driven over to the general store for his newspaper and a couple of things, he asked Pop Crawford—Pop was a good fifteen years younger than Jorgensen, but since everybody else called him Pop, Jorgensen did, too—if he might use the phone.

"Local call?" Pop wanted to know.

"One of those eight-hundred numbers," said Jorgensen. "Same thing."

Pop looked at him suspiciously, but handed over the phone. Jorgensen dialed the toll-free operator and asked if she had a number for the American Autism Association, or anything like that.

He waited a moment while she looked it up.

"Would you like the listing for emergency road service," she asked, "or travel assistance?"

He tried for another minute or so, but it was obvious they were having two different conversations, and the twain were not about to meet. He thanked her for her trouble and hung up.

"What is it you're trying to find out?" Pop asked him.

"Autism," said Jorgensen, "information about autism. It's a disease where—"

"Yeah, yeah," Pop cut him off. "I know what it is. They say Nellie Strock's boy has it. Used to bite folks when he was young. Zack!"

"Zack has autism?" That suprised Jorgensen. "I thought he was just a rotten kid."

"No, no," said Pop, "not Zack. Nellie's kid is Donald. Zachary here is my nephew." And as though on cue, a skinny, bespectacled youngster appeared from the back room. "He's staying with me till his momma gets back from up north. Right, Zack?"

The boy nodded shyly, but said nothing, serving only to perpetuate Jorgensen's confusion. He looked to be about seven or eight, standing no more than four feet tall and weighing maybe fifty pounds, all of it knees and elbows. The kind of kid who got picked last whenever sides were being chosen for a ball game.

"Zack," said Pop, "do me a favor. Take the judge here with you and help him look up some stuff. He used to be a smart man, but he doesn't get out much anymore."

Jorgensen was about to take issue with the comment, but the boy had already turned and was headed back to wherever he'd materialized from.

"Go on." Pop shooed him away with a dismissive wave. "Unless you're too proud to learn from a ten-year-old."

"If he's ten," said Jorgensen, "how come he's not at school like he's supposed to be?"

"And for his first lesson," Pop called to the boy, "why don't you teach him the days of the week?"

Jorgensen looked down at his newspaper, saw it was Saturday. "I knew that," he mumbled, and headed to the back room.

He found Zachary sitting at an old rolltop desk, his feet dangling a foot above the floor, his face lit up by the blue glow of a television screen. In front of the TV was a keyboard, but the boy seemed to pretty much ignore that. Instead, his right hand rested on a gadget that had a wire sprouting from it, connecting it to a big plastic box. Every once in a while he'd move his hand a tiny bit, and images on the screen would jump around.

"A computer," said August Jorgensen.

"How old *are* you?" asked the boy.

It turned out to be easy, amazingly easy. Zachary needed a little help spelling *autism* to start him off, but that was about it. Once he'd typed the correct letters into a little box and pressed the ENTER key, the machine seemed to take over and do the rest.

Not that Jorgensen didn't know about computers, or what they could do. He lived in a lighthouse, after all, not on another planet. He'd seen people using computers in banks and department stores, and looking up listings at the Motor Vehicle Department and the Social Security office. He knew everyone was on-line these days, exchanging E-mails instead of letters, and that you weren't anybody unless you had *.com* after your name. It was just that he'd never actually seen anybody doing research on one before, the kind of stuff you used to have to go the library for, lug all sorts of books around, and spend forever trying to zero in on what you were looking for.

Suddenly, it was all right there at his fingertips—okay, their fingertips, the white-haired octogenarian and the nerdy ten-year-old with the Coke-bottle glasses.

Autism, Jorgensen was surprised to find out, wasn't a disease at all. It was a pervasive developmental disorder that occurred in as many as one in every five hundred individuals, or as rarely as one in every five thousand, depending upon the diagnostic criteria one chose to use. Symptoms usually appeared during the first three years of childhood, and continued throughout life. They typically included problems with communication (particularly verbal skills), conceptualization, social interaction and, occasionally, motor skills. Austistic children seemed removed; they often failed to respond to other peoples' voices, and tended to avoid eye contact. Endless and obsessive repetitive motions were common, such as rocking, spinning, stroking and hair-twirling. In extreme cases, biting or head-banging occurred. People with autism often exhibited unusual responses to light, sounds, smells, or other sensory stimulation. Paradoxically, they could be relatively impervious to pain, while exquisitely sensitive to touch.

Autism was an equal-opportunity disorder, in that it affected people of all geographic, racial and social groups; but it discriminated between the sexes, choosing five males for each female it selected.

In terms of causation, autism has long defied easy analysis. Once thought of as the manifestation of flight from poor parenting (particularly frigid mothering) or early psychological trauma, the disorder was now recognized as having an array of physiological components. No unique biological marker had been discovered, and no single gene "caused" autism, although several had been identified as contributors. Families with one autistic child had a 5 percent risk of having a second child affected, far greater than the normal expectation. Recent neurological studies had uncovered abnormalities in a number of areas of the autistic brain, most prominently the cerebellum and hippocampus. In at least some cases, these changes could be attributed to diseases—among them rubella, fragile X syndrome, PKU (phenylketonuria), tuberous sclerosis, Rett's syndrome, encephalitis, and hydrocephalus—contracted either *in utero* or during the early months of childhood. There was some evidence pointing to chemical imbalances, and heightened or depressed serotonin levels had been found, as well as abnormalities in various other "signaling" molecules. But these anomalies might eventually prove to be more effects than causes.

Whatever the particular causal agent of the damage might be, the effect seemed to manifest itself as a disruption of the normal circuitry of the brain. Specific areas could be left relatively intact, but integration with other areas might be greatly diminished or even totally absent. The result was that complex behavior—such as language skills, social interaction, conceptualization, and the development of a sense of personal identity—became difficult, if not altogether impossible.

Over the years—and although autism wasn't fully identified and classified until the 1940s, the condition most likely predated recorded history—there had been no shortage of "miracle cures." Psychotherapy, diet, vitamin and mineral regimens, and various sorts of behavior modification had all been tried, and all had failed. Most recently, advocates of "facilitated communication" had boasted that profoundly autistic children could "type" intelligent and coherent thoughts when assisted by a "facilitator" holding the child's hand over a keyboard. But controlled studies had cast serious doubt on the claims, suggesting that they reflected no more than suggestiveness (whether deliberate or unconscious) on the part of the facilitator.

In terms of intelligence, it had long been assumed that the majority of autistic children were retarded, with the debate centering on the question of degree. But recent thinking had begun to cast new light on the issue. One complicating factor was that autism was often accompanied by other abnormalities, and clinicians tended to be guilty of attributing deficits to the autism, when in fact some other condition might be responsible. Additionally, it was likely that much of what presents itself as retardation could be explained by the close connection that existed between language facility and intelligence testing. As more sophisticated testing methods were employed, relying less on the subject's verbal ability, IQ levels tended to rise rather significantly.

Occasionally—and only occasionally—autistic children displayed enormously prodigious aptitudes, and when they did, the phrase "idiot savant" was sometimes used to describe them. Examples of such behavior included the ability to perform complex mathematical calculations with computer-like speed, or to unerringly predict what day of the week a particular date will fall on centuries into the future. Kim Peek, the man upon whom the movie *Rain Man* was based, had such talents. Other autistics were musically gifted. In Civil War times, a blind negro boy (for those were the terms in favor back then, "sightless" and "African-American" still more than a century away from coming into vogue), described as an "idiot" in all other ways, mastered the piano without any training, to the point where he could perfectly re-create any piece he heard. Blind Tom, as he became known, astounded audiences by playing one song with his left hand and another with his right, all the while singing a third. He was also known to play with his back to the piano and his hands held upside down. Leslie Lemke, at age fourteen having heard Tchaikovsky's Piano Concerto No. 1 once, sat down and played the piano part flawlessly. Tony DeBlois, a blind autistic jazz improvisationist, quickly learned to play fourteen musical instruments, twelve of them proficiently.

But as impressive as these accounts of autistics with mathematical or musical skills were to Jorgensen, of even more interest were the artistic savants. Nadia, a girl of three and a half, began drawing animals and other objects in a manner described by developmental psychologists as "not possible." Unlike children three and four times her age, she displayed a sense of proportion, perspective and light that was not only technically accomplished, but appeared to be entirely intuitive. A man named Alonzo Clemons could glimpse a fleeting image of a horse on a television screen and, given twenty minutes, could sculpt a perfect three-dimensional replica of it out of clay or wax. Richard Wawro was an autistic who was also a world-renowned landscape painter. Many autistic artists (*many*, of course, being a relative term) concentrated on a single subject matter to the point of fixation. An autistic boy known as Jonny specialized in drawings of electric lamps; the autistic Japanese artist Shyoichiro Yamamura focused on insects; while the American Jessy Park was first obsessed with radio dials and heaters, then weather anomalies and constellations in the night sky, before moving on to renditions of houses and churches. And Oliver Sacks (perhaps best known as the psychologist who worked with post-encephalitic patients and became the model for Robin Williams' portrayal in the movie *Awakenings*) had described in detail the case of Stephen Wiltshire, a black, autistic English boy whose drawings from memory of London architecture were said to be nothing less than breathtaking.

Jorgensen came away from the session ten dollars poorer. It was all Pop Crawford would permit him to pay Zachary for three full hours of research assistance.

"Give him any more'n that, and he's liable to go out and find himself a woman, blow it all on her. Right, Zack?"

Zack yawned. He seemed pretty noncommittal on the subject, and was anxious to get back to the more important stuff he'd been doing on the computer, before he'd been sidetracked by the old man who pretended he was a hacker, but barely knew how to click a mouse.

The other thing Jorgensen came away with was a hunger to learn more about the paradox presented by the autistic savants, particularly the artistic ones. How could young children—some of them so profoundly impaired that they couldn't respond to their own names, or carry on a conversation or be taught to read a single rudimentary sentence—nevertheless create stunning visual depictions of things they'd only glanced at? And that they could do so without the least bit of training, practice or (at least it seemed) concentration, made it all the more stupefying.

"It truly boggles the mind," Jorgensen said aloud.

Jake, sitting beside him in the pickup truck, his nose stuck out the far window, contributed no more than a wag of the tail. Small boys and dogs, apparently, were not so easily impressed.

That night, Jorgensen sat in front of his stove, reviewing the notes he'd made and the pages young Zachary had printed out for him. Boyd Davies' lawyers were probably right in acknowledging that their client wasn't retarded, at least not in the sense that the courts might be interested. And in focusing on Boyd's failure to comprehend the logical link between his act (murder) and the resulting sentence (death), they'd somehow managed to stumble upon what seemed to Jorgensen to be the very essence of his disorder: the utter inability of the autistic brain to put things together and form a concept out of them.

But where did that leave them? Boyd had murdered an eleven-year-old child, and likely raped her, as well. At the time, he'd been on parole for an earlier sexual assault of a child. Was William Rehnquist really going to concern himself with whether or not Boyd could make the connection between his crime and his punishment? Was Antonin Scalia looking to broaden the reach of the Eighth Amendment, so that every defendant who stood up and said, "Look, I don't understand why you're killing me," would get his sentence commuted? Did Clarence Thomas give a hoot about damaged cerebella and hippocampi, or abnormal serotonin levels?

The answers seemed painfully obvious, just as they had to have seemed obvious to those who'd reached out to Jorgensen and drawn him into their circle, so that he could lead them into a hopeless battle against overwhelming odds.

As his thoughts wandered, so did his concentration, and at one point he had to yank the steering wheel sharply to the right, in order to keep the old truck from drifting off the road and into the marsh.

Why was it he'd wanted to know more about autism? He tried to remember. It had been only this morning, but it seemed so long ago. Ah, yes—it had been because he wanted to understand more about Boyd Davies, to get to know him better, so he could humanize him for the Court.

But Zachary's computer hadn't humanized Boyd at all. It had spat out long lists of statistics and Latin words and case histories and unproved theories; but in the end, all of the autistic savants he'd read about seemed *less* human, if anything. They were freaks, is what they were, sideshow performers. Somewhere along the line, some genetic accident or mutant virus or playful god had reached into their brains, lifted out the essence of whatever it was that made people human, and replaced it with some weird and extravagant talent. They belonged right between the fire-breather and the sword-swallower. *"Step right up, folks! See the amazing picture-drawer! Snatched from his parents at birth and raised by rats in the basement of the Smithsonian! Only one dollar!"*

It was starting to get dark as Jorgensen crossed over the narrow bridge to the barrier island, and already the fog was beginning to settle into the low spots. He thought of Boyd Davies, sitting alone in his cell in Brushy Mountain. Poor Boyd. Except for a handful of drawings, his whole life was probably nothing but fog.

TWELVE

Jorgensen spent a couple of days getting ready for winter. That meant mending the shrimp nets, folding them up, and putting them into barrels; carrying in a week's worth of firewood, in order to keep it dry; shutting off the water to the outside hose, draining the pipe to it, and pouring in a little antifreeze to keep anything he might have missed from bursting the fittings; and doing some caulking around the portholes—at least those he could reach from the ground, or with a stepladder.

That left the biggest job of all, dragging the catboat out of the water. But he wasn't quite ready to do that yet—not only because it was backbreaking work that would take him half a day, but because, even though it was already November, he was determined to get in one last sail before mothballing her.

His chance came one morning at the end of the week when, even before he'd stepped outside, he knew from the spray on the windward portholes that there was a crisp offshore breeze blowing. With the wind coming directly out of the east, it would be something of a struggle to get out past the breakers. But there'd be a payoff: once he was beyond them, he'd be able to pick his course at will, without having to worry about getting back in; the same breeze he'd have to fight going out would carry him home safely.

He found Jake nosing around at a crab hole in the sand. "You up for a sail, mate?"

If the old dog didn't really understand, he sure did a good

job of pretending. Tail wagging, entire body wagging (if indeed a body can wag), he all but knocked the old man over, rushing past him on the narrow pathway that led through the spartina grass and down to the dinghy.

It took them a series of tacks to get out. The one-sail design of the catboat made for poor pointing upwind, and they were forced to zigzag—first to port, then to starboard, then back to port—over and over again. Each time they came about, they'd lose a little headway: The sail would luff for a moment, and the waves would slap against the hull, stopping their momentum and occasionally even pushing them back toward shore. But the cat had a fixed keel, with a leaded core for ballast. It was shallow enough to let them glide over the shoals and sandbars without running aground, but long and heavy enough to minimize drifting. Bit by bit, tack by tack, they made headway, and gradually Jorgensen was able to see that the shoreline was receding behind them, and the lighthouse was getting smaller.

Once safely over the breakers, Jorgensen swung the tiller one last time and set a north-northwesterly course, or at least a pretty good approximation of one. He carried no compass, other than the internal one he'd inherited from his Scandinavian ancestors, and that had always proved pretty accurate. In fact, he had nothing on board more sophisticated than a folding knife, a screwdriver, and a bailing can. Marge had been after him for years to buy a little outboard motor, but doing so would have meant registering the boat, and registering it in turn would have meant insuring it. So instead he paid attention to the wind and the weather and the tides, and they hadn't let him down yet. And if they ever did, if some monster squall suddenly appeared from out of nowhere and knocked them over, or some rogue wave decided to crash over their bow and swamp them? Well, to August Jorgensen's way of thinking, there were worse ways to die.

But today there would be no monster squalls to knock them over, no rogue waves to swamp them. Only a long starboard reach in the morning sun, followed by a good run back to shore—a satisfying end to the season.

And that afternoon, while there were still a couple of hours of daylight left, he rigged a bowline to the winch he'd welded to the front of his truck, and let Thomas Edison do the work dragging the old catboat out of the water and up onto her winter cradle.

He spent the following morning chocking the hull so she wouldn't slip. He removed, cleaned, folded, and stored the sail. He scraped a season's worth of barnacles and algae from the keel and the underside. He thought about putting on a coat of anti-fouling paint, but decided he'd be better off waiting until spring, when the surface would be good and dry and take the paint better. Finally, he draped her with plastic tarps and secured them with nylon cord, leaving only the mast uncovered. With the boat no longer swinging free at her mooring to show him the direction and strength of the wind, her landlocked mast would serve as his winter flagpole, its red pennant the only telltale he'd need.

His work done, he whistled for Jake and took a drive to the post office. His electric bill was a month or so past due, and even though the folks over at Santee Cooper had learned to put up with his irregular payments, he didn't like to abuse their kindness.

Edna Coombs, the postmistress who'd been retiring for at least eleven years, kept lollipops for the kids and treats for the dogs behind her window, so Jake was always the first one through the door. Jorgensen waited while he and Edna got reacquainted, then handed over his envelope.

"Thirty-four cents," said Edna.

"Thirty-*four*? What happened to thirty-*three*?"

Edna reminded him that it had gone up a penny, way back in January. Jorgensen nodded absently. It seemed only yesterday that stamps were purple, and it cost three cents to mail a letter. Or you use a one-cent green one and stick it on a post card. Penny post cards, they used to call them. A nickel would get you a whole Coke, one that came in a bottle made out of real glass, not that plastic stuff they used today. And a dime? A dime would get you into the picture show, where you could hunker down and spend half a day watching a newsreel, a couple of Tom and Jerry cartoons, a Bill and Coo short, and a double-feature.

"Thirty-four cents," Edna was saying again.

He fished around in his pockets until he came up with two quarters. "Put the change in my account for next time," he told her, "and make sure you keep track of the interest. Got anything for me?" They both understood that his *anything* meant any mail worth opening. Edna had long ago taken it upon herself to weed out the catalogs, credit card offerings, sweepstakes announcements, and other junk mail Jorgensen had no patience for.

"As a matter of fact, I do," said Edna. She pretended to search around for it, but Jorgensen knew that was just for show, to impress him with how busy she was, and how much stuff she had back there. "Ahh," she said after a minute, "here it is." And handed him a package.

But this was no ordinary package, Jorgensen could see; this was how packages used to be. The size of a shoebox, wrapped in well-used brown paper, and all tied up in white cotton string with lots of knots. Instead of bearing one of those postage meter stickers, it had real stamps, a whole row of them. And his name and address hadn't been typed or printed on a label by one of those machines. No, it had been written by hand, and—if he was any judge—slowly and meticulously, the work of someone to whom writing was definitely not second nature.

"You been expectin' it?" Edna asked him. She was a bit of a busybody, as they used to say, who liked to know whatever there was to know about her customers.

"No," said Jorgensen, "can't say that I have been." He tucked it under his arm.

"Well, don'tcha want to see what's in it?"

"I probably will," allowed Jorgensen, "I probably will." And opened the door for Jake.

Back home, he placed the package on his kitchen table and studied it. There was no return address, and the postmarks (there were several, to cover all the stamps) were all too smudged to read.

Back when he'd been on the bench, a federal agent had come around, from Postal Inspection or Secret Service, or maybe ATF, warning Jorgensen and his colleagues to be on the lookout for suspicious-looking packages. It seemed some district judge over in the Fifth Circuit had had three fingers blown off when he'd opened up a box mailed by a defendant who hadn't been too pleased with his sentence.

Well, if ever anything looked suspicious, thought Jorgensen, this certainly fit the bill. But then again, who on earth would want to blow him up? Just about everyone he'd ever sentenced had finished doing their time long ago, or died trying to. He found a pair of scissors, snipped the string, and slit open the paper.

Inside, just as he'd guessed, was a shoebox, an old beat-up one with the name THOM McCANN printed on the lid. He remembered Thom McCanns well. No-nonsense shoes, folks used to call them. He tried to remember if they were the same as Buster Browns, or different.

> *Hi, my name's Buster Brown,*
> *And I live in a shoe.*
> *This is my dog, Ty—*
> *He lives here, too.*

Or something like that.

He lifted the lid off the box. No flash of light blinded him; no deafening explosion shattered his eardrums. Instead, he found himself looking down at a letter, a single-paged letter written in the same hand that had addressed the package. Using the tips of his fingers (all ten of which had somehow managed to survive the opening of the package), he lifted it up, noticing as he did that underneath it lay a stack of more letters, older ones from the look of them, tied together with faded blue ribbon.

Dear Mr Judge,

They tell me you are the new lawer for Boy. I am his sister. My name is Nell. First of all I want to thank you for help my brother. Even if he did what they say and I gues he must of he is not a bad person. He never lern to read or rite. He try but his brane is no good at lest it is not the same as other fokes.

Ever since our mama got sick and cant travel no more I am the onliest one to visit Boy at Brushy Mt. I use to go ever month so I can rite a letter and tell Mama how her one sun is. After mama pass I dont go ever month but I still go when I cans.

When Mama pass and my sisters and I clean out her things from her closit we find all the letters I ever rite her about Boy in a shoe box all tie up just like this. I dont no if they help you but may be so. I hope so.

Please do not contack me as I have a new husban and he do not no about Boy and I am a fraid he will leave me and my babys if he find out and I can not a ford that.

Ever nite I pray to Jesus to bless Boy and now I will pray for Him to bless you to for helping Boy.

Nell McDaniel Ashworth

He read the letter twice through before replacing it in the shoebox. What kind of a man, he wondered, would leave his wife because of sins committed by her afflicted brother? Plenty, he decided. And what good would a stack of old letters do him? None that he could think of. The fact was, they were all hearsay, the words not of Boyd Davies himself, but of one of his sisters. Boyd Davies had no words. And August Jorgensen had no appetite for reading a bunch of old letters assuring an ailing mother that her autistic son was doing just fine on death row. He laid Nell's "Dear Mr. Judge" letter on top of the rest of them, and replaced the lid on the box. "Save them for a rainy day," his mother used to tell him.

Well, there'd be plenty of those.

And this business about Nell's praying for Jorgensen to be blessed? He had to chuckle at the thought of that. A lifelong atheist in a state full of Southern Baptists, he'd been forced to answer a lot of pointed questions at his confirmation hearing, when subjects like abortion, creationism, and separation between church and state had come up. And now Jesus himself was being asked to bless Jorgensen's appearance before the Supreme Court.

Hell, he figured. *Why not?* Or as folks liked to say nowadays, *What's the down side to it?*

There was none, of course.

Then again, if Jorgensen's memory served him, that Jesus fellow hadn't fared too well in his own battle against the death penalty, had he? If you wanted to look at it that way.

Three days before Thanksgiving, Jessica Woodruff received a telephone call from Linda Greenhouse. Like Jessica, Linda was a lawyer who'd managed to find employment on the other side of the bar: Linda made her living covering the United States Supreme Court for *The New York Times.* But "covered" hardly did justice to Linda's reporting. Her analyses and commentaries—which often began at the top of Page One—were so informative and insightful that she'd long ago become required reading for most of the nation's constitutional scholars.

On top of that, Linda had been a friend of Jessica's since law school days.

"I just thought you might like to know," she said now, "the Court's scheduling order came out today."

"Oh?" said Jessica.

"And oral argument on the Davies case has been set down for April tenth."

"How much are they giving us?" Jessica asked.

"Each side gets forty-five minutes."

"Not exactly *Bush versus Gore,* huh?"

"No," Linda agreed. "But it could have been worse. A lot of them get only half an hour."

"I guess you're right."

"Are you going to argue it?"

"Me? No way."

"Larry Tribe?"

"No," said Jessica. "And you have exactly one more guess."

"David Boise."

Jessica did her best impersonation of a buzzer, signifying a final wrong answer.

"How about telling me off the record?" Linda asked.

One thing about Linda: When she said off the record, it was off the record. Still, Jessica said, "Promise?" It was her way of letting Linda know she really didn't want this to get out.

"Honest Native American," said Linda.

"Okay," said Jessica. "We've reached deep into the retired judges' geriatric ward."

A silence on the other end told her Linda was stumped. Supreme Court justices tended to die, rather than retire. "I give up," Linda said.

"August Jorgensen."

"August Jorgensen? Is he still alive?"

"I think so," Jessica said. "Though every once in a while, I'm tempted to check for a pulse."

"Where'd you dig him—, I mean, where'd you find him?"

"I've got to tell you," said Jessica, "it wasn't easy. He lives all alone in this dilapidated, falling-down lighthouse, halfway into the ocean. Heats the thing with logs. And get this: The guy doesn't have a phone. Can you believe it?"

"So what's your thinking?"

"Are we still off the record?"

"You know we are."

"Linda, what do you think our chances are on this one?"

There was only the briefest of pauses before Linda answered, "Somewhere between slim and none."

"I think you're being charitable with the slim part."

"So you've decided to go down to defeat with venerable dignity?"

"Something like that," said Jessica.

"Well, good luck."

"Thanks. And I appreciate the heads-up."

April tenth. That was early in the term but still almost five months away. Jessica toyed with the idea of dictating a letter to Jorgensen, so he could circle the date. But then she decided against it: There was simply no need at this point. It wasn't like he was carrying a caseload, like other lawyers, and might have a scheduling conflict. No, they'd let him know a month or so ahead of time, give him enough time to leave a bowl of food out for his dog.

For August Jorgensen, the next rainy day came sooner than expected. He awoke two mornings later to what he considered a medium fog. (A medium fog was one you could actually see in, and occasionally even see through. By way of contrast, a heavy fog was one that obscured absolutely everything, so that when you looked out one of the lighthouse's portholes, you had the sensation that someone had draped a gray blanket over it from the outside.)

Within the hour, the fog had become supersaturated with moisture, which had begun to precipitate out as rain. When that happened, the fog dissipated to a certain extent, and the visibility became better. But if you went outside, instead of just getting damp from the fog, you got good and wet from the rain, and—this time of year, at least—good and cold, as well.

So Jorgensen cracked the door open just enough to let Jake

slip out. When you were a Labrador retriever, damp was okay, but wet and cold—they were your briar patch.

Then the old man slid another log into the stove, gave it a poke to get it going, and reached for the Thom McCann shoebox. Settling into the chair closest to the stove, he lifted off the lid of the box, put Nell's cover letter to one side, and removed the rest of them, the ones tied together with the faded blue ribbon. None of the letters was dated, and it took him a moment to figure out that the most recent were on the top, so after he'd untied the ribbon, he turned the stack over, so that he could start at the beginning.

Dear Mama,

I went to the prison yestaday at Brushy Mt. It is a scary place when you first see it with a grate big wall. But onst you get use to it it is ok I guess. When they fond out I was ther to see Boy they was nice to me. I think they like him cause he is so quite and he dont give them no truble.

Boy is ok he reely is. He dont say nuthin but I can tell he recanize me. In a way I dont think been in prison will be as hard for Boy as it wood be for most fokes if you no what I means. They give him food and close and look after him. He was pretty clean to. Acourse Boy is never to clean if you no what I means. Ha. You rememba the time he came home afta plane in the mud down by the riva and alls you cood see of him was his 2 eyes. Rememba how we laff and laff. Even Boy laff that time.

O Mama there bees to much pane in this worl. I miss you and send you my love.

Your dawter Nell

Too much pain, indeed. Jorgensen put down the letter. He'd intended to work his way through the entire stack, hoping that in the process he'd somehow get to know Boyd Davies a little better. Already he was beginning to realize he might have been wrong, that there simply might be no getting to know Boyd at all. Maybe the most you could ever come away with was an image of a young man so covered with mud that only his eyes were visible. But then again, he'd laughed; or at least Nell had remembered him laughing. That was something, wasn't it?

And as he sat there that morning by his stove, it occurred to August Jorgensen that, sooner or later, he was going to have to give it another try. He was going to have to go back to Brushy Mountain and somehow get through to Boyd Davies, whatever it took.

A single bark brought him out of his thoughts. He pushed himself up from the chair, walked to the door, and opened it. Jake, ever thoughtful, shook himself off before entering. Jorgensen found a dry towel. Jake obediently buried his nose between the old man's legs, as if to suggest that while he had no use for the rubdown that was about to come, he'd suffer through it nonetheless just to please his master. Jorgensen's own private suspicion was that Jake absolutely loved it, but was too embarrassed to let the smile on his face be seen.

"Better get some rest," he told the dog. "As soon as the weather clears up, you and I are going to be hitting the road again."

THIRTEEN

The Wall at Brushy Mountain was every bit as imposing as it had been the first time. Jorgensen was waved through to the parking area, and found a spot for the truck in the visitor's section. Walking through the main gate, he tried his best to look straight ahead or down at his feet; still, he couldn't help noticing the gun towers and the coils of razor wire looming above him.

He went through the sign-in procedure, the metal-detector drill, and the waiting. Again it took almost an hour before he was finally ushered into the counsel visit room. But August Jorgensen was a good waiter. Over the course of his eighty-plus years, he'd come to learn that the longer you had to wait for something, the more you appreciated it when it finally happened. All of a sudden, you were so grateful that the waiting was over, you completely forgot how annoying it had been.

Boyd Davies sat in the same chair, at the same table, as he had the first time they met. If he recognized Jorgensen, or even remembered their earlier visit, he gave no sign of it. And yet, thought Jorgensen, this was the same young man who, from nothing but memory, had created a likeness of the older man that was absolutely photographic in its accuracy.

In fact, Jorgensen had brought the drawing along, and now, withdrawing it from his folder and smoothing out the creases, he placed it on the table between them, in such a way as to face Boyd Davies. And although Boyd didn't look down at it, as anyone else might have been expected to do, Jorgensen was quite certain that he took it in just the same, with the most fleeting of sidewise glances.

"This is very good," said the old man, speaking slowly, the way one might speak to a child, or to one whose grasp of English was severely limited. "Very, very good."

There was no reaction from Boyd, no indication whatsoever that he'd even heard the words, let alone understood their meaning. No hint of a smile at the fact that his achievement had been appreciated, his talent recognized. Jorgensen turned the paper over, exposing its blank side. He took a pencil from his jacket pocket, pushed it across the table. "Can you do it again?" he asked.

He half-thought he saw Boyd shrug his shoulders ever so slightly, but he might have been wrong—it might have been nothing more than a tic, a tiny involuntary muscle spasm. Or it might even have been Jorgensen's own imagination, engaging in an exercise of wishful thinking. "Do it again," he said, this time turning what had been a question into an instruction. Then he turned his face away to one side, as if to soften the imperative aspect of his words just a bit.

They sat like that for a full fifteen minutes, a period of time that would have been an absolute eternity in any normal human relationship. But in a sense, August Jorgensen was no more normal a human than was Boyd Davies. He'd spent more than eighty years on the planet, but his closest companions had come to be the sea and the wind and the fog. His only living friend had four legs, a wet nose, and a tail. He'd chosen to live a monk's life in a modern world. And somewhere along the way, he'd gained a capacity for patience. He could wait out blackouts, whiteouts, storms, entire seasons. He could sit at that table for an hour, if he had to. Hell, he could sit there at the visiting table for a week, if they'd let him.

But they wouldn't have to.

Boyd Davies had picked up the pencil. He was drawing.

At first, Jorgensen was afraid to look, or even move. But he needn't have been. As he gradually turned back to the table, he realized that Boyd was paying him no attention: It was as though Boyd were sitting there alone, with only the paper and pencil. Jorgensen could have been a million miles away, for all Boyd seemed to care.

But down on that tabletop, on that piece of paper, something extraordinary was happening, something just short of a miracle. When Jorgensen had sat in front of the computer with young Zachary, in the back room of Pop Crawford's general store, the boy had fiddled with the keyboard and clicked away with that mouse thing of his, and images had appeared on the screen. Some of them had popped up right away, but others—color photographs, for example—had developed more slowly, from top to bottom or left to right, until they were complete. Now that same electronic process was occurring on the piece of paper. A likeness of Jorgensen was appearing—materializing was the only word to describe it—materializing from the tip of the pencil, and spreading out from the upper-left-hand corner to the rest of the page.

It took only ten minutes, fifteen at most. When he was done, Boyd simply laid the pencil down and looked away. Jorgensen had to reach across the table for the completed drawing and slide it toward himself. It was quite remarkable: Without once turning it over to make reference to the earlier drawing, Boyd had somehow succeeded in replicating it, almost perfectly.

But not quite.

For August Jorgensen was looking at a likeness of himself that was distinctly less world-weary than the one on the flip side. He wasn't quite smiling, but there was something more upbeat about him, more resolute. Though, as he turned the sheet over and over, comparing his two faces, he'd have been hard-pressed to point to a single detail that had contributed the change.

"I'm going to come back tomorrow," he told Boyd, "and I'm going to ask you to draw some more."

And though Jorgensen might not have been willing to stake

his life on it, he was almost certain that some part of Boyd shifted or moved ever so slightly, as if to tell him that would be all right.

Jorgensen went back the following day as promised, and asked Boyd to draw pictures of his mother and his sisters, and Boyd did. And although Jorgensen had never seen so much as a photograph of any of the subjects, and therefore had no idea what they looked like, he had no doubt he was looking at them now, through Boyd's eyes, exactly as they'd once appeared to him.

In one of the drawings, Hattie McDaniel looked to be about twenty years old, her eyes clear and her skin so smooth and youthful that Jorgensen had to fight the impulse to reach out and touch her cheek. Thinking about her that night, back at his motel, it occurred to him that if he was right about Hattie's age in the drawing, it meant that at the time she'd looked like that, Boyd himself could have been no more than two or three. Yet somehow that image of his mother had seared itself into his memory at that tender age. And now, a third of a century later, because of some freakish accident to his brain, he was able to tap that memory as though it had been only yesterday, and effortlessly and flawlessly recreate it on a piece of $8^{1}/_{2} \times 11"$ paper.

Jorgensen had planned to drive home the following morning, a Friday, and had even told Jake as much—not that he was convinced the dog understood him. (Then again, no one could convince him the dog didn't; and when it came to Jake, he was strongly inclined to place the burden of proof not upon the believer, but upon the doubter. So he kept telling Jake things, the way a young mother might speak to her newborn, or an expectant one to her belly.)

But the implications of that one drawing kept tugging at him, denying him sleep. What were the limits of Boyd's memory? Or were there none? Could he recall the moment of his birth? Could he reach back even further, to when he sat coiled *inside* his mother? Too bad the lighting conditions were so poor in there; but for that, Jorgensen might have been able to test his hypothesis.

He felt Jake shift his weight at the foot of the bed, and heard an exaggerated, long-suffering sigh, the dog's way of letting Jorgensen know that his insomnia was contagious.

Discovering Boyd's earliest possible memory was interesting, but only in the most academic sort of way: It did nothing in terms of helping Jorgensen argue on behalf of his client. What was the issue again? Ah, yes, Boyd Davies' ability—or inability—to connect his crime to his punishment. Suppose Jorgensen were to go back to Brushy Mountain once more in the morning, and ask Boyd to draw what it was going to be like to be strapped down to a gurney, to feel a needle inserted in his arm, and to hold his breath as long as he could, in a doomed attempt to fight off the poison they were pushing into his vein and toward his heart.

The old man looked to the foot of his bed, causing the dog to raise his head and open one eye expectantly. "What say," Jorgensen asked, "we put off leaving until tomorrow afternoon?"

He was answered with another sigh, even more mournful than the first.

Boyd was at a loss. He looked at the blank sheet of paper Jorgensen had placed in front of him, reached for the pencil and picked it up. But unlike the exercises of the past two days, this was one he evidently couldn't fathom. To Jorgensen, it was almost as if the pencil had no more drawings in it; it had finally run dry.

So Boyd wasn't going to be able to help himself with his talent, after all. He couldn't picture his punishment, because he'd never glimpsed it in real life. It was an idea, something still off in the future, an abstraction. And in Boyd Davies' universe, there were no abstractions.

If Boyd had no way of comprehending his punishment, he certainly had no way of comprehending its connection to his crime. But how did Jorgensen go about demonstrating that to the court? He couldn't very well show them a blank piece of paper and say, "See, he can't even visualize what they're going to do with him." It would be contrived—contrived and pointless.

The trip back had been a waste of Boyd's time and his. In fact, the whole trip had been a waste. He'd ended up with some nice drawings, but nothing more. No insights, no breakthroughs, no ammunition. He looked across the table, imagined he saw disappointment on Boyd's face, realized it had to be his own projection. People like Boyd didn't feel disappointment. Disappointment was a construct of emotions, a concept, and was therefore beyond them. Still, he *looked* disappointed, the corners of his mouth turned down, what, maybe a millimeter? And why shouldn't he be? Jorgensen had come back to visit him, and had asked him to draw again, and he couldn't. What a cruel way to be left.

Later on, Jorgensen would look back and recall his own thought process at the time. He'd needed to let Boyd down easy, he realized, if not for Boyd (whose disappointment had almost certainly been a figment of Jorgensen's imagination), then for himself (whose guilt over causing it had been real). So he'd tried to come up with a remedy, the way he used to do as a judge, once a litigant had proven that there had been a wrong committed. The remedy he'd decided on was to ask Boyd to draw something he *could* draw, something he'd actually seen. Originally, he'd wanted a drawing of Boyd's punishment; that had turned out to be impossible. He rubbed his eyes, played a quick game of word association with himself.

Punishment?

Crime.

But surely that would be too painful, too cruel. Then again, would it really be? Only, he decided, if Boyd was capable of experiencing guilt. But guilt was a complicated concept, one that required a blending of understanding, responsibility, and regret. Guilt had to be every bit as alien a notion to Boyd Davies as quantum theory was to August Jorgensen.

Or so he convinced himself.

And turning back to Boyd, he'd leaned forward and lowered his voice. "Draw me the day the little girl died," he said. "Draw the killing for me, Boyd."

"Draw up a proposal for me," Elizabeth Algren told Jessica Woodruff over martinis. Elizabeth Algren was rumored to be the daughter of the writer Nelson Algren. And if she wasn't, she was smart enough not to deny it. Her married name was Cippolini, but she retained Algren as her business name. And since her business was running a literary agency, she figured it didn't hurt.

"Draw up a proposal," she said again. "You know, a summary, a first chapter, and a rough outline of where you want to go with it."

They were sitting at a corner table at Anglers and Writers, a fitting enough selection to discuss a book idea. Jessica had been working on it off-and-on for nearly a year, but until now she'd been afraid to tell anyone about it. It struck her as, well, just a wee bit unseemly, at this point. So she'd confided only in Brandon Davidson (who'd assured her it was nothing less than a brilliant idea) and one or two others. But with oral argument already scheduled, she'd decided it was time to start putting out feelers. Five months was a blink of the eye. Besides, Liz Algren was more than a literary agent; she was a friend. She could be trusted.

"I absolutely love the concept," Liz was saying, "and if we time the release right . . . Well, let me put it this way: The publicity could be an absolute windfall for us. What are we going to call it again?"

Jessica took a sip of her martini, regretted that she hadn't ordered a sea breeze or a continental. But this was a book meeting, and she hadn't wanted to come off like a wimp. "Actually," she said, "I haven't come up with a title yet."

"How about 'Drawings from Beyond,'" Liz suggested, "or 'Drawings from the Grave?'"

"Not bad," said Jessica. "Or maybe, 'Dead Man Drawing.'"

"I'm afraid you're too late, sweetie. That was a movie. Sean Penn, Susan Sarandon—"

"Exactly," said Jessica. "Only that was '*Dead Man* Walking.' 'Dead Man *Drawing*' would be a play off it. See, in prison, a guy on death row, they refer to him as a dead man walking. You know, like he's still walking around, but he's already dead?"

"You can do better," said Liz. "But don't worry about it. The publishing house will end up calling it whatever they want, they always do. They've got focus groups and all that kind of stuff to help them know what'll make Oprah happy, what'll work with the book clubs, what fits on the best-seller lists. Listen, hon, what do you say we order? I'm absolutely famished."

August Jorgensen stared at the drawing in front of him. He'd asked Boyd to draw him the killing, the day the little girl died. And to a certain extent, Boyd had complied. What Jorgensen was looking at was a picture of a man, a man carrying the lifeless body of a child in his arms.

The first thing that struck Jorgensen was the perspective. Boyd's sense of perspective was always flawless, just like that of the other autistic savants Jorgensen had read about on Zachary's computer screen. In fact, had this been a photograph—and, like all of Boyd's drawings, it very much resembled a photograph, except for the fact that it was done in pencil, and on regular paper—Jorgensen would have guessed that it had been shot from slightly below, say from ground level, looking upward at the subject.

The next thing that got his attention was the man's face.

Although his eyes were hidden behind mirrored sunglasses, Jorgensen could still feel the pain on his face. His lips were slightly parted, his teeth visibly clenched beneath them, and though there was no real way to tell if his grimace reflected the horrible sorrow of the moment or simply the physical weight of the burden in his arms, Jorgensen *knew*. And neither pain nor sorrow began to describe it. It was anguish Jorgensen was looking at, torture, pure undistilled agony.

And there was one other thing about the man's face that struck Jorgensen.

It was white.

Not white, as though it were wintertime and he'd been spending too much time indoors, or had just that moment thought he'd seen a ghost.

White, as in Caucasian.

Had Boyd misunderstood what Jorgensen had asked him to draw? Instead of drawing the moment of the killing, had he drawn the recovery of the little girl's body? And if he had, what did that say about him? That he was still too racked by guilt to picture—either for Jorgensen or for himself—what he himself had done sixteen years ago?

The implications of that were at once comforting and frightening. Comforting, because experiencing guilt made Boyd Davies human and frail and pitiable. But frightening, because if Boyd could feel guilt, it meant he was capable of making the connection between his act and its consequences. From there, what a tiny step it would be for the state to argue persuasively that he could also connect his act to his punishment.

Jorgensen wanted to tear up the drawing, crumple it up into a ball, but he was afraid to do so in front of Boyd, its creator. He'd wait until he was outside. This much was certain: There was no way he could let it fall into enemy hands.

He tried to remember from his reading of the file they'd left him, or of the narrative account they'd told him, just who it was that had found the body of young Ilsa Meisner. There'd been a bloodhound, he recalled, that had led some deputy sheriff or other member of the search team to the grave site. That must be the man whose tortured face he was looking at now. Rural areas weren't like big cities when it came to stuff like this, Jorgensen knew. Chances were, the deputy had known the Meisner family, might have sat next to them in church each Sunday. Perhaps his daughter had baby-sat for little Ilsa, or had been in her class at school. Things had a way of getting personal in small towns, of hitting home.

Maybe, thought Jorgensen, it might not be a bad idea to save the drawing after all, see if he could find out who the deputy was. If Boyd Davies had seen him well enough to draw him from memory sixteen years later, carrying the little girl's body like that, didn't that mean the deputy would have had to have seen Boyd at the very same moment? Mightn't he be able to describe Boyd's reaction at seeing the result of his acts? The deputy didn't look that old in the drawing, thirty-five or forty, at most. Maybe he was still alive. Maybe he could help. Nothing else seemed to be helping, that much seemed sure.

FOURTEEN

The deputy who had dug up the body of little Ilsa Meisner had been a man named Whitey Alverson. He'd been sixty-one years old at the time, with a beer belly and a head of hair to match his nickname. The highway officer who had taken over for Alverson and carried Ilsa out to the coroner's station wagon had been Rufus Catterson, a dark-skinned black man. At all times thereafter, the body had been transported on a stretcher. All this Jorgensen found out over the course of three weeks and a dozen trips to Pop Crawford's pay phone. The only thing he didn't know was where it all left him.

Pop used his fax machine to make copies of the drawing, and Jorgensen sent one off to Boyd's sister Nell, being careful not to refer to the murder, just in case Nell's husband were to see it. She wrote back that she had no idea who the man in the picture was.

He sent another copy to Jessica Woodruff. He got a letter back from her (actually, from some intern at the studio), in which she questioned the relevance of the man's identity to the issues in the upcoming argument. But she promised to have one of their investigators try to track him down, if that would make him happy.

He hunkered down for winter, spent a fogbound Christmas day, and brooded. He knew the Supreme Court's scheduling order should be out by now, but nobody had told him.

Nobody ever told him anything.

He dug out the envelope in which he kept all of Boyd Davies' drawings—the ones Jessica had first left with him, the two of himself, the ones of Hattie and Nell, and the latest one, of the man carrying the lifeless body of Ilsa Meisner. He spread them all out on the table in front of him, looking for clues, searching for messages.

"Speak to me," he said, "help me." But no answer came. And if someone had happened to be in the lighthouse at the time, standing over his shoulder, August Jorgensen would have been hard-pressed to explain whom he was addressing— the drawings, the faces depicted in them, Boyd Davies, or some god whose very existence he doubted.

Jessica Woodruff was beginning to doubt her sanity for having enlisted August Jorgensen in the first place. "He sent me a copy of some drawing he got from Davies," she told Tim Harkin and Ray Gilbert on a conference call. "He wants us to tell him who carried the deceased's body after they discovered it."

"Why should he think that has any relevance?" Harkin wanted to know.

"Exactly."

"Are we sure this dude's still got it together?" Gilbert asked. "I mean, it's beginning to sound like you picked someone who's got an advanced case of old-timer's disease."

"Don't you do that to me, Ray," snapped Jessica. "You guys signed off on him, remember. You said he'd add a measure of *gravitas* to it."

"Don't worry," said Harkin, "he'll be okay. So what did you tell him?"

"Tell him? The old coot has no phone, remember? I can't tell him anything. I had Ginny send him a letter, told him we'd do our best to identify the guy for him."

"Good, good," said Gilbert. "Humor him, stroke him. And when we get a month or so away from the argument, we'll reevaluate the situation, see if he's up to it. If not, there's plenty of names out there who'll jump at the chance."

"To argue a case like this?" asked Jessica. "On two weeks notice?"

Professor Gilbert laughed into the phone. "On two hours notice," he said. "Not everyone's senile, you know. Or living in some godforsaken lighthouse, surrounded by fog."

The only fog surrounding August Jorgensen at that particular moment was a mental one. Outside, the air and water temperature were close enough to produce an equilibrium, a truce of sorts that would more or less hold until early spring. Then dry, warmer breezes would drift over the still-cold ocean, producing an instability where the two met, an instability that would set the stage for a whole new season of fog.

Was he deluding himself? Was he so taken by the intricacies of Boyd's pictures, so fascinated by the paradox of one who couldn't speak but could draw like a camera, that he'd convinced himself the images could tell him a story when in fact they couldn't? They were drawings, after all. Nothing more, nothing less. Drawings done by a man who was incapable of conceptualizing, editorializing, or imparting hidden messages. What you saw was what you got, as the saying went. And yet, he couldn't stop staring at them. Particularly the one of the man carrying the girl.

Jorgensen had always wanted to be a pilot. As a boy, he'd dreamed of flying fighters in the war. Not to bomb civilians below, or knock out MIGs or Zeros, but just to *soar*. His dreams were always about climbing, banking, rolling and diving; the killing was never a part of them. But he'd been too young for Europe, too nearsighted for Korea, and too old for Vietnam, and he'd had to settle instead for the cockpit of his living room, devouring every aviation book he'd been able to get his hands on. Of all the things he'd come across, one had stuck with him the longest. He'd been reading a study about young pilots who'd been shot down by enemy aircraft they'd never seen. The common denominator in each case had been this: The pilot had been so intent on scouring the horizon for planes approaching in the distance, that he'd failed to notice one almost on top of him until it had been too late to react. As incredible as it sounded, it kept happening over and over again, often with fatal consequences. *Relax,* was the lesson the trainers learned from the phenomenon and passed on in flight school, relax and take in the whole picture. The older pilots—the ones who'd somehow learned to do it—swore it worked like magic. And they had their lives to prove it.

So Jorgensen tried relaxing. Looking at the drawing, he stopped squinting, instead opened his eyes wider, allowing the muscles around them to slacken. Stepped back from the table a foot or so, took a deep breath. Exhaled. Took another. Stood there for five minutes like that, trying not to miss anything by looking for it too hard, doing his best to take in the whole picture.

And, like magic, it worked.

At first, he thought his eyes might be playing tricks with him, thought maybe he'd made it up. He looked away, then back again. Counted once, twice, a third time, just to make sure.

He was right, and it was the drawing of the man carrying the girl. If you looked too hard, you missed it every time; but if you relaxed it was plain as day: The way the man was carrying the girl, both of his hands were completely visible. If you squinted and peered and concentrated too hard, you ended up thinking that part of his right hand was obscured by her clothing. But when you stepped back, you saw that simply wasn't so.

And the thing of it was this: The man's right hand—the one that seemed to be partially covered by the girl's clothing, but in fact wasn't—had only three fingers.

––––––––

Jorgensen's first reaction, upon satisfying himself that he was correct, was to wonder if maybe Boyd Davies hadn't simply made a mistake. But as he considered the likelihood of that, he realized that for that to have been the case, it would have had to have occurred in one of three areas: an error in perception at the time, a lapse of memory over the years, or a failure to accurately reproduce an image on paper. But to Jorgensen, none of those possibilities seemed plausible. Boyd had trouble with all sorts of tasks; you could write a book about the myriad of things he couldn't do, like speaking and reading and writing and conceptualizing the way other people could. But in terms of seeing something, remembering what he'd seen, and drawing it later on, Boyd had no match among mortals. When it came to those three things, the gods themselves had to be envious.

No, thought Jorgensen, Boyd hadn't made a mistake; he wasn't capable of it. If Boyd said so—and his drawing was his way of saying so—then some unidentified, three-fingered deputy sheriff (or state trooper, or other member of the search team) had carried the lifeless body of Ilsa Meisner as Boyd had watched from nearby, crouching or lying on the ground. Sure, all of that had happened sixteen years ago. But how hard could it be to track down a man with three fingers on his left hand, to see what light he could shed on Boyd's understanding of what he'd just done to the poor girl.

If indeed Boyd had had any understanding at all.

Jorgensen wished he could get in touch with Nell, Boyd's sister. She'd been around at the time the body was discovered; maybe she could be of some help here. But Nell had specifically asked Jorgensen not to contact her, and he'd done so once already. He didn't want to further risk jeopardizing her marriage to her new husband by letting him know there was a murderer lurking in the family.

So he found Jake and took another ride to the general store. He was beginning to regret not having a phone in the lighthouse, but imagined it would take a good two weeks to get the folks from Horry to come out and install one. By that time

he'd no doubt be ready to have it disconnected. He decided
he'd just have to keep making do with the one on Pop Crawford's wall, at least until he'd exhausted Pop's patience and his
own supply of quarters.

"He's driving me crazy, Brandon."

"He?"

"The judge."

"What now?"

"He just called me from a pay phone. He's carrying on like
he's *The Fugitive,* on the trail of some three-fingered man."

"Calm down, Jessica. You told me yourself, he's a harmless
old man."

"I know, I know. But all we asked him to do was to stand up
in court for forty-five minutes and look dignified. Instead he's
plugging into the Internet, researching the entire history of
autism, running back and forth to that prison, getting Davies
to draw all sorts of pictures for him, and God knows what else.
Where's it all going to end?"

"It's going to end," said Davidson, "when they uphold the
Court of Appeals decision, vacate the stay, and tell some war-
den to pull the switch."

"The IV."

"What?"

"There's no switch any more," Jessica explained. "Virginia's
joined the ranks of the lethal-injection states."

"How come?"

"I don't know. Too many heads bursting into orange
flames, I guess."

"Do you know," said Davidson, "that we're the only civilized nation in the world that still has the death penalty?"

"Actually, you're wrong about that."

"Oh?"

"*No* civilized nation still has the death penalty."

"Now *that*," said Davidson, "sounds more like the Jessica Woodruff I know and love. The *fighter*. Listen, don't worry about Johannsen—"

"Jorgensen."

"—Jorgensen. Let him get his rocks off, running around playing Perry Mason. He'll get tired of it soon enough. You didn't lose your cool with him, or anything, did you?"

"No, no," said Jessica. "In fact, I told him I'd put one of our investigators on it, see if he could track down the mysterious three-fingered man."

"Good. He'll be fine, you'll see."

But August Jorgensen was anything but fine. He'd found Jessica Woodruff rather dismissive on the phone. When he'd first gotten through to her—he'd reached her on her cell phone, while she was in the back of a cab on the Queensboro Bridge—she'd had trouble understanding the importance of his new discovery. Then, when Jorgensen had explained how finding the man could shed new light on whether Boyd Davies was able to connect his act to its consequences, she'd turned patronizing, promising to assign an *investigator* to check it out.

Well, Jorgensen didn't need some *investigator* to tell him how many fingers the man had; he'd counted them himself, a hundred times already. She was giving him lip service, is what she was doing.

One of August Jorgensen's admitted shortcomings as an appellate judge had been his inability to delegate responsibility. His budget had allowed him to maintain a staff consisting of two law clerks and a secretary, all full-time employees. A two-year clerkship for a United States Court of Appeals judge was a plum job, and each January graduating law review seniors from Harvard, Michigan, Yale, Columbia, DePaul, and the rest of the country's top law schools had flooded him with more résumés than he could read. He'd tried his best to hire the best and the brightest, while keeping an eye out for women and minorities (a practice unheard of among his all-male, all-white colleagues). They'd turned out to be genuine scholars—almost every one of them—talented researchers and gifted writers. And yet, somehow Jorgensen had always ended up in the stacks himself, hunting down some elusive precedent or arcane footnote, or hunched over his typewriter, putting his personal touch into a decision or a dissent (and there'd been no shortage of dissents), long after everyone else had been home in bed.

He just hadn't been able to help it.

Any more than he could help it now.

It wasn't that Trial TV didn't have good investigators; he was quite sure they did. They certainly had enough money to go out and hire retired FBI agents and CIA sleuths and big-city homicide detectives. The best and the brightest, just like Jorgensen's law clerks. But as capable as they were, they lacked one thing. And that one thing was passion, fire. To everyone else, whether it came down to a matter of writing a legal opinion or picking up a trail grown cold over sixteen years, it was just a job.

To Jorgensen, it would become a mission.

He would go back up to Virginia. He would do it himself. With winter socked in as solid as any fog, what better did he have to do with his time but read and pass the days? He would go to the hill country, to the place where little Ilsa Meisner had had the life choked out of her one September afternoon, long ago. To the place where Wesley Boyd Davies had been arrested, tried, convicted, and sentenced to die. To the place where folks tended to grow old under the same roof where they'd grown up, and would be likely to remember a law enforcement officer missing two fingers on his right hand.

FIFTEEN

Virginia is not so much a single state as many smaller states passing themselves off as one. To the northeast, it is a network of suburbs serving Washington, D.C., going by names like Arlington, Alexandria, Annandale, Reston, and Falls Church. Due south lies Richmond, the state capital, at the hub of crisscrossing interstates. From there, one can continue south through Petersburg and Emporia all the way to the North Carolina border, or east-northeast over to Charlottesville. But a more tempting route lies to the southeast, past Tallysville and Williamsburg and on to where the land meets the ocean. Here lie cities with grander names, like Newport News, Norfolk, Portsmouth, Hampton, and Virginia Beach, guarding the gateway to Chesapeake Bay. Here billionaires do business over lunch at outdoor cafés, gazing out across an azure sea, while hired captains tend their yachts.

And far to the west, there is another Virginia, a Virginia of aromatic spruce and cedar, and breathtaking mountain ranges that together comprise the Appalachians, but whose names invite not so much listing, but singing: Blue Ridge. Cumberland. Allegheny. Black Creek. Shenandoah.

That leaves the south-central part of the state, an expanse that many Virginians would just as well forget about altogether. Here one discovers towns bearing names that are somewhat less pretentious, like South Boston, Red House, Horse Pasture, Motley, Mike, Henry, Mayo, Hurt, Dry Fork,

Union Hall, and Pittsville. There are no fancy capitol buildings here, no azure seas, no majestic mountain ranges. Instead there are dirt farms, trailer parks, feed stores, and filling stations, peopled with poor whites, and even poorer blacks.

This was the part of Virginia that August Jorgensen came to, his red pickup truck bouncing along and kicking up dust behind it. He stopped at three different motels along a twenty-mile stretch of Route 29, but none of the proprietors was interested in putting him up once they heard he had a dog. Finally, just outside of a place called Gretna, he spotted a small sign in front of a blue frame house.

CLEAN ROOMS
SOME WITH BATHS

A black woman answered the door and looked him up and down through thick glasses. "How come the white folks wouldn't take you in?" she asked.

"I'm not too sure," said Jorgensen. "Maybe it's because my dog's black."

She chuckled at that, and said her name was Ruby Mason, and he knew he'd found a place to say. He paid her sixty dollars in cash, to cover the first two nights of his stay, and was pleasantly surprised to learn that breakfast was included, "as long as you can get yerself into the kitchen by eight." He assured her that would be no problem.

They followed her up a well-worn staircase lined with photos of smiling children.

"Dog don't bite, does he?"

"Not once in all the years I've had him."

"You don't think maybe he's been *savin' up,* do you?"

The room was small but, as promised, clean. And it was one of those with a bath, not too far down the hall. Right before she left them alone, Jorgensen removed a piece of paper from his jacket pocket and unfolded it. "Any chance you might recognize this fellow?" he asked her. "Picture's close to twenty years old, but if you look closely you can see he was missing a couple of fingers on one hand."

"Then he most likely still is," said Ruby. "They don't grow back, you know."

"No," he said, "I guess they don't."

She studied the drawing for a minute. "Nope," she said. "Anyway, this here is farm country. Lotsa folks around here be missin' fingers. Toes, too. Them machines, they eat 'em up. Jus' like that."

He spent a day and a half getting the lay of the land, driving from Gretna to places like Pittsville, Sandy Level, Dusty Hill, and Little Hollow. Everywhere he went, he brought along Boyd Davies' drawing of the three-fingered man, and showed it to anyone willing to take the time to look at it. By the afternoon of the second day, he'd grown bold enough to tell a few people that he was working on a case from sixteen years ago, in which a young girl had been murdered, her body buried in a shallow grave.

What he found was that the older folks—the ones who'd been living there back at the time—remembered. Not Boyd Davies' name, or Ilsa Meisner's, either, but the case itself. And those who remembered either tried hard to be helpful, or tried hard not to be, depending pretty much on the color of their skin.

As a result, he learned about a good half-dozen men who had lost this finger or that to a piece of farm machinery, cut a hand off with a chain saw, or been mangled by a bumper jack. But every last one of them was a black man. It was beginning to seem to Jorgensen that the Good Lord was decidedly not an equal-opportunity amputator.

He made the rounds of the local police departments, the county sheriff's office, and the state police barracks. No one he spoke to remembered any law enforcement personnel with missing fingers.

"Impossible," said one highway patrolman. "I mean, how's he gonna fire his weapon with nothin' to pull the trigger with? His *pecker?*"

"Good question," agreed Jorgensen, biting his tongue to refrain from mentioning that, over the years, he'd actually encountered some officers who'd had two hands.

He stopped in every diner, restaurant, and fast-food joint he came across, drank more cups of coffee than he'd had in a lifetime, and over-tipped every waitress who would talk to him. But he made it a point to steer clear of the food, which—as best as he could judge—ran the entire gamut from totally inedible to downright dangerous. Instead he made a deal with Ruby Mason, promising her an extra ten dollars a day if she'd agree to make him dinner as well as breakfast. It turned out to be the best investment of his life: Ruby was a terrific cook and, living alone and having no other takers for clean rooms at the moment, she was more than happy to oblige. The first night of their new arrangement she served him like a maid, donning an apron and ladling pork chops, stewed tomatoes, and rice onto his plate.

"No, no," he explained. "My offer's only good if you'll sit down and eat at the table with me."

She pondered that for a moment, but by the second night she'd gotten rid of the apron and set a place for herself, across from his. But not without giving him a hard time about it.

"You are one strange old white man," is how she put it.

He couldn't have felt more honored.

On the fourth day, Jorgensen caught a break. He'd struck up a conversation with a man stacking pallets of two-by-fours at a lumberyard over in Leesville.

"You handle that forklift pretty good," Jorgensen said.

"Ain't a forklift," said the man.

"Oh?" It sure looked like a forklift to Jorgensen. But he was looking for information, not an argument.

"This here's a hi-lo," the man explained. "See the way I can raise the platform all away up, like this?" And he demonstrated, by pushing forward a lever that proceeded to lift the two-by-fours a good ten feet off the ground, threatening to return them to the very treetops they'd come from.

"Dang!" said Jorgensen. "I guess that shows you how much I know."

"Shucks," said the man, but he was obviously pleased to show off his superior knowledge. "I prob'ly don't know much about whatever it is you do, know what I mean?"

"Could be," said Jorgensen.

"So what line a work you in, anyway?"

"Me? I settle claims for an insurance company," Jorgensen lied. "It's my job to track down people who are owed money from accident settlements, but haven't claimed it." He reached into his jacket pocket and took out Boyd Davies' drawing, which by this time was showing signs of wear.

"Sheeeet," said the hi-lo operator. "I hope my name's on that list."

"Ain't a list," said Jorgensen. "It's an old drawing of a man I'm looking for right now." He unfolded it and showed it to the man.

"Nice pitcher."

"Know him?" Jorgensen asked. "Bear in mind, it's been some years since this drawing was made." He was talking to a white man, so he was purposefully vague about the length of time. "They say the guy mighta been a law enforcement officer of some sort. And if you look real close there, you can see he's missing two fingers on his right hand."

"That what the accident was about?"

Jorgensen pointed a finger at the man, a gesture meant to equate him with a rocket scientist.

"Shucks," the man said again.

"Know him?"

"'Fraid not. There's a lot a *nigras* runnin' around shorta fingers," he said, effectively combining *negro* and *nigger* into a

single word. "But the only white man I know like that is
Clement Brownlee, over in Rocky Mount."

"Clement Brownlee?"

"Yeah, but don't ask for him by that name. No one'll know
who yer talkin' about."

"Okay then," said Jorgensen. "What name should I use?"

"His nickname."

"And that would be—"

The man smiled mischievously, before delivering his carefully orchestrated punch line. "Why, *Three-finger Brown,* a
course!"

Jorgensen's polite smile evidently failed to satisfy the man,
who promptly launched into an elaborate explanation. "See,
there was this feller, Mordecai Peter Centennial Brown. That
was his true name, swear to Jesus. Lost two fingers to a
thresher, he did, when he was a young'un. But a cause a that,
he was able to break off a wicked curve on a baseball, right offa
the stub where his fingers had used to a been. So guess what
they called him?"

Jorgensen shrugged, as though he still had no idea.

"Three-finger Brown!"

This time, Jorgensen laughed heartily.

Rocky Mount turned out to be almost an hour's drive to the
west, just off State Highway 40. Three-finger Brown turned
out to be something else.

Over the years, Clement Brownlee had lost more than a
couple of fingers. A diabetic who prided himself on shunning
insulin ("That stuff's for AIDS patients and faggots," he
explained to Jorgensen), he'd miraculously lived into his seventies. But along the way, he'd parted company with his eyesight,
one kidney, six fingers, and all of his toes. Presently confined
to a wheelchair ("I can still walk, but I fall over a lot"), he
seemed happy to have someone to talk to.

"Nope," he told Jorgensen, "I never carried the little girl's body. Remember the case, though. It was the talk of the county at the time. Nineteen eighty-one, wasn't it?"

"Right around then." It had actually been 1985.

"Horrible thing, horrible thing. Family never did get over it, from what I heard."

"Oh?"

"Older brother got hisself kilt in a car crash, and their mama just wasted away till she died. Wouldn't eat nuthin' after the killin.'"

"And the rest of the family?" Jorgensen realized he'd shown little concern for the surviving Meisners. It was an occupational hazard of working for the defense, he guessed: You had only so much sympathy to spread around.

"Other two kids moved away, up North or out West somewhere, I dunno." He shifted in his wheelchair, grimacing as his body settled itself into a slightly different position.

"And the daddy?"

"The daddy," said Brownlee. "He took it worst of all."

Jorgensen tried to imagine what could be worse than killing yourself in a car accident or starving yourself to death. He expected to hear that Kurt Meisner had blown his brains out, slit his wrists, or worse. It was the *worse* that had him worried.

But Brownlee surprised him. "Last I heard, he was livin' up in Ro-noke," he said, "in some kinda rest home."

That surprised Jorgensen. From what he'd read in the file, he had the impression that Ilsa's father had been around forty at the time of the tragedy. That would put him in his mid-fifties now. Then again, maybe Jorgensen's memory was failing him. That happened more and more these days, it seemed.

"How old is he?" he asked.

"The daddy?"

"Yes."

"I dunno," said Brownlee, shifting his weight again. "Sixty?"

"You know the name of the rest home?" Jorgensen asked. Roanoke was no more than twenty miles north of Rocky

Mount. It might be worth the drive, to show Kurt Meisner Boyd Davies' drawing, see if he remembered a three-fingered lawman. Of course, there was no way Jorgensen could show him the entire drawing; doing so would force him to look at the recovered body of his daughter all over again, and likely set him back another sixteen years.

Talk about cruel and unusual punishment.

"So far as I know," said Clement Brownlee, "ain't but one rest home up there. Ro-noke ain't exactly the capital of the world, you know."

Tim Harkin had the feeling he'd reached the very edge of the world. The first time he'd come out to the lighthouse, Ray Gilbert had done the driving, with Jessica Woodruff beside him in the passenger seat. That had left Harkin in the back seat, with his view obstructed, and he hadn't paid much attention to what was ahead of them. Now, alone behind the wheel of his own car, he'd been forced to concentrate carefully as he crossed the rickety bridge and followed the narrow road as it snaked its way through the dunes and finally down to the ocean's edge.

Only to find no sign of the old man, his pickup truck or his dog.

The lighthouse itself was unlocked, and Harkin swung the heavy door open and leaned his head inside. "Hello!" he called. "Anybody home?"

The only answer was the echo of his own voice, bounced back to him by the hard walls of the structure. Harkin had grown up on a farm outside of Memphis, and the lighthouse reminded him of nothing more than a silo that had had the corn cleaned out of it.

Cavernous, cylindrical, and empty.

He sat down against the outside wall and waited for an hour, and another hour after that. He'd driven four hours to get there, and the drive home would take even longer in the dark. He needed to see Jorgensen, needed to let him know what he himself knew. If the judge still wanted in, so be it. But he had a right to know. An informed decision, wasn't that what they called it?

But by now the sun was casting long shadows over the dunes, and Harkin was leery of driving back to the mainland in the dark. He gave it another half an hour, then found a sheet of paper in his glove compartment and penned a note to the old man.

Judge Jorgensen:
Sorry I missed you. I'm one of the people who talked you into joining the Boyd Davies defense team. Please call me as soon as you can. There are some things we need to talk about. My number is (405) 555-1284.
Tim Harkin

He thought of leaving the note inside the lighthouse, but decided against it. He was a son of the South, Harkin was, and he'd been taught manners long before he was old enough to read and write. You didn't walk into another person's home uninvited, even when the door was unlocked. So he folded the paper in half, and wedged it between the door handle and the frame, where the old man would be sure to find it.

That evening an onshore breeze would freshen from the southwest, tearing the paper and soon after dislodging it altogether. It would blow around aimlessly for a bit, drifting this way and that, gradually finding its way down to the beach, where the dampness would weigh it down, causing it to rest a while in its travels. Eventually, the rising tide would reach it and lift it up, and the flow of the Gulf Stream would begin to carry it northward. In a few minutes' time, the ink on the paper would begin to blur and run in the salt water, and soon the writing would fade completely.

Tim Harkin would know none of that, of course, any more than the old man would.

By the time Jorgensen got to Roanoke, it was getting dark, and he decided he'd better look for a motel, and put off searching for a rest home till morning. None of the places he stopped at allowed dogs, but since it wasn't supposed to get below forty-five degrees or so overnight, he figured Jake would be all right in the cab of the truck, with an old wool blanket he carried around for just such exigencies.

He found a diner and ordered the rib eye steak special, $11.95. Not because it was something he'd ordinarily eat, but because he knew there'd be enough left over to keep Jake happy. And while he waited for his meal, he used the pay phone to call Ruby Mason, let her know he wouldn't be back till the following evening.

"You make sure you eat proper," she told him.

It was something Marge would have said, and it caught him up short. He wondered just how long you could go on missing someone so much it physically hurt, and decided the answer was probably forever. He thought about what had brought him to western Virginia, and to Roanoke. And the more he thought about it the more the notion of looking for help from the father of Boyd Davies' victim struck him as absurd, perhaps even unfair. Better to skip it, he decided. He'd get a good night's sleep, then head back to Ruby's first thing in the morning. He suddenly felt tired, and a very long way from home.

But when morning came, he woke up feeling different about things. He'd come this far, after all, and as long as he was tactful with Kurt Meisner and didn't reveal the true nature of his business or let him see the drawing containing the body of his daughter, what harm could come of it? Assuming, that was, that he could find Meisner in the first place.

It turned out Three-finger Brown had been wrong: There were actually three rest homes in Roanoke, even though none of them called themselves rest homes. There was the Roanoke Assisted Living Center, the Phyllis N. Smythe Residence for Seniors, and the Twylight Passage Rest and Hospice Facility (a pretty enough name, thought Jorgensen, but one that hinted that the staff might not be entirely focused on the recuperative powers of rest).

But it didn't matter; Jorgensen never got past the second of the three, the Smythe Residence for Seniors. A pleasant woman greeted him at the door to a red brick building that looked more like a schoolhouse than a, well, an assisted care center. Yes, she said, they had a Kurt Meisner in residence. And as long as Mr. Meisner was willing and up to it, Mr. Jorgensen—he seldom identified himself as *Judge* Jorgensen, and certainly wasn't about to break the precedent now—could visit with him as soon as eleven o'clock rolled around.

That gave him an hour, and he spent it walking the grounds with Jake. And since the grounds consisted of a six-foot-wide apron of grass surrounding the building, they covered every inch of it, several times over, in both directions. When it seemed as though an hour had to be almost over (Jorgensen never wore a watch, preferring to rely on the sun, the stars, and his own internal clock for guidance), he walked Jake back to the truck and himself back to the seniors residence. According to a clock just inside the entrance, it still wasn't quite eleven, but the same pleasant woman didn't make an issue of it; she simply called over an orderly (or perhaps the young man was a nurse—Jorgensen wasn't certain) and asked him to take Jorgensen to Mr. Meisner's room.

They rode an elevator to the second floor, then walked down a long corridor fashioned of cinderblock and painted a pale green. There were no paintings in evidence, no photographs, not so much as a table with a vase of dried flowers. The walls were interrupted at regular intervals by numbered doors, all of which were slightly ajar. Jorgensen caught occasional glimpses of patients (or occupants, or seniors, or whatever they called them) propped up in bed, hunched over in wheelchairs, or standing at walkers. They all seemed to be alone, except for the ubiquitous companionship of their television sets.

Jorgensen's guide stopped at Room 238, and ushered him inside. The interior was small—*tiny* might have described it better—and every bit as sparse as the corridor. A white-haired man sat propped up in bed, staring out a window. A faded blanket covered the lower half of his body.

"Mr. Meisner," said the young man, "your visitor's here." And with that, he backed out the door, leaving them alone.

Jorgensen navigated his way around the bed until he ended up by the window, cutting off Kurt Meisner's view of it. What he saw was a ghost, a shadow of a man. His hair was snow white, his skin not far from it. His face was gaunt: eyes that were blue, but a *chemical* blue, deep-set and ringed with dark circles. Hollow cheeks that suggested a complete absence of teeth beneath them. Arms that were nothing more than bones, draped with skin. To Jorgensen, he had the look of a man whose life was being slowly sucked out of his body. Though he looked to be tall, he couldn't have weighed a hundred pounds, and had Jorgensen not known something of his age, he'd have sworn he was past ninety.

"My name is Jorgensen, August Jorgensen."

"Yes, they told me. Do I know you?"

"No, you don't. But I'm hoping you'll speak with me for a few minutes."

Meisner lifted one hand out from underneath the blanket and pointed vaguely at a plastic chair, except for the bed the only piece of furniture in the room. Jorgensen lowered himself onto it and said, "Thank you."

"Are you here about the case?" Meisner asked.

Jorgensen hadn't expected that. "What case?" he asked, feeling like a small child caught at the cookie jar, able to come up with nothing better than a "Who, me?"

"The murder case," said Meisner. "My daughter." His voice was dry and flat, but at least it wasn't the voice of a ninety-year-old. Jorgensen found that by looking over the man's shoulder just a bit, and focusing on a crack in the plaster on the wall beyond him, he could imagine he was talking to someone much younger than the one presented to his eyes.

Jorgensen flirted briefly with the idea of denying the true reason for his visit, but thought better of it. It was one thing to pass himself off as an insurance adjuster when rummaging around for leads, quite another to utter a bald-faced lie when confronted. So he said, "Yes, I'm here about the case."

"They must be getting ready to kill the boy again," said Meisner. "Every time they get ready to kill him, somebody or other comes here to see me."

"He's not a boy anymore," said Jorgensen. "He's a man in his thirties."

"To me, he'll always be a boy, and my daughter will always be eleven. You see, my life ended back then. The day before it happened, I was a young man. The day after it happened . . ." His voice trailed off.

"I'm very sorry," said Jorgensen.

Meisner smiled ever so slightly. "When I woke up the next morning, I looked in the mirror. My hair," he said, lifting his hand and motioning toward the top of his head, "my hair had turned white, just like this. Overnight."

Jorgensen had heard of such things happening to people; he'd just never seen evidence of it before now. "I'm sorry," he said again, sounding foolish, but feeling the need to say something.

"That's all right," said Meisner, "it wasn't your fault. So tell me, what can I do for you? You can't be a reporter, I know, you're too old. Are you from the clemency board, perhaps?"

"No, no. I'm looking for a man," said Jorgensen, "a man who had something to do with the case, back when, when it happened." He took Boyd Davies' drawing from his pocket. Carefully he folded it so that the lifeless body of Meisner's daughter couldn't be seen. Only the man's face showed, albeit hidden behind mirrored sunglasses.

He held the folded picture out for Meisner to see. "I believe," Jorgensen told him, "that he was a peace officer of some sort." He'd meant to say *police officer* but had inadvertently lapsed into legalese. Technically, he was right: All police officers were peace officers in the eyes of the law, but not all peace officers were police officers. It had mattered when he'd had to apply the *Miranda* rule, or decide some search-and-seizure case. It didn't matter now, though, certainly not to Kurt Meisner, and Jorgensen regretted using the term. But he'd used up two "sorrys" already.

Meisner studied the face for a long moment. Jorgensen wasn't sure, but at one point he thought he saw a smile begin to form on the man's thin lips. But if it had happened at all, it was gone the next instant.

"Do you know him?" he asked.

Meisner drew a deep breath. "I used to," he said.

"Oh?"

"He's dead." He leaned what weight he had left in his body back against his pillows and allowed his eyelids to close. "He died sixteen years ago."

"Can you tell me his name?" asked Jorgensen.

Meisner opened his mouth as if to speak, but coughed instead. It was a hacking cough that seemed to dislodge stuff deep inside him. Marge had coughed like that at the end, bringing up big globs of green and yellow phlegm from her chest. A *productive* cough, the doctors had called it, a good thing. But all it had *produced,* all the *good* it had caused, was her death.

Meisner continued coughing, fighting for breath. His hand sought a device off to one side of him, and he pressed a button. A moment later, a nurse came in. As Jorgensen rose to get out of her way, she placed both her arms around Meisner's waist and lifted his body forward. Then she freed one arm and pounded him soundly on the back, hard enough, to Jorgensen's thinking, to break the poor man's ribs. Gradually, the coughing subsided, and Kurt Meisner regained his breath.

"I think we'll let Mr. Meisner rest now," the nurse said, directing the remark to Jorgensen without looking at him. "Perhaps y'all can resume your visit tomorrow?"

"Yes, of course," said Jorgensen. Then, turning to Meisner, he added, "If that's all right with you."

Meisner shrugged.

Jorgensen took a step toward the bed and said, "Thank you, sir." The *sir* came easily, almost automatically, to a lifelong Southerner. So, too, did his the extension of his right hand. Kurt Meisner looked at it for a moment, almost as if he'd expected there to be something in it. Then, slowly, he worked his own right hand free from the blanket that had until then covered it, and they shook.

So that even before August Jorgensen saw it, he felt it. Kurt Meisner's right hand was missing two fingers.

SIXTEEN

Even under the best of conditions, sleep doesn't come easily to men in their eighties. Noises that go completely
unheard during daylight hours suddenly become deafening.
Aches that were barely noticeable hours earlier ripen into
cramps demanding constant kneading, stretching, and changing of position. The bladder somehow manages to shrink to
the size of a shot glass, allowing only the barest interval to pass
before refilling itself and requiring that immediate attention
be paid.

But that night, sleep wouldn't come at all to August Jorgensen. In addition to the usual suspects, there were a few
newcomers he was still adjusting to. For one thing, in spite of
the curtains Ruby Mason had thoughtfully hung over the windows in his room, a full moon bathed everything in bright,
white light. Closer to home, Ruby's meatloaf, hush puppies,
and gravy had gotten together and were conducting a protest
of sorts, holding a *sit-in* somewhere between his esophagus
and his stomach. While off in the distance, some kind of animal was practicing a half-howl, half-snort call that Jorgensen
couldn't place for the life of him. A dog? A pig? A wild boar,
maybe? Did they even have wild boars in these parts? Zachary
might be able to look it up on his computer.

But what would keep Jorgensen most from sleeping this
night didn't fall under the heading of ambient noise, cramping

muscles, filling bladder, full moon, meatloaf, or even wild boar. What would keep him awake was the discovery that the three-fingered man was none other than Kurt Meisner.

No less than four times would Jorgensen climb out of bed, turn on the light, find his reading glasses, and stare at Boyd Davies' drawing. And each time—in spite of the mirrored sunglasses that hid the man's eyes, in spite of the dark hair that fell across his forehead, and in spite of the fact that the man in the drawing couldn't have been a day over forty, while the one sitting in bed at the Smythe Residence for Seniors looked to be at least twice that—Jorgensen would nevertheless know they had to be one and the same.

And yet that couldn't be. Both the police reports and the trial testimony made it quite clear that Kurt Meisner hadn't seen his daughter's body—let alone carried it—until he'd identified her the following day, when she was draped in a sheet and lying on a gurney at the county coroner's office. So how on earth could Boyd Davies had gotten a glimpse of Meisner carrying her, lifeless but still clothed?

Unless . . .

And when you came right down to it, it was precisely that *unless* that would keep August Jorgensen awake all night.

What kept Jessica Woodruff awake was much simpler. After putting it off for as long as she felt she could, she'd finally decided to get word to August Jorgensen that the Supreme Court had issued a scheduling order, and that the Davies case would be heard the second week of April.

Normally, getting word would have meant picking up the phone and calling, or having some intern at the station do it for her. But Jorgensen's lack of a phone made that impossible. Ditto for e-mailing him or faxing him. She could send him a letter—regular, overnight, priority, registered, certified, whatever. But she was already on notice that he paid little attention to his mail, and often threw envelopes away without opening them.

Not wanting to take chances, she'd had a letter typed, and then had the station dispatch a courier from its Charleston affiliate to hand-deliver it. That way, a human being could present it to Jorgensen, stand there to make sure he not only opened it up but actually read it, and get him to sign an acknowledgment that he understood it.

Jesus, she thought. It was like dealing with a *child.* But she'd done it anyway. Better safe than sorry, she'd decided.

That was four days ago. Now her secretary had buzzed her to tell her the courier was on the phone, waiting to speak with her. Didn't he understand that wasn't necessary, that all he had to do was forward the signed acknowledgment to her?

"It sounds like there's some kind of problem," the secretary explained.

"*Jesus,*" she thought again, this time out loud. "Put him through."

There was some clicking on the line, then a male voice. "Hello?"

"Hello," said Jessica. "Are you the courier?"

"Yes, ma'am."

"What's the problem?"

"He's not home."

"So wait for him. He doesn't go far."

"I've been waiting for him all day, ma'am."

Christ, she thought. Maybe the old guy had an embolism, or a heart attack. His body's probably in there, rotting away. "Is his dog there?" she asked.

"I don't think so."

"Have you looked in the windows?"

"There *are* no windows, ma'am. Just these little round things. Can't hardly see nothin' through 'em, neither."

"How about his truck?"

"I doubt it would fit through the door, ma'am."

"No, no. Do you see it parked outside?"

"What does it look like?"

"Like a TRUCK," Jessica shouted. "*Red*. Full of rust. About a thousand years old."

"Where does he keep it?"

"Right there. You'd see it."

"Then I guess it's not here, ma'am."

"*Great*." She lit a cigarette, inhaled deeply. "Listen, can you go back tomorrow?"

"Yes, ma'am, only there'll be an extra charge for re—"

"Go back tomorrow!" shouted Jessica, slamming down the phone and stubbing out the cigarette. Maybe the judge was at the doctor's, she decided. Old people were always going to the doctor. Or to the vet, maybe, or to get his truck serviced, or the hairs in his ears and nose trimmed. Leave it alone, she told herself; it could be almost anything.

What worried her, of course, was that it might not just be anything. It might be that August Jorgensen was off snooping somewhere.

Well, let him snoop all he wanted to. When you came right down to it, what were the chances of his actually finding anything? And if it turned out she was wrong, if he happened by pure dumb luck to stumble onto something that wasn't his business, well, they'd deal with that, too, if they had to. That's the way things worked in television. Every problem, no matter how perplexing or annoying, had a solution. The bottom line was the story, and getting that story out to the viewers, whatever it took. Anyone or anything that got in the way of that was expendable. That's simply the way it had to be.

And if that sounded tough, so be it.

It was a tough business.

It was a bleary-eyed August Jorgensen who climbed out of bed the following morning, slipped into the same clothes he'd worn the day before, and got behind the wheel of his truck. Sitting next to him on the drive to the Smythe Residence, Jake shot him a sideways once-over and snorted. Over the years, he'd grown used to the same-clothes-as-yesterday routine and the two-day stubble; Jorgensen cared little about clothes and often went a week or more without shaving. No, thought Jorgensen, the snort must be a reaction to the odors. In his haste to get back to Kurt Meisner's bedside, he'd completely forgotten to wash his face, shave, or even brush his teeth.

"Sorry, old boy," he told the dog. "This is what it must be like to grow old."

The ride took fifteen minutes, the wait to see Meisner the usual hour. Hurrying up was evidently not high on the list of protocols at the Smythe Residence for Seniors.

By the time Jorgensen was led to Room 238, someone had gotten Kurt Meisner up out of his bed (which was now freshly made) and placed him in the chair. At least Jorgensen assumed that someone had done those things; he couldn't imagine that Meisner possessed the strength to do them for himself.

"How are you feeling?" Jorgensen asked, once the two of them had been left alone.

Meisner shrugged.

"You had a bit of a coughing spell there," Jorgensen reminded him, "right before I left yesterday."

"Oh, that. I'm all right, thanks. Sit down if you like. I'm sorry . . ." He motioned vaguely, as his voice trailed off in midair.

Jorgensen took it as an apology for the lack of furniture in the room. He found a spot on the edge of the bed and lowered himself onto it. It gave him a profile view of Meisner, though no eye contact: The other man's gaze was directed out the window, just as it had been the day before. But unlike the first day, when Meisner's right hand had been hidden under his blanket until the last moment, today it rested on the arm of his chair, the arm closest to Jorgensen. And it was still missing two fingers. More than once during his sleepless night, Jorgensen had thought back to their parting handshake. Was it possible he'd only imagined the missing fingers? He'd played the scene over in his mind, again and again, trying to feel the deformed hand in his own, trying to recreate the strange sensation of the stub—

Mordecai Peter Centennial Brown

—until the only thing he'd known for sure was that he couldn't be sure at all.

Now, at least, he could see for himself. He could be sure.

By this time, Jorgensen had had an entire night and half a morning to frame his next question. He'd thought up a hundred opening lines and rehearsed a dozen little speeches, without once settling on a satisfactory way of wording it. So now, for lack of anything better, he simply came out with it. "That's you in the picture, isn't it?"

Meisner seemed to think a minute, then nodded.

"Carrying your daughter's body."

Another nod.

"Before she was found."

This time, nothing. Perhaps Meisner hadn't heard him; Jorgensen knew he himself had trouble picking up conversation when he wasn't looking at the speaker's mouth. Then again, Perhaps Jorgensen was getting close to something, uncomfortably close. "Do you happen to know who drew the picture?" he asked.

"Yes."

"Can you tell me why he seems to be looking up at you? Could he have been lying down, do you think, or kneeling?"

A sideways shake of the head.

"What, then?"

Meisner's words came slowly, deliberately, as though it caused him physical pain to recall and recount the memory. But recount it he did. "He was standing in the hole," he said.

"The hole?"

"The grave he'd dug."

Jorgensen had heard the words, and he was trying to digest them, but a loud pounding in his temples made it all but impossible for him to think. It took him a moment to recognize the pounding as his own pulse, his own heartbeat. He closed his eyes and rubbed the sides of his head with the palms of his hands. He had the sensation that he was standing on the edge of some great abyss, and that any moment the ground at his feet might give way, causing him to plunge downward. He opened his eyes and lowered his hands, reached down with them for support, felt the bed beneath him, took a deep breath. "I don't understand," he said. "Why are *you* there? Why are *you* in the picture?"

Slowly, very slowly, the man in the chair began turning his head. By the time his face had swung fully around, Jorgensen could see there were tears running down both of his cheeks. No sound, no sobbing, no wrenching. Just two steady, unchecked rivers of tears.

"Boyd Davies buried your daughter. Right?"

"Yes."

"But he didn't kill her."

"No."

A chill ran up the length of Jorgensen's spine. He suddenly felt light-headed, thought he might actually faint. He gripped handfuls of blanket with each of his hands, fought to anchor himself, to find solid holding ground. He should have slept last night, he told himself, should have had breakfast, should have showered. This was far too important for him to be confused about, to miss. He tried taking another deep breath, but the light-headedness persisted, and now tiny black dots appeared and began dancing before his eyes. *Get a hold of yourself,* he told himself. *Don't let this opportunity slip away because you're old and tired and can't think straight. Say something. Anything.*

"So," he said, forcing the word out, letting the sound of his own voice reassure him, convince him that he could do this. "So," he said again, more assertively. "So it was *you* that killed her?"

Meisner stared at him for a while, then smiled one of his fleeting smiles. "Is that what you think?" he asked.

The black spots were still there, now rising and falling, but he no longer felt faint. "I don't know what to think," Jorgensen confessed. "I very much wish you'd tell me."

"Why?"

"Why? Because I'm one of Mr. Davies' lawyers, that's why. Because I've been asked to speak for him on some obscure, technical issue that even I, who was once a lawyer and a judge, have been having trouble understanding. And now all of a sudden it occurs to me that my client might be completely innocent. So I, as his lawyer, have to—"

"He's not completely innocent," said Meisner. "He helped me bury her, didn't he?"

"Yes, he did," Jorgensen agreed. "But last I checked, not even the Commonwealth of Virginia executes grave-diggers."

"Does that mean I'm safe, too?"

"That," said Jorgensen, "depends."

"Depends on what?" The tears had dried, leaving twin vertical stains where they'd run down Meisner's cheeks. His look was less emotional now, more calculating. "I wasn't a lawyer or a judge," he said. "Me, I was just a dumb tobacco farmer."

"It depends," said Jorgensen, "on what you did. If it was you who killed her, I'm afraid I can't tell you you're *safe,* as you put it."

"I didn't kill her," said Kurt Meisner.

"Then you're safe."

"How about helping to bury her? How about not telling the truth, lying, covering up for—you know—for whoever did do it? How about all those things?"

"It's been sixteen years," Jorgensen said. "For all of those things, the statute of limitations has run. Even if they wanted to prosecute you, they couldn't. It's too long ago."

"That's what the law says?"

"That's what the law says."

"You wouldn't lie, now, would you? You know, to help the boy?"

"I might," said Jorgensen. "But I'm not."

"Well, maybe you're right. The others said pretty much the same thing."

"The others?"

But if Kurt Meisner had heard, he gave no sign of it. He'd swung his head away, and his gaze was once again fixed on the window. Although to Jorgensen, it didn't look as though he was focusing on the things that were outside, as much as he was on the things that had been, sixteen years ago.

SEVENTEEN

Wesley Boyd Davies, if you listened to Kurt Meisner tell it, had been nothing but a nuisance. He hadn't worked, he hadn't gone to school, he hadn't even helped his mother out with chores. Not like Meisner's own children, who from the time they'd been old enough to walk and talk were required to do their share, whether in the fields, around the house, or both. Farming—at least the grim business of trying to run a small family tobacco farm in the soil-poor hill country of southwestern Virginia—was something that required everyone to pitch in. The Davies boy never would have survived in the Meisner household, no way. Instead of having provided a helping hand, he'd have been nothing but a mouth to feed.

"Had he been an animal born in the wild," Meisner observed, "he woulda just died off, leaving more food for the stronger ones to survive. Ain't that a fact?"

Jorgensen was prepared to admit there might be some truth to that. He had his own thoughts on the wisdom of tampering with natural selection, but he didn't want to go off on any tangents, certainly not now, not with Meisner on the verge of telling him what had actually happened sixteen years ago. "You're probably right," he said. "Go on."

Farming was a tough life, Meisner explained again. You woke up before the sun, worked all day, and pretty much collapsed after supper. The problem was that a schedule like that didn't leave you much time to spend with your family. Sure, you might work beside them in the fields for hours at a stretch, but that didn't mean you were conversating. And it didn't mean you knew what was new at school, or what was really going on with them.

What was going on with Kurt, Jr., was that he'd just turned sixteen. He'd shot up six inches over the past year, had developed a man's pair of shoulders, and had suddenly started to notice girls. "All them hormones jumpin' around in his body. That testerone stuff, you know. It can be a problem." Meisner's solution was to keep young Kurt as busy working as he possibly could. "I figured if I wore him out real good, he'd be too tired to get into trouble when he was outa my sight."

He figured wrong.

The only thing was, almost all of the girls young Kurt noticed proved off-limits to him. As soon as the school day ended, he was expected to rush home and get out in the fields. Evenings, a strict nine o'clock curfew effectively deprived him of a social life. And weekends, except for two hours out for Sunday services, it was back to the fields. The pretty young girls who flirted with him at school or winked at him in church raised his *testerone* level to the boiling point, but because of the demands the farm placed on his time, the poor boy had no outlet for the strange and discomforting stirrings going on inside his body.

No outlet, that was, except for his sisters.

Katrinka was just a year younger than Kurt, but she was a solidly built fifteen-year-old who took after her mother and was fully capable of defending herself. When her brother made crude advances toward her—once exposing himself, another time lifting her sweater and grabbing her breasts, she slapped his face and let him know in no uncertain terms that if he did anything like it again, she'd go straightaway to their father. At least that's how she related the incidents to Kurt, Sr. Only it took her more than two years to get around to it. By that time, it was too late for her younger sister.

Ilsa was only eleven at the time, and small for her age, at that.

Unlike Katrinka, she was hopelessly outmatched by her brother, physically and in every other way. However he may have approached her, she must have been helpless to defend herself.

"I have no idea what, you know, what actually went on, or how long it went on for," Meisner told Jorgensen. "Maybe there were signs, but my wife and I, we never saw any, not even when we looked back after."

After.

"How did it end?" Jorgensen asked.

"Peter found her." Peter was the other son, thirteen at the time. He'd been walking home from school, cutting through the woods, when he'd entered a small clearing and all but stumbled over Ilsa's body. At first, he thought she was asleep. But when she wouldn't answer him, he rolled her over. Her lifeless face brought a scream from him, the last sound he'd make for three days.

He ran and found his father in the barn, and—literally unable to speak—began tugging at him. Meisner, annoyed at being distracted from whatever task he was doing, raised a hand as if to strike Peter, and might have done so. But at that instant, he saw the wild expression on the boy's face, and knew something was terribly wrong. With Peter leading the way, the two of them took off, Meisner with a shovel in his good hand.

"Why a shovel?" Jorgensen asked.

"I happened to be using it when Peter ran into the barn. I don't remember if I just held onto it, or if I figured I might need it. At that point, I didn't know what had frightened my boy. For all I knew, it mighta been a bear, a mountain lion, an escaped convict, anything. I guess I didn't want to be empty-handed, is all."

They ran all the way to the clearing—or at least to the edge of it. There Peter stopped abruptly, and would go no further. Kurt Meisner slowed to a walk, and continued. A hundred yards away, there was something on the ground. From fifty yards, he could see it was a person. From twenty, that it was a young girl. At ten, Meisner dropped to his knees, crawling the rest of the way on all fours. When he reached the spot, he stared in disbelief and horror at the two things on the ground in front of him.

The first was the body of his youngest child. Her head was thrown back as if her neck had been broken. Her eyes were wide open, but her pupils weren't visible, and where the whites of her eyes should have been, there was bright red. Her dress was pulled up above her waist, and there was blood on the front of it, where it would have covered the part where her legs came together.

The second thing Kurt Meisner stared at was also on the ground, ten or twelve feet from Ilsa's body. Meisner recognized the second thing almost as easily as he'd recognized the first. It was a work glove. Not just any work glove, though. It had reinforced stitching and a real leather patch on the palm. And on the cuff, it said, WRANGLER II. It was one of a pair he'd given Kurt, Jr., for his sixteenth birthday.

For the next five minutes, Kurt Meisner fought back waves of sobs, and tried desperately to regain control. When finally he could trust himself enough to speak, he turned to face Peter. The boy was still at the edge of the clearing, his arms hugging a tree trunk.

"Go home," Meisner told him. "Go home and go to bed. You're sick. You never saw this. Understand?"

The boy said nothing.

"*Understand?*"

A nod.

"Go!"

Peter gradually loosened his grip on the tree, turned, and then ran off toward the house.

"And?" Jorgensen asked.

"And he never said a word. Ever."

For what seemed to him to be a long time, Kurt Meisner continued to kneel beside his daughter's body. No matter how hard he tried to come up with explanations that someone other than Kurt, Jr., had killed her, he couldn't. Gradually, his sorrow gave way to anger, an emotion he was more familiar with. But even as his anger simmered, another reaction was occurring in him: a parent's natural inclination to protect his child. And in the end, that was the inclination he yielded to.

Summoning the strength to push himself up from the ground, Meisner picked up the glove and stuffed it into his belt. Next he lifted the body of his daughter and carried it deeper into the woods. He didn't stop until he got down to the edge of a stream that ran through the forest nearby. His first thought was to lay Ilsa in the water, face down, to make it look as though she'd drowned. But he knew that wouldn't fool anyone, not with the red eyes and the blood on the dress.

Then he remembered the shovel.

He walked back to the clearing and retrieved it. He even had the presence of mind to look around for other evidence that might point to his older son. Finding none, he brushed leaves over the area where Ilsa's body had laid, and used a branch to cover his own tracks—the way he'd seen Indians do it in Westerns—as he made his way back to the stream.

The ground by the stream was damp and soft, and at first the digging was easy. But then, as he began hitting rock, the going got tougher.

"Did you really think you could hide her body so it wouldn't be found?" Jorgensen wanted to know.

"*Think?* I wasn't *thinking*," said Meisner. "I just did what I did, cause I didn't know what else to do. All I knew was, I'd lost a child, and I wasn't about to lose another one. Can't you understand that?"

Jorgensen allowed that he could understand that.

Meisner kept digging. He was a farmer, used to hard work, but the rocks and stones wore him out, and he was forced to rest from time to time. "The stream must've changed course over the years," he explained. "It was like I was dredging up a river bottom."

He was maybe a foot and a half deep when he suddenly sensed a shadow looming over him. He spun around, grasping the shovel in both hands, ready to do battle with whatever man or beast had sneaked up behind him.

It was Boyd Davies.

Meisner let out a little laugh, much as he had at the time, sixteen years ago. Of all the people he knew on the face of the earth, he'd been surprised by the only one his secret would be safe with. Boyd didn't even look at him; Boyd never looked at anyone. Nor did he look at Ilsa's body, lying nearby. In fact, he gave no sign that he'd noticed it at all. Instead, he stared at the stones Meisner had dug out of the ground and piled at the edge of the hole, and the stones still remaining in the hole.

Meisner decided it was safe to ignore the boy (even though Boyd was twenty, Meisner would always think of him as a boy), and he resumed digging. But his arms were heavy by that time, and he felt like each shovelful of wet dirt and rock might be his last. It was right around then that he decided to put Boyd to work. "I figured if I could trust him to *watch*," he explained now, "why couldn't I trust him to *dig?*"

It took some demonstrating and coaxing, but eventually Meisner had Boyd down in the hole with him, on his knees. Each time Meisner loosened a stone with the shovel, Boyd would pick it up and place it in the pile on the rim of the hole. "The hard part was getting him to let go of the stones," Meisner recalled. "Each one, he'd want to roll it around in his hands, or rub it up against his face. But he finally got the hang of it, and between the two of us, we got the thing dug."

At that point, Meisner climbed out—by this time he could barely lift his arms—and gathered up Ilsa's body. He managed to lift her one final time, and carry her to the newly dug grave, in which Boyd Davies continued to kneel, still captivated by the smooth stones. As Meisner approached, the limp body of his youngest child in his arms, a look of anguish on his face, something must have caused Boyd to look up from his stones, and in that instant,

Click!

The image of father and daughter was burned into the young man's retinas, imprinted in some faraway corner of his damaged child's brain, to rest there like some old forgotten photograph in the bottom of an attic trunk, waiting for August Jorgensen to utter the magic words that would unlock it and summon it forth sixteen years later.

By this time, it was already late afternoon, and Meisner did his best to cover Ilsa's body with the stones and dirt they'd unearthed from the hole. Where his boots had left impressions in the soft ground, he used the shovel to obscure them. If he was somewhat less careful with the prints Boyd's larger boots had made, he attributed the difference to exhaustion, rather than design.

Stepping back from the grave site, Meisner surveyed their work. Other than the fact that the newly turned earth was a shade or two darker than that surrounding it, there was nothing remarkable about it. And, he figured, the earth would dry some overnight, blending the colors until they wouldn't be noticeably different.

That left the shovel.

It was Meisner's shovel, an old one with duct tape wrapped around a portion of the handle, where a crack had developed. He tried to peel the tape off, but his fingers were too cramped and tired to do it. He carried it across the stream and further up into the woods until the ground began rising. He continued on until he came to an outcropping of rock and boulders. He found a hollow spot behind one of the boulders and, after wiping the handle clean of any fingerprints, hid the shovel. He turned around, only to see for the first time that Boyd Davies had followed him.

"For a moment, I thought about killin' him," Meisner admitted, "I really did. But then I realized he wasn't goin' to say nothin.' He never said nothin' to nobody, that boy."

Jorgensen wondered if perhaps Meisner wasn't giving himself enough credit for guile. While a dead Boyd Davies might have been something he could have explained without too much difficulty, a living Boyd Davies presented the perfect murder suspect, totally unable to explain what had really happened. "I simply told Boyd to go home to his mama," said Meisner. As for his own son, Meisner found him in the barn. By that time, Ilsa was overdue from school, and Kurt, Jr., had been asked by his mother to look around for his sister. When he saw his father, young Kurt went wild-eyed with fear.

"I knew right then," said Meisner. "I mean I'd pretty much known already, but now I *knew*. He started backin' up from me, like I was goin' to beat him. Each time I'd take a step toward him, he'd back up two. Finally, I stopped, and opened up my arms to him, and motioned him to come to me. 'It's okay,' I told him, 'it's okay.' I kept tellin' him that over and over, but I guess he didn't believe me. He must've been scared I was going to give him a beating, or something. Around then, I remembered I still had his work glove stuck in my belt. So I took it out and tossed it to him. It landed on the ground, right at his feet. He looked down at it for a long time, like he was trying to figure out what it meant. Then he came into my arms and began sobbin' like a baby. We musta stood like that for twenty minutes, huggin' each other and sobbin', until someone came in and found us. I don't remember who it was, but they musta just figured we was upset cause Ilsa was missin' and all. And that's when I knew it was goin' to work out."

"How about when the police picked Boyd up?"

Meisner said nothing.

"And arrested him?"

A shrug.

"And how about when they took him to trial and convicted him?" asked Jorgensen. "And sentenced him to die?"

For once, Meisner met Jorgensen's glance. "Are you a father?" he asked.

"No," said Jorgensen, "No, I'm not."

"Then you wouldn't understand. You couldn't possibly understand. I had to choose, you see. I had to choose between my son—my firstborn son—and, and some *retard*. So I chose my son. I chose my family. Do you know the price I've paid for that?"

It was Jorgensen's turn to remain silent.

"I lost my daughter. I lost my son. I lost my wife. My other two children are . . ." He waved an arm in the air, as if to shoo away a fly. "And look at me."

"They tell me you're a Christian man," said Jorgensen.

"I was. Once."

"Do you believe in redemption?"

Meisner shrugged. By this time, he'd broken off eye contact again, and was busy staring out the window.

"Your son is dead. You're protected from what you did by the statute of limitations. It's time for you to come forward now, to tell this story to the authorities."

Meisner shook his slowly. "I can't do that," he said.

"Why not?"

Meisner mumbled something in response, but Jorgensen couldn't make it out. "What?" he asked. Marge had been after him for years to get a hearing aid, but he'd refused. Hearing aids were like canes and walkers and umbrellas, he'd told her; they were for *old* people. "What?" he said again, leaning forward and cupping his hand over his ear.

Again Meisner mumbled, and this time it sounded almost like, "They'd kill me." But when Jorgensen said, "What?" a third time, Meisner looked up at him and replied, "I can't, I just can't. That's all."

Jessica Woodruff heard from the courier shortly after five o'clock that afternoon.

"Still no sign of him, ma'am."

"*Fuck* him."

"What was that, ma'am?"

"Nothing. Okay, just leave the envelope for him."

"It'll get wet, ma'am."

"What is it, *raining* there?"

"No, ma'am, but there's all this mist and stuff, and it might as well be raining, if you know what I mean."

"So slide it under his door."

"I already thought of that, ma'am, but there's no room."

"Then wrap it up in plastic, and just leave it on the doorstep. You do have plastic, don't you?"

"No, ma'am. But don't worry. I'll find something."

"You do that," said Jessica.

If Jorgensen hadn't realized it at the moment, Kurt Meisner's "That's all" didn't simply mean he couldn't fully explain his reasons for being unable to go public with the true story of Ilsa's death. It meant, as Meisner soon made clear, that the visit was over, and that Jorgensen was not welcome to return.

Jorgensen found this out in stages. First, Meisner said he was tired, and asked him to leave, which Jorgensen did. Then, when Jorgensen returned after lunch, he was told that Meisner didn't want to see him. Jorgensen figured the man was worn out from the effort of unburdening himself. Tomorrow was another day, he decided. He went back to Ruby Mason's, showered, shaved, put on clean clothes, spent some time with a much-neglected Jake, had dinner, and got his first good night's sleep in as long as he could remember.

The following morning, he got up and returned once again to the Smythe Residence for Seniors. He was kept waiting at the front desk while a staff member, a young man with a harelip, went to inform Meisner he had a visitor. But when the young man returned, he was shaking his head.

"Mr. Meisner," he reported, "says no more visitors."

"There must be some mistake," Jorgensen said.

"No mistake," he was told. "Just no more visitors."

He left a note, he tried calling from a pay phone, he went back once more that afternoon—but all to no avail. He realized he should have pressed Meisner into continuing the day before. Then he cursed himself for not having had the fore-thought to secretly tape their conversation, and for not having brought along a witness to hear the man's confession. Without proof, he knew, he didn't have a chance. Better than anyone, August Jorgensen understood the rules under which appellate courts operated. They'd have no interest whatsoever in his uncorroborated account of what Meisner had supposedly told him, even if he were to reduce it to affidavit form and swear up and down to it. The man was still in his fifties and living in a senior's residence, for God's sake, talking to someone who probably ought to be there, too. And now he'd clammed up.

"Damn!" he shouted to no one in particular. "Damn, damn, damn, damn!" Five "damns" were about as profane as he got.

The following morning, after breakfast, he squared his account with Ruby Mason and thanked her for her hospitality. Then he and Jake climbed into the red Chevy pickup truck and headed home.

He'd come as close as one could come to saving Boyd Davies, and he had only himself to blame for failing to pull it off. And fail he had. He would have been better off if he'd never gone to see Kurt Meisner in the first place. That way, someone else—someone younger and cleverer—might have had a chance. Or at least a tape recorder.

Maybe that's what happened, he thought, when you sent a man to do a boy's job.

Boyd Davies was innocent, completely innocent. He'd spent the last sixteen years in prison, waiting to die for a crime he'd never committed. Jorgensen had stumbled across the truth, but then he'd managed to destroy any chance of proving it. And what did he have to show for his trip to Virginia? Noth-ing. All the Supreme Court wanted to hear was whether or not Boyd's possible inability to connect his crime to his punish-ment meant the Commonwealth couldn't kill him. Well, how was Boyd supposed to connect something he couldn't under-stand to something he hadn't done? Jorgensen hadn't come up with a thing to tell them, not a thing. He pictured Justice

Rehnquist leaning forward to interrupt him before he could get two words out of his mouth.

"So tell us, Judge Jorgensen. Exactly where in the Eighth Amendment does it say it's 'cruel and usual' for a state to execute a murderer who's concededly competent, but who can't quite reconcile in his mind his offense with his punishment?"

"He's not a murderer, your honor."

"Excuse me?"

"He didn't do it."

"Well, thank you so much for sharing that little insight with us. Call the next case, Mr. Clerk. And then please see to it that Judge Jorgensen is permitted to have a warm glass of Ovaltine and take a nap before returning home."

Jorgensen found the entrance ramp to the interstate and pulled the truck into traffic, causing three faster cars and an eighteen-wheeler to swerve into the passing lane to avoid hitting him. The driver of the eighteen-wheeler pulled on his horn as he roared by.

"FUCK YOU!" Jorgensen shouted, easily exceeding his previous personal best. In the passenger seat, Jake lay down and covered his ears with his paws.

EIGHTEEN

The old lighthouse never looked so good as it did to August Jorgensen, rising from the salt flats and the marsh grass against blue sky and bluer ocean. He'd made the drive straight through, fueled by anger and frustration and a single pit stop, just long enough to fill the truck's tank and empty theirs.

As it always did, coming home had a soothing effect on him. There was something about sand and salt and sea air that calmed his nerves, ironed out the wrinkles of life, and allowed him to remember just why it was he'd chosen years ago to drop out and leave the mainland behind. He belonged here; he fit in. He'd grown out of touch with the rest of the world, and was no longer a match for its vagaries and complexities, if ever he had been. Here, things stayed the same. The seasons changed, storms came and went, the beach shifted a bit. But the shifts and changes were natural ones, incremental ones, and afterward everything pretty much returned to the way it had been before, the way it had always been.

Forget about Kurt Meisner, he told himself. Forget about little Ilsa and young Kurt, Jr. Forget about Boyd Davies. Other than some freakish accident that had left him able to draw like the lens of a camera, he was what he was. The world would barely notice his passing, and his suffering would finally be over. When the time came, Jorgensen would pack a bag, go up to Washington, and argue the case. How hard could it be to stand at a podium and tell nine old men and women that yes, of course it mattered that Virginia wanted to kill a man who was powerless to understand why. They'd interrupt him and ask him questions, and he'd do his best to answer them. Then he'd sit down, and they could do whatever they wanted, whatever they were going to do in the first place. Hell, they'd gone and decided a presidential election, hadn't they? They hadn't worried too much about what the Constitution said when they'd done *that*; why on earth should he expect them to now?

He pulled the truck between two dunes where a dozen storms had been kind enough to carve out a parking space. As soon as he killed the engine and opened the door, Jake jumped across him and bounded out. Jorgensen watched as the dog raced around in circles, the puppy in him rejoicing at being home again.

"You and me both," said Jorgensen. "You and me both."

There was an envelope on his doorstep, an envelope wrapped up in one of those little plastic bags they kept in rolls at the supermarket, the ones he could never figure out which end you were supposed to open. Rather than bending down to retrieve it, he simply slid it across the floor with his foot. Only when he'd put down his bag and fed Jake did he get around to picking it up and examining it. His name was typed on it, in large capital letters. THE HONORABLE AUGUST LARS JORGENSEN. Hell, it had been years since anyone had accused him of being honorable. The return address told him it was from Trial TV.

They've changed their minds, he told himself. They've fired him and gotten Lawrence Tribe to argue the case instead. Well, good for them. Larry'll give Boyd a run for his money. And Jorgensen? Well, it was almost March. Soon enough, it'd be time to put the boat in the water, do a little sailing.

He tore the envelope open. Inside was a letter, neatly typed, the right-hand margin as straight as the left. If he lived to be a hundred, Jorgensen would never understand how they did that.

The Honorable August Lars Jorgensen
One Lighthouse Lane
Old Santee Island, South Carolina

—BY HAND—

Dear Judge Jorgensen:

I hope and trust that this letter will find you in good health and spirits. We have received word that the United States Supreme Court has set the matter of *Davies v. Virginia* for argument the second Tuesday of April, the 10th, at 10:00 A.M. According to the scheduling order, each side will be given forty-five (45) minutes to argue the issue. Under the Court's rules, as Petitioner, we have the option of reserving up to fifteen (15) minutes of that time for rebuttal.

Within the next several weeks, you will be contacted by a representative of a briefing team, headed by Professor Reynaldo Gilbert, whom you have previously met. The team will be setting up a series of practice sessions to bring you up to speed and fill you in on the nuances of any recent decisions you may have missed.

Very fondly,
Jessica Woodruff

Even before he'd finished reading the letter, Jorgensen felt the rush of adrenaline. Not five minutes ago, he'd been telling himself to forget about the whole thing, that Boyd Davies would be better off dead than languishing in prison. As for Jorgensen himself, he'd fantasized about being rescued by Lawrence Tribe. Anything to get off the case.

And now this. This harmless little single-page, two-paragraph letter, informing him of nothing more than a few ministerial details—a date, a time, and a length of argument— assuring him of assistance, and wishing him well.

So why did reading it suddenly cause his heart to race as though he were back in high school, rounding the final turn of the cinder track in the half-mile run, leaning forward and shortening his stride for the final hundred-yard kick?

What was it about April tenth, or ten o'clock A.M., or forty-five minutes, for that matter, that made him forget he was eighty-something, and feel instead like he was eighteen all over again? What was it about the patronizing references to a *briefing team* that he could laugh at and forgive? He had no answers to those questions, only the vaguest notion that it had to be about *him,* and about whatever it was that had driven him to the law in the first place, some sixty years ago. April tenth wasn't just a day, then, or even *the* day; it was *his* day. Not Larry Tribe's or David Boise's or Alan Dershowitz's. *His.* His day to stand up and speak for Boyd Davies, to summon up every ounce of strength and knowledge and wisdom he possessed, in order to do whatever he possibly could to try to save another man's life.

His *life.*

He looked at the letter again, but the words on the page kept jumping in and out of focus, and it took Jorgensen a moment to realize that his hands were trembling. He folded the letter and placed it on the table, walked across the room to the weather porthole, and looked out. In the foreground, the cattails and tall spartina grass bent before the breeze. At the water's edge, sandpipers scurried up and down the sand, emboldened by each receding wave, only to retreat a moment later, just before the next one's advance. Farther out, herring gulls wheeled and dived and disappeared between the white-caps. And in the distance, where the breakers marked the outer banks, a string of pelicans flew single-file just over the water. With their long beaks and jointed wings, they looked absolutely prehistoric to Jorgensen; they might just as well have been pterodactyls, gliding on the very same currents, above the very same ocean, as they had a hundred million years ago.

———

He drove to the post office the following morning. There were a couple of bills, a solicitation from the local volunteer fire company, and half a dozen pieces of assorted junk mail—nothing he couldn't have done without. But it was nice to see Edna Combs, just the same.

"Yong man was here the other day," she told him, "snooping around, looking for you."

"Oh?"

"Yep. Had some letter for you. Said he had to give it to you hisself, *personal delivery.*"

"Thanks," said Jorgensen. "I got it."

"Musta been real important."

Jorgensen pretended not to have heard her. With each passing year, it was something he found he could get away with more and more.

"Not bad news, I hope." This time too loudly for him to ignore.

"No," he assured her, "not bad news."

"Nothing you'd like to *share,* I suppose."

But by that time, he'd developed a sudden coughing fit that completely drowned out her voice. It subsided after a moment or two, but by that time he was safely out the door.

From the post office he walked over to Doc Crawford's, where he bought a few things and exchanged small talk. A brief silence followed.

"I s'pose you'll be wanting to use the phone," said Doc.

"Well," said Jorgensen, "now that you mention it . . ."

He removed a piece of paper from his pocket and glanced back and forth at it as he dialed the number, beginning with its 917 area code.

Jessica Woodruff picked up her cell phone on the first ring, hoping to catch it before it woke the man lying in bed next to her.

"Hello," she whispered.

"Miss Woodruff?" It sounded like an old man on the other end, an old man with a hearing problem.

"Yes."

"I can barely hear you. This is August Jorgensen, down in South Carolina."

"Yes, hello, Judge. How are you?"

"I'm fine, thanks." He sounded awfully chipper for the middle of the night. But she'd heard about old people and their insomnia. She had a grandmother who claimed not to have slept a wink for the past fifteen years.

"What time is it down there?" she asked him.

"I don't know, a little after nine?" It sounded as though he were guessing. She tried to place South Carolina on the map, couldn't remember if it went above or below Georgia. But she was pretty sure they were in same time zone. She looked around for her robe, hoping to take the conversation into the next room, but it was too late: The body next to her was already stirring, and she felt an arm circle her waist.

"What can I do for you?" she asked Jorgensen.

"First of all," he said, "I wanted to thank you for the letter, and assure you I'll be *up to speed* by April tenth."

The letter, April tenth. Suddenly she remembered. Remembered, in fact, how the courier had been unable to find him, and had ending up having to leave the letter on his doorstep.

"Good," she said, leaning her weight back against the body, allowing its arm to shift and its hand to find its way between her legs.

"And something else," he said. "I took a little trip."

"Oh?"

"Yup. Jake and I took a ride on up to Virginia."

The hand was spreading her legs apart, and she was having trouble concentrating on the conversation. "Jake?" she asked.

"You remember Jake. He's my dog."

"Right," she said, not remembering, but not caring, either. She relaxed her thighs, allowing the hand to open her, feel her wetness. "So where in vagina did you go?"

"*Virginia.*"

"Right. Virginia."

"We went to Roanoke."

Jessica sat up, nearly spraining the wrist that connected the hand to the arm. "Roanoke? What were you doing in Roanoke?"

"Investigation."

The hand was trying to work its way back. Jessica pushed it away. "Investigation?" she repeated, turning it into a question.

"Yup," said Jorgensen.

"So did you learn anything?"

"I did indeed. I learned that Boyd Davies is completely innocent."

"You're kidding," said Jessica. She reached for her cigarettes on the nightstand. "That's incredible."

"You want to hear about it?"

"No," said Jessica. "I mean, yes. But not now, not over the phone." She lit a cigarette. "What's today, Saturday?"

"Yup."

"I can be down there tomorrow afternoon," she said. "Monday by the latest. I want to hear everything, okay? Before you breathe a word of this to anyone else."

"Not to worry," said Jorgensen. "I'll make Jake take an oath of silence."

She hung up and snapped her cell phone closed. "That was Judge Jorgensen," she said, rising and beginning to pace the bedroom, momentarily forgetting her nakedness. "He's been doing *investigation.* He thinks he's got it figured out that Wesley Boyd Davies is innocent. I told him to keep a lid on it, that I'd fly down and talk to him in a day or two."

The man shifted his weight to one elbow, using his recently rejected hand for a headrest. *God, he's one good-looking man,* thought Jessica, *even at nine o'clock on a Saturday morning.* She suddenly became self-conscious, turned her back to him. He'd often made a point of telling her it was her best side, anyway.

"Why don't you take Duke Schneider with you?" he said.

"Duke Schneider? Wasn't he a football player?"

"Something like that," he said. "The guy I'm talking about is Mickey Schneider. But everyone calls him the Duke."

"I was going to take someone from video with me. You know, to shoot some footage of Jorgensen in his lighthouse or against the ocean, for a 'Retired-Judge-Comes-out-of-Seclusion-to-Argue-a-Death-Penalty-Case' bit. Why should I take this Duke guy along?"

"He's from our security department. They do investigations. It sounds like this thing is rapidly turning into one, right? I just heard you say so yourself."

"I guess so," said Jessica, exhaling smoke. "Anyway, you're the boss. Whatever you say."

"I say get that cute little ass of yours back over here where it belongs," said Brandon Davidson.

Jorgensen paid Doc Crawford for the call, thanked him, and headed to his truck. He felt good about his conversation with Jessica Woodruff. He'd half expected her to react with skepticism to his claim about Boyd Davies being innocent, to demand to know what proof he had. And, of course, he had none.

But instead, she'd seemed to have taken him seriously—so seriously, in fact, that she wanted to come down and talk about it. And not next month or in a couple of weeks, but right away—tomorrow or Monday.

He was nothing but an old man, an old man who hadn't been smart enough to think of bringing along a tape recorder when he'd gone to talk with Kurt Meisner. But Trial TV? They had to be a huge outfit, he was quite sure, with all sorts of money and employees and technical equipment at their disposal. Someone there would be clever enough to figure out how to finish the job he'd started, and how to do it right.

Jorgensen knew one thing: He was going to sleep well that night, confident in the knowledge that he'd set things in motion that, one way or another, were going to lead to Boyd

Davies not only avoiding execution, but being completely exonerated and freed.

God, Marge would have been proud of me, he thought, as he climbed into his truck, fired it up, and pulled out onto the road. As soon as they were up to speed—which in this case meant doing a shade under the posted twenty-mile-per-hour limit—he turned to Jake and began booming, "Free at last! Free at last!" in the deepest, most resonating baritone he could summon. "Thank God almighty, he'll be free at last!"

The dog promptly turned his back, stuck his face out the far window, closed his eyes, and opened his mouth wide, to drink in the salt air. Or perhaps to yawn.

NINETEEN

Jessica Woodruff didn't show up until Tuesday afternoon, and when she did, she had two men with her again, although different ones from before. One was a cameraman (or, as Jessica referred to him, a *video technician*). Although Jorgensen kept telling Jessica he had important stuff to share with her, she was insistent that it wait until they'd *shot some footage*. The cameraman was a nice young fellow who, at Jessica's direction, aimed his camera at Jorgensen—first standing in front of his lighthouse, then walking along the beach with Jake, and finally explaining (to a microphone attached to the camera) why he'd been willing to come out of exile to argue Wesley Boyd Davies' case. Then the young man took footage of Jessica asking questions, but only after making sure to get the sun lighting her face and the breeze blowing her blonde hair just the right way.

"Back at the studio, we'll splice everything together," the cameraman explained. "That way it'll look like she's asking the questions in front of one camera, and you're answering them in front of another. Neat, huh?"

"Neat," Jorgensen agreed. Although he'd always thought the word neat was reserved for either orderly or without ice, he figured it was never too late to learn.

But as much as he liked the cameraman, it was the second man who interested Jorgensen. He was a beefy guy with a pasty complexion, a droopy mustache, and a green-checked sport jacket. Jorgensen didn't quite catch his last name, but as the day wore on, he gathered that the guy was a private investigator of some sort, and answered variously to "Mickey," "Duke," or even "the Duke."

It was warm outside, and while the cameraman went off to take a long walk on the beach—Jorgensen had the distinct feeling that the idea hadn't been his own—the rest of them sat down on an old park bench Jorgensen had scavenged from the town dump some years back. He finally got a chance to show them Boyd Davies' drawing of the three-fingered man (by this time it was well worn and faded), and tell them about his trip in search of him, and how it had led him to a seniors' residence in Roanoke. He described his meetings with Kurt Meisner, including Meisner's confession that he'd been the one who'd dug most of Ilsa's grave, and that Boyd had only happened along and helped out—because to Boyd, helping out meant arranging and rearranging big piles of smooth stones.

"So you think Meisner killed his own daughter?" Jessica asked him.

"No," said Jorgensen, "but his son did." He told them about the work glove Meisner had found near the body, and how he'd known for certain whose it was, and about young Kurt's reaction when his father returned it to him later that afternoon. He spoke for nearly half an hour, Jorgensen did, his voice growing scratchy from the effort, but his eyes alive with excitement.

"But the shovel," said Jessica. "How was it Boyd was able to lead them to the shovel? It was found quite a distance from the grave, as I recall."

"Meisner hid it," Jorgensen explained. "Boyd just happened to follow him, and saw where he put it. Later on, he remembered what the place looked like."

"Wow," said Jessica, sitting back on the bench. "That's quite a story."

"Did you get any of it on tape?" asked the Duke.

"No," said Jorgensen. "And now I'm afraid Meisner won't talk to me anymore."

"Did you get him to sign an affidavit?"

"No."

"A statement of any kind?"

"No," Jorgensen admitted. He hadn't even thought of doing anything like that. The man had been so cooperative, so—

"Did you take notes?"

"No."

Jorgensen felt more inept than ever.

Jessica wanted to know if he'd told anyone else about Meisner's account. Jorgensen said he hadn't.

"Well," she said, "this is huge. This is absolutely huge."

The Duke nodded solemnly in agreement.

It struck Jorgensen that neither of them had taken notes during their conversation with him. But he let it pass; he didn't want to seem overly defensive. Instead he asked, "So what do we do now?"

"Well," said Jessica, "for starters, as soon as we leave here we're going to fly right up to Roanoke, see if we can't get Mr. Meisner to talk to us."

"Want me to come along?" Jorgensen asked. "I can—"

"No," they replied in unison.

"What makes you think," Jorgensen wondered aloud, "that he'll talk to *you?*"

"Oh, dontcha worry," the Duke assured him. "He'll talk to us."

Jorgensen had forgotten that they'd never seen Meisner. No doubt they pictured him as a healthy, robust man in his mid-fifties, someone with normal fears, whom the Duke could always rough up a bit, if it came down to that. He found himself wondering about why the guy had kept his sport jacket on, when it had to be close to ninety degrees in the sun. Maybe it was to conceal a gun. He imagined a shoulder holster, containing a nine millimeter, or a .357 magnum, or maybe a small rocket launcher. The guy was so beefy, there could have been just about anything under there.

"Lissen," the Duke was saying now. "Zit okay fwee take that pitcher with us?"

Jorgensen looked around for a pitcher, failed to spot one.

"That one there," said the Duke, pointing at Boyd's drawing of Meisner. "It could help us to get the guy to tawk to us, fya know what I mean."

"Sure," said Jorgensen, handing over the drawing. As far as he was concerned, it had already served its purpose for him. If it helped them, fine. "So what do we tell the Supreme Court in the meantime?" he asked. "Do we make an application to have the argument postponed to a later term, because we're considering going back into state court and filing a motion for a new trial? And don't you think we should be sending a letter to the Virginia Attorney General's Office, letting them know we've got newly discovered evidence? You know, so later on they can't claim any lack of due diligence on our part?"

Jessica raised both hands, then lowered them several times, palms down, the way a third-base coach might signal a runner to slide. "Slow down," she said, "slow down. We don't do a thing until we've nailed down Kurt Meisner's story—"

"On tape," added the Duke.

"—so that nobody else can get to him first, and talk him into changing it."

"Or clammin' up alltagedda," was the Duke's contribution.

Jorgensen had never been to Brooklyn, but he imagined that's where the Duke had to be from. Not just New York, but *Brooklyn*. Who else used expressions like *dontcha worry, clammin' up,* and *alltagedda?* But what did it matter? The important thing was that they got to hear Kurt Meisner's story firsthand, believed it, and memorialized it—preserved it in some form that could be used to get them a hearing on Boyd Davies' innocence. Something that August Jorgensen himself had conspicuously failed to do.

They left just before dark, turning down an invitation to stay for dinner and spend the night. Had the weather been bad, and the fog been rolling in, Jorgensen would have insisted. But a nearly full moon was already visible, and he figured they'd have enough light to navigate the road back to the mainland. Besides, he liked the idea that they seemed in a hurry to get on with what they had to do next.

"Time is of the essence," explained Jessica.

"When da goyne gets tough, da tough get goyne," is how the Duke phrased it.

It was only after the cameraman had returned from his walk and the three of them had driven off that Jorgensen realized that, in their haste, they'd forgotten to ask him the name or address of the seniors' residence in Roanoke where Kurt Meisner was living. Well, Jorgensen figured, if he'd managed to find the place, so would they.

For a week, Jorgensen busied himself with chores in and around the lighthouse. Spring was in full cry, and he took advantage of the longer, warmer days to do some caulking and painting, and some pointing around the brickwork. He washed those portholes he could reach, leaving the upper ones for the weather to take care of. He repaired a wooden fence that had taken a beating over the winter, and pulled some weeds from a patch where wildflowers had begun to bloom. And while it was still a few weeks too soon to put the boat in the water, there was plenty to do to get her ready. He removed the tarps from her, and gave her hull and keel (from which he'd scraped the barnacles before he'd wrapped her up at the end of last season) a good sanding. This he did by hand; at the boatyards, he knew, they had these huge electric sanders to do the job. But August Jorgensen had never been much of a believer in power tools. They worked much faster, to be sure, but time was one thing he had an abundance of. Besides which, hand-sanding not only took less of the precious wood off the surface; in the end it left her smoother to the touch—so smooth he could run the palm of his hand across her without picking up a single splinter.

When he'd finished sanding her, he washed her down real well, to make sure he got all of the sawdust off. Then, after she'd dried overnight, he applied a coat of antifouling paint. Once the boat was in the water, the paint would serve to inhibit the growth of barnacles, snails, algae, and other marine hitchhikers, so as to reduce drag and let her slip more easily through the water.

Each day he waited for news from Jessica Woodruff. He assumed from her silence that she and the Duke had had no trouble finding Kurt Meisner; otherwise they would have contacted him, for sure. But had Meisner been willing to talk to them? Had he *clammed up* only when it came to Jorgensen, or did his sudden silence extend to others, as well? He cursed himself for not having a phone, then reminded himself that they knew how to contact him when they needed to.

It had long been Jorgensen's routine to drive to the mainland every several days, stopping at Doc Crawford's general store to pick up a paper and whatever he needed in the way of groceries. From there he'd walk over to the post office, to see if Edna Coombs had any mail for him. Now he made the trip each morning, using Doc's phone to call Jessica Woodruff. But each time he'd succeed only in reaching her answering machine. "Please leave your name and number," her voice told him, "and I'll get right back to you." But, of course, he had no number to leave—except for Doc's, which finally he asked her to call and leave some word for him about what was going on. But she hadn't even done that. Not yet, at least.

Then he'd walk over and check with Edna, to see if a letter might have come for him from New York City. But each day, the answer was the same: nothing. The only break in the routine came on the fifth day, when the moment he walked in and closed the screen door carefully behind him—to avoid letting it bang and fall off its rusted hinges—Edna had some news.

"Hello, Mr. Bigshot Celebrity!" was how she greeted him.

Jorgensen could only frown in confusion.

"Don't tell me you didn't you see yourself on the *tee*-vee," she said.

"Don't *have* a TV," he replied.

"Oh, that's right. I forgot. Well," she said, "that Trial TV program says you're going to be arguing a big case in front of the Supreme Court. That a fact?"

"Could be," Jorgensen admitted, "if they say so."

"You looked real good, you did. And Jake, too."

Jorgensen cleared his throat. Accepting compliments had never been one of his strengths.

"So how come you been holding out on us?"

He shrugged. "It's no big deal, really. I get to stand up and talk for forty-five minutes, that's all. Hell, you do that every time I see you."

"Well," said Edna, "I think it's a right nice thing you're doing, speaking for that colored boy. Of course, not everyone feels that way."

Jorgensen raised an eyebrow.

"I mean," said Edna, "there's no excusing what he did to that poor little white girl, is there?"

"No," Jorgensen agreed, "there isn't."

"But then I guess somebody has to take his side, right?"

"Right," said Jorgensen. And as far as he was concerned, Edna Coombs had pretty much hit the nail on the head. "Any mail for me?" he asked.

"Fraid not," said Edna. She knew he'd been expecting a letter or a package for almost a week now, but she'd refrained from teasing him about it. Something in the way he'd been stopping in each morning and asking had told her it was too important for that. "But I'll keep an eye out," she promised him.

Edna Coombs was a smart woman.

———

August Jorgensen was a patient man, ordinarily. But this silent treatment he was getting from Jessica Woodruff was getting to him. He knew full well he wasn't part of the brain trust on this appeal, and no one had ever led him to believe he'd be a charter member of the inner circle responsible for making tactical decisions. His role was pretty much limited to that of a figurehead: They'd give him words to mouth, prep him on recent decisions and developments, and run him through a series of practice sessions, until they were satisfied he could hold up his end. Then, when the time came, they'd bring him up to Washington and he'd argue the case. After that, he'd be done; it would be up to others to continue the fight, if there was any fight left to continue.

For a time, he'd been okay with that arrangement. But now things had changed, and changed hugely. Boyd Davies was innocent, and Jorgensen had been the one who'd figured things out. That had to count for something, didn't it? And yet they continued to ignore him, to leave him completely in the dark. He had no way of knowing if Kurt Meisner had told Jessica and the Duke the same things he'd told Jorgensen, before he'd suddenly *clammed up*. He could only hope that they'd gotten Meisner to tell his story again, and that they'd either got it down on tape or convinced him to sign an affidavit swearing it was true.

He just needed to know, one way or the other.

On the morning of the eighth day, a storm blew up from the south, bringing torrential rain and keeping Jorgensen inside his lighthouse for a full two days. He took it as an omen of sorts, a sign that when the rain finally subsided and he was able to drive to the mainland, there'd be a letter from Jessica waiting for him at the post office. Every few hours he'd crack the door open and let Jake slip out or back in. (Jake loved the rain; to him it was nothing but a giant sprinkler, custom-made for him to play in.) At one point it occurred to Jorgensen that he himself was some sort of a modern-day Noah, riding out

The Flood, and Jake was his dove, whom he dispatched every so often to see if the waters had begun to subside. But he dismissed the idea as far too grandiose: Noah had been summoned by God to save all the creatures who inhabited the earth's land, while Jorgensen had been enlisted by some folks at a television station to help save one poor soul.

Still, a week and a half of *not knowing* was driving him absolutely crazy.

In the end, it only seemed as though the storm lasted forty days and forty nights. In fact, it ended on the evening of the third day. With the overhead sky nearly black from the last of the rain clouds and the approach of night from over the ocean, the western horizon suddenly cleared and lit up, revealing a band of orange light and a glowing red sun. To Jorgensen, there was something about the effect—as strikingly beautiful as it was—that was positively eerie. Just before the sun disappeared from view, it sunk low enough in the sky to light the undersides of the clouds above him, casting a purple glow to everything. Then, moments later, it was dark.

The following morning, Jorgensen rose and made the trip to the mainland, driving slowly through a thin mist created by the evaporation of more rain than the ground could soak up. It was after nine by the time he got there, so he decided to stop at the post office first, figuring that in the three days since his last visit, a letter from Jessica simply *had* to be waiting for him.

"Nothing," said Edna Coombs.

Which meant, since it was Saturday, nothing until Monday, at the earliest.

At Doc Crawford's, he used the phone once again to call New York City. "Hi," said Jessica's voice, but immediately he recognized her recorded message; he'd certainly had enough practice. "You've reached Jessica Woodruff of Trial TV. Please leave your name and number, and I'll get right back to you."

Without bothering to leave a message, he placed the headset

back on the cradle of the wall phone. By this time he'd already left her half a dozen messages, more than enough to let her know he wanted to speak with her, needed some word from her, however brief, however discouraging. He imagined she had to be very busy; TV folks probably worked hard, dealing with deadlines and updates and breaking stories and all sorts of other stuff he couldn't even begin to imagine. No doubt she'd get around to calling him one of these days. Leaving another message was only going to annoy her.

Jessica Woodruff heard the ring of her cell phone and flipped open the cover. The numbers and letters that came up on its LCD screen were by this time familiar to her. They told her that the incoming call was from Crawford's General Store in Cumberland, South Carolina.

"It's him again," she said to no one in particular, although she was seated at a conference table with six men and two other women.

"Him?" someone asked.

"Jorgensen."

"Who's Jorgensen?"

"The judge," she said, "the old retired judge who's going to argue the Eight Amendment case before the Supremes next month."

"Oh, Larry Lighthouse?"

"Yes," she said, "Larry Lighthouse."

"Call him later, Jess. These Nielsen numbers are important."

She closed the cover of the phone.

For a long moment, August Jorgensen's hand continued to rest on the phone's cradled headset, as though there were some magnetic pull that was making it impossible for him to let go of it. He could feel Doc's gaze on the back of his neck, and though he knew Doc was far too kind to ever say anything harsh, Jorgensen didn't need to be told that he was being played for a fool.

After a time, he picked the headset back up, put it to his ear, and listened for a dial tone. Then he punched in another number. He listened as it rang three times before being answered. Then a woman spoke to him, a woman with a pleasant voice, who asked if she could help him.

"Yes," he told her. "I'd like the number for American Airlines."

TWENTY

The big jet touched down on the runway and bounced slightly, its engines roaring, before settling into its deceleration run. August Jorgensen loosened his death grip on the armrests of his seat a bit, and finally allowed himself to breathe.

He hadn't always been a white-knuckle flyer; it was simply that he was out of practice. The flight from Charleston to New York's LaGuardia Airport, all two hours of it, marked the first time he'd set foot in a plane in almost ten years. He knew how safe flying was supposed to be, had heard all the statistics, and had no doubt that the pilot was well-trained and experienced. Still, he hated the feeling of being so terribly out of control. In a boat, when a situation came up, you dealt with it. You eased up on the sheets, you reefed the main, you doused the jib, you ran a radar reflector up the mast, you dragged a storm anchor—whatever it took. Sitting in the passenger compartment of a plane, you were completely powerless. All you could do was tighten your seat belt, grab onto those armrests, and pray. So for two hours, he'd done his share of all three.

And it wasn't just the flight; his anxiety had been compounded by several other things. He was worried about Jake, who'd be looked after by a neighbor (*neighbor* being a decidedly relative term on a barrier island), but nevertheless wouldn't quite be himself until Jorgensen's return. Beyond that, Jorgensen had neglected to reserve a hotel room in New York, figuring that wouldn't be much of a problem, given all the hotels there had to be in the city. Marge had always taken care of that sort of thing. But now he began to wonder: Suppose there was some huge convention going on—or three or four of them, simultaneously—and all the rooms had been booked? He imagined himself sleeping in some doorway, or bedding down in that big park they had, until he heard the pilot announce that it was twenty-two degrees in New York, and snowing lightly. So much for camping out.

Finally, he was worried about locating Jessica Woodruff. Getting to Trial TV should be no problem; he'd copied down the address of their headquarters from a letter Jessica had sent him, back when she'd been sending him letters. But suppose when he got there, she wasn't around? Suppose she was out of town? Suppose she'd picked this very week to fly down to South Carolina and meet with him?

Still, he'd decided against leaving word for her that he was coming north. Two weeks of calling her had convinced him she was deliberately avoiding him, for whatever reason. Maybe Kurt Meisner had refused to talk to her and the Duke, and she was too embarrassed to say so. Maybe Meisner had changed his story, dug in and decided to protect himself and his son— or at least his son's memory. On the other hand, maybe Meisner had repeated for Jessica everything he'd told Jorgensen, and now all the folks at Trial TV were scurrying around madly, drawing up papers to get the Supreme Court argument put off while they went into state court to move for a new trial. Whatever it was, Jorgensen was determined to not give her another opportunity to duck him. Better to take his chances showing up unannounced. That way she'd have to let him know what was going on, whether it was good news or bad.

The plane seemed to taxi for almost as long as it had been in the air. When it finally reached the gate and pulled to a stop, an audible *"Ping!"* signaled the passengers to stand and fill the aisle, and Jorgensen rose, too, only to find himself pressed in from all sides by a sea of people in a terrible hurry to get somewhere, but unable to budge.

"Welcome to New York City," said the pilot.

The cab driver dropped him off at Madison Avenue and Fortieth Street, but only after relieving Jorgensen of $26.50 for the fare, $3.50 for the tunnel toll, another $3.50 for a tip, and a $1.50 surcharge occasioned by the driver's having had to walk all the way from the front seat to the trunk, where he stood by and watched as Jorgensen lifted out his bag. If the ride had set him back $35.00, Jorgensen shuddered to think what a hotel room might go for. He shuddered, too, from the cold, although the light snow forecast by the pilot had thankfully failed to materialize.

He found the building with numbers that matched the address on Jessica's letter, a huge mass of glass and steel that filled an entire block and had too many floors to count. Inside, it was like a city, with hundreds, perhaps thousands of people crisscrossing the lobby. There were restaurants, newsstands, boutiques, a shoeshine, a barbershop, even a subway entrance. Jorgensen made a mental note that if he couldn't find a hotel room, this might be as good a place to stay as any: A person could easily spend a week here without attracting notice.

A huge glass-covered directory informed him that Trial TV occupied more than a single floor of the building. RECEPTION was on the forty-eight floor, as opposed to RECEIVING, which could be found on forty-nine, apparently not too far from SHIPPING. But Jorgensen had no interest in announcing his arrival, whether by being received, receipted, or shipped. PERSONNEL, meanwhile, was down on forty-seven, along with MARKETING & DEVELOPMENT and MEDIA RESEARCH. In the end, he opted for EXECUTIVE OFFICES. Jessica Woodruff had to be an executive, he figured; his best chance of finding her ought to be there. Besides, the number was the easiest to remember: an even fifty.

He found the elevator bank marked 45–60, hoping it referred to floors, rather than the age group of passengers permitted. The ascent took only seconds, followed by a slightly longer period for his stomach to catch up to the rest of him.

He found himself in a plushly carpeted area roughly the size of Delaware, with hand-rubbed wood (no anti-fouling paint here) and indirect lighting. There were several doors to choose from, all bearing numbers, but only one with raised bronze lettering spelling out

TRIAL TV
EXECUTIVE OFFICES

He tried the knob somewhat tentatively, having heard that New Yorkers unfailingly secured themselves behind multiple deadbolt locks. To his surprise, the door swung open. A large black man, wearing a military-type uniform, sat behind a handsome wooden desk. Jorgensen, who knew something about wood, recognized it as mahogany, probably Philippine.

"May I help you?" the man asked.

"Yes," said Jorgensen. "I'm Judge Jorgensen. Miss Woodruff, Jessica Woodruff, is expecting me, sort of." He looked at his watch, or where his watch would have been, had he been wearing one. "Though I'm afraid I'm running a bit late," he added.

"They're all across the hall," the man said. "Screening Room One." He reached for a phone. "Your name again, please?"

"Jorgensen. And do you happen to have a rest room I could use first? I've been traveling, and—"

"Down the hall on your left."

"Thank you," said Jorgensen. Then, setting his bag down on the floor, he added, "I'll just leave this here for a moment, if I may." He turned to leave, and was a step from the door, when he was stopped in his tracks by a "Sir?"

"Yes?"

"You'll need this," said the man, extending a key attached to a large wooden tag with the word GENTLEMEN carved into it.

The door to Screening Room One was unlocked, too. So much for rumors of fearful New Yorkers; they were actually turning out to be considerably more friendly than advertised. He stuck his head into the room. Except for a movie screen on the far wall, it was dark. Jorgensen mumbled, "Sorry," closed the door behind him, and slipped into the nearest seat. It was the kind they used to have in the movie theaters of his youth: red velvet, padded arms, and cushiony soft. It even reclined a bit as you leaned your weight against the backrest.

Once his eyes had adjusted to the darkness, he looked around. A half-dozen people sat in chairs identical to his, in rows in front of him. He thought he recognized Jessica Woodruff's blonde hair in the front row, but it was hard to be sure, from just the back of her head.

His attention moved to the movie screen, which, he could now see, was actually a television monitor, only about a hundred times bigger than any he'd ever seen before. It showed a man, seated behind a metal table, talking into the camera. He looked vaguely familiar, though at first Jorgensen couldn't quite place him. But when it came to him, it came like a punch in the gut, knocking the wind out of him.

He was looking at Kurt Meisner.

But it was a Kurt Meisner who seemed better, much healthier than he had just a couple of weeks ago. And they'd combed his hair, made it look thicker somehow, and managed to get him out of that dreadful room of his.

". . . the Davies boy," he was saying, "he just came along at the wrong time. He helped me bury her, he did that. But he didn't have nothin' to do with, you know, with what happened before."

"And you know it was your son that did that?" The voice was that of a woman, coming from somewhere off-camera.

"Yes, ma'am."

"And how do you know that?"

"Like I told you," Meisner was saying. "The glove. The dirt on his clothes. His reaction when I saw him after. It wasn't any one thing, you know. It was, it was everything."

"No question in your mind?"

"No question."

By God, they've done it! Jorgensen wanted to shout out at the top of his lungs, to jump up and leap for joy. Why hadn't they gotten word to him? Why were they all sitting around so quietly, instead of whooping it up, as he was on the verge of doing?

A technician was rewinding the tape now, in fast motion, with a squealing noise. Jorgensen decided to postpone his celebration; he figured if he kept quiet, he might get to see the thing from the beginning.

"What about the date and time?" the blonde woman was asking, and now he definitely recognized Jessica's voice. "Can that be changed?"

"Absolutely," said the technician, stopping the tape and letting it resume playing, this time without the sound track. For the first time, Jorgensen became aware of writing superimposed on the lower left-hand corner of the image.

JULY 11, 2000   3:38 P.M.

"Show us," said a man, seated next to Jessica, one arm draped over the back of her seat.

"What would you like?" the technician asked.

"Can you go earlier?" the man asked. "Say, to January?"

The technician pressed some buttons on a keyboard in front of him. The writing disappeared for a moment. When it returned, it read

JANUARY 11, 2000   3:38 P.M.

Even as they watched, the 3:38 changed to 3:39.

"How about later?" the man asked. "Can you go into next year, for example?"

The technician played with his keyboard again. Jorgensen remembered Doc Crawford's nephew Zachary, and the magic he'd been able to do with one of those things.

JANUARY 11, 2002   3:39 P.M.

"Beautiful," said Jessica. "Why don't you leave it there for now. *Lights!*"

Jorgensen froze as the room suddenly brightened. Those in the front rows were already rising from their seats, a few of them even turning his way. He pushed himself up and tried to pivot toward the door, but his knee locked, causing him to momentarily lose his balance and pitch forward. He put out his hands to catch his fall (a reflex known all too well by roller skaters and their orthopedists), landing awkwardly on the padded carpeting.

The others in the room let out a collective gasp, and rushed over to offer assistance.

"Are you all right?" a woman asked.

"Don't move him!" shouted a man. "Someone call nine-one-one."

"Stand back," said another man. "Let him breathe."

But the others paid no attention, instead crowding around Jorgensen's fallen body so tightly that the last person to reach him was forced to peek between two others in order to get a glimpse of his reddened face. When she did, she managed to confine her reaction to a single word.

"Fuck," is what Jessica Woodruff said.

"Would you like some more water?" someone asked him. "Some ice for your forehead, maybe?"

"No," said Jorgensen, "this is fine, thank you."

From Screening Room One they'd adjourned to Conference Room One. It was every bit as nice as the first room, but in place of the giant monitor and the rows of theater seats, there was a large wooden table (teak, was Jorgensen's guess this time), surrounded by a dozen chairs. Jorgensen had been helped into one of them, at one end of the table. Half the others were occupied now, presumably by the same people who'd been at the screening moments earlier. Jessica Woodruff—it *had* been her—sat at the opposite end. Jorgensen recognized Ray Gilbert, one of the two men who'd accompanied Jessica on her first visit to the lighthouse, though the other one, Tim Harkin, was nowhere in sight. The man who seemed to have been in charge of things during the screening was there, as well as several others Jorgensen couldn't place. The technician appeared to have been excused.

"Are you certain you're all right?" asked In Charge. He looked to be fifty or so, and very handsome, in a corporate sort of way. "We have a physician on call, and a—"

"Thank you," said Jorgensen, "but not to worry, I'm really fine. A bit embarrassed, but fine."

"I'm Brandon Davidson, by the way. I'm a big fan of yours. Though I must say, I'm surprised to see you here in New York. Jessica—you remember Jessica from—"

Jorgensen nodded.

"—Jessica was just getting ready to fly down to, to—"

"South Carolina."

"Right, along with Ray here, to begin prepping you for the oral argument."

"And I can assure you I was very much looking forward to it," said Jorgensen.

"Perhaps," Davidson suggested, "they can even join you on your return flight, if you wouldn't mind."

"I wouldn't mind at all," said Jorgensen. "But if you'll permit me—"

"Yes?"

"—I mean, will there still *be* an oral argument?"

Jorgensen thought he noticed Jessica shifting her weight uncomfortably in her chair.

"I'm not sure I follow you," said Davidson.

"*The screening*," said Jorgensen. "*Kurt Meisner*. Everyone in this room now knows Boyd Davies is a hundred percent factually *innocent*. Don't we have an obligation to ask the justices to take the case off its docket while we pursue our remedies in the Virginia courts?"

"I'm afraid it's not quite that simple," said Davidson.

"What's not simple about it?"

"Plenty," said Davidson. "For one thing, you're making the assumption that Mr. Meisner was telling the truth."

Jorgensen rubbed his eyes. Maybe the fall had affected him more than he realized. "Why on earth," he asked, as calmly as he could, "would he be lying? Why would he suddenly claim that his own son was the murderer, if it weren't true? And why would he acknowledge that he's known it all along and covered it up, allowing an innocent man to spend sixteen years on death row? Those are pretty damning admissions, wouldn't you say?"

"Okay," said Davidson. "Let's assume for just a moment, for the purpose of argument, that Meisner *was* telling the truth. Who says he's going to be believed?"

"He *has* to be believed," Jorgensen fairly shouted. "Other than it being the truth, what other explanation can there possibly be for it? That he's suddenly decided he likes Boyd Davies? That he wants to reward him for killing his daughter, by setting him free?"

"Remember also," said Jessica Woodruff, "that his statement is hearsay. There was no opportunity for cross-examination."

"But you have to start somewhere," Jorgensen explained. "The tape, along with a written transcript of it, will get us into court. Some judge will have to order an evidentiary hearing, where we'll subpoena Mr. Meisner and have him testify. That's when the state will get its chance to cross-examine him. That's how it's done."

None of them said a word; all they did was exchange glances across the table. It occurred to Jorgensen that he might have overestimated these people. Weren't they lawyers, though? Didn't they know anything about criminal procedure, and how the rules of evidence worked?

"There are a few things you evidently don't know," said Brandon Davidson.

"*I* don't know?"

"Yes," said Davidson. "In the first place, no one's going to need to cross-examine Kurt Meisner."

"I don't understand how you can say that."

Jorgensen interpreted the pause that followed as a sign of contemplation on the part of his hosts. But as the seconds ticked off, it began to dawn on him that they were simply giving him the silent treatment. He looked from one face to another, hoping to spot someone on the same wavelength as he was—the way he used to look around for a fellow judge on the bench whose reaction to an appellate argument might be the same as his. But not one of them would even make eye contact with him, and eventually he gave up trying. Across from him, at the far end of the table, Jessica Woodruff appeared to be engrossed in studying her shoes, or perhaps the carpet beneath them, and now she began to shake her head slowly from side to side. At last she looked up, sighed, and said, "I'm afraid this isn't working." She spoke the words softly, without emotion, as though she were suddenly very tired after a long day. Turning to Brandon Davidson, she said, "May I?"

Davidson shrugged, and waved his hands slightly. Jorgensen couldn't quite tell if that was his way of granting Jessica permission of some sort, or washing his hands of the whole thing. Jessica seemed to take it as the former.

"Judge Jorgensen," she began, giving him the distinct impression that he was in for a speech, "if you had to name the single driving passion that unites everyone in this room, what would you come up with?"

"The single driving passion?"

"Yes."

Jorgensen thought for a moment, wondering if it might be

a trick question, before deciding to play it straight. "Justice?" he answered.

"Not bad," said Jessica. "Can you be a little more specific?"

"Justice for Boyd Davies?"

"Try going in the other direction for a moment," she suggested. "Boyd Davies is only one man. Try thinking *big*, why don't you."

Jorgensen leaned back in his chair. He wanted to tell this television woman that as driving passions went, justice was a pretty big thing, even justice for one man. Particularly when that man had been wrongly convicted and spent the past sixteen years of his life on death row for a crime he hadn't committed. But he sensed that Jessica Woodruff wasn't really looking for a debate on that point. She was going somewhere else with this, somewhere else entirely. Somewhere *big*, as she'd put it. So he held his tongue and waited.

"Why did you retire from the bench, Judge?"

Jorgensen smiled. "I was getting old," he said. "It was time to make room for some younger men. Younger women, too."

"Be honest," Jessica told him. "It was more than that. I've read some of your writings. I think everyone in this room has."

"I was tired."

"And what was it you were tired of?"

Years ago, Jorgensen had been a chess player. He'd never played enough to get really good at it, but he'd liked the game, the way you had to plan five, six, sometimes seven moves ahead. The thought that came to him now was that he was badly overmatched and caught in an endgame, with the enemy pieces closing in on him, with each move backing him slowly but surely into a corner.

"The caseload," he said, "and the constant bickering with colleagues."

Buying time, slipping out of check for a moment.

"Which cases?" she pressed him. "And bickering over what?"

Check.

"You must know," he said.

"Yes, I know. But I'd prefer for you to tell us."

Check.

He closed his eyes, but it was no use. He could see them still, the endless line of petitioners, each with three names, which were almost always easily identifiable as black or Hispanic. Their all-too-familiar stories of alcoholic parents, broken homes, and physical abuse. Their pitiful I.Q. scores, forever hovering somewhere in the range between 60 and 70.

"The death cases," acknowledged August Jorgensen.

Mate.

"Every single person in this room," Jessica was saying, "is a committed, passionate foe of capital punishment. Because it's immoral, because it's invariably applied in a racist manner, because study after study has demonstrated that it has absolutely no deterrent value whatsoever. And because it defines us as an uncivilized nation that places a higher value on vengeance than on compassion. Sound familiar?"

Eyes still closed, Jorgensen nodded.

"It should," said Jessica. "If I'm not mistaken, those are your own words."

He'd actually said it a little better, as he recalled, a little more succinctly. But she was pretty close.

"Why do you think it was," she asked, "that we sought you out in the first place?"

He opened his eyes, blinked a couple of times at the unexpected brightness. "You told me so yourself," he replied. "It was my good looks and deep voice." A ripple of polite laughter spread around the table. "That, and your claim that I'd bring a bit of dignity with me, a degree of gravitas, I think you called it."

"All true," said Jessica. "But you're overlooking the biggest requirement of all, the *sine qua non*."

"That being?"

"That being your longstanding principled opposition to executing fellow human beings."

Jorgensen smiled at the mouthful. He knew there was a reason he had no use for television.

"So," said Jessica, "here's what we need to know. Do you still feel the same way you felt when you stepped down from the bench in protest and wrote those words? Are you one of us? Can we trust you?"

"Can you trust me?"

"Yes." The voice was that of Brandon Davidson. "What Jessica means, I think, is that we're about to share a confidence with you, a very important confidence. We need your assurance in advance that you'll treat it as such. In other words, we need to know we can trust you with it."

"And I'm supposed to give you my word in a vacuum, before I hear what this confidence is."

"I'm afraid so."

"And if I won't?"

Davidson looked him hard in the eye. "If you won't," he said, "we'll get someone else who will."

Jorgensen sat for a moment, pondering that. Once, as a small boy, when he'd been tagging along with a group of older boys, they'd pulled him aside and asked him if he could keep a secret. Wanting to hear it, he'd promised that he could. So the older boys had told him they planned to set fire to the barn of a farmer who'd chased them off his fields. Bound by his promise, young Augie Jorgensen had stood by helplessly as the barn burned to the ground. It had been a hard thing to watch, and an experience he hoped he'd learned from.

Slowly now, he placed the palms of his hands on the arms of his chair and began pushing himself up. When he reached a standing position, he said, "If you're truly satisfied that I'm as principled in my opposition to the death penalty as you are, that should be all the word you need. If it isn't, then by all means get someone else."

There was an embarrassing silence. Finally someone said, "That's good enough for me." That was followed by a, "Me, too," and a, "He's okay." Only after everyone at the table had voiced approval in one way or another did Jorgensen lower himself back down into his chair.

No barns would burn this day.

"Several years ago," began Jessica, "we received a report about a man living in Virginia by the name of Kurt Meisner. Meisner was said to be in poor health, and staying by himself in a rest home. According to our source, he was troubled by a burden that he'd been carrying around for almost fifteen years, a burden that might be of particular interest to us at Trial TV. Our research department did some digging, and came up with the fact that back in the mid-eighties, a child named Ilsa Meisner had been murdered, and that court records from that time listed her father's name as Kurt.

"Through Social Security records, we found Kurt Meisner, at the very same seniors' residence where you yourself visited him not too long ago."

"Which explains," said Jorgensen, "why you didn't have to ask me where he was."

"Correct," said Jessica. "In any event, back when we first spoke with him, Mr. Meisner was uncooperative. He denied carrying around any sort of a burden, and insisted he had no idea what we were talking about. But we persisted."

Jorgensen wasn't sure he liked the emphasis she placed on the word *persisted,* but he let it go. There were times in life, after all, when the end truly did justify the means.

"Eventually, after assuring Mr. Meisner that the statute of limitations had long run on any crimes he might have committed—"

"And in the interest of full disclosure," broke in Ray Gilbert, "we also provided him some modest financial assistance, defraying some of the costs of his care at the facility."

"Right," said Jessica. "There came a time when he finally broke down and told us his story."

"His story," echoed Jorgensen. A part of him was beginning to see where this was going; another part was having great difficulty digesting it.

"Yes," said Jessica. "The same story he told you."

Jorgensen rubbed his eyes. Maybe he'd hurt himself more than he'd thought when he'd fallen back there in the screening room. He kept remembering how a couple of weeks ago, back at the lighthouse, Jessica, the Duke, and the cameraman had said they were going to see Meisner as soon as they left. Wasn't that when they'd found him, and made the videotape of him? All of a sudden, everything seemed confusing, as though a fog bank had settled in. He rubbed his eyes again. "When was this?" he asked.

It was Brandon Davidson's turn. "A year ago," he said, "a little more, maybe. Eighteen months, tops."

The fog parted momentarily. Jorgensen leaned forward, straining to see, fighting to comprehend. "You all have known all this for a *year?*" he asked.

Nods all around.

"And the videotape?" He waved in the direction of the screening room.

"What about it?" Jessica asked.

"When was it made?"

"About eight months ago."

Eight months ago. Of course: That explained the younger, healthier Kurt Meisner, the one with more hair on his head. Jorgensen suddenly felt very old and very foolish. Here he thought he'd performed a minor miracle, running around like some Don Quixote with Boyd Davies' drawing, until he'd stumbled upon Kurt Meisner and succeeded in prying the truth out of him. And now they were telling him they'd found Meisner a year and a half ago, and had had his story down on videotape before they'd ever sought Jorgensen out. The fog was rolling in again, thickening, threatening to overwhelm him.

"So," he said, forcing himself to fight it back, "so you all have known for a year and a half now that there was an innocent man sitting on death row in Brushy Mountain. And for eight months, you've been in a position to prove it."

"That's true," said Davidson, "to a certain extent."

"Did you go see Boyd?"

"Yes," said Jessica. "At least we sent someone in to see him. And we did a lot of fact-checking on him, too."

"And what *facts* did you come up with?"

"That he can't read, can't write, and doesn't speak. That he has no visitors, no family that cares about him, no friends in prison or out, no comprehension of what he's there for, no ability to distinguish between one day and the next. Nothing."

"But you knew he was innocent," said Jorgensen, "you've said so yourselves. You had no choice but to—"

"Stop . . . right . . . there," said Jessica. "That's precisely where you're wrong. In fact, the more we thought about it, the more we realized we *did* have a choice, one we'd be forced to make. On the one hand, we could save Boyd Davies. If we did that, we'd be patted on the back and told we were heroes. But what would we really have accomplished? Davies would be taken out of Brushy Mountain. But with nobody to care for him and nowhere to go, he'd still be a ward of the state. He'd trade in his prison cell for a bed in the psychiatric wing of some dreadful state hospital, where he'd probably be worse off than he is now. He'd languish there until the day he died."

"Which, in all fairness," said Ray Gilbert, "would then be later, rather than sooner. In other words, if we chose to save him, he'd live longer."

"*If* you consider that a blessing," countered Jessica. "But that's not the worst of it. The worst part is that if Meisner's story were to come out in time to save Davies, the opposition—the pro-death forces—will get a chance to put their own spin on it, and claim it as a victory. 'See,' they'll all say, 'the system works; an innocent man has been set free.' And all we'll have succeeded in doing is to hand them the ammunition they need to shoot us down with."

"But," Jorgensen protested, "the alternative—"

"The alternative," said Jessica, "is simply to wait."

"Until?"

"Until after. If we do that, the state will have the blood of an innocent man on its hands, in full view of the rest of the nation."

"The rest of the *world*," added Davidson.

"What's more," explained Jessica, her eyes brightening with the fire of a true believer, "the timing couldn't be better. People are worried like never before about innocent men being executed. A moratorium's been declared in Illinois, by a Republican governor, no less. Other states are considering similar measures. Look at the polls, study the statistics, examine the trends. Every indicator shows an erosion of support for the death penalty. Don't you see? Years from now, historians will look back and point to this case as the pivotal moment, the turning point, when America was forced to face the fact that we'd killed an incontrovertibly innocent man. Don't you see? If we pull this off, we can bring the whole system crashing down, once and for all."

Jorgensen shook his head, trying to clear it, trying to push away the fog. "So all we've got to do is play God," he said, "and sacrifice one of his children."

"*We're* not sacrificing anyone," said Jessica. "The Commonwealth of Virginia is doing that. All we're doing is the math. Boyd Davies dies, in order that hundreds of others won't."

"Thousands," said Davidson.

"So what's the purpose of the videotape?" Jorgensen asked. "If you're not going to use it."

"Oh, we're going to *use* it," said Jessica. "After."

"But people will be outraged that you sat on it."

"People," said Jessica, "aren't going to know."

The date, Jorgensen realized. Of course: They'll simply change the date on the video and make it look like they found Kurt Meisner too late to save Boyd. "You've got it all figured out," he told them. "Don't you?"

"We thought we did," said Davidson. "Until you had to go and play detective."

Jorgensen allowed himself a smile. "I guess I wasn't supposed to find Kurt Meisner, was I? I was supposed to be a good boy, sit home, and stay out of trouble."

Several of them returned the smile.

"And now I've rather complicated things for you, haven't I?"

"I certainly hope not," said Brandon Davidson. "I'd like very much to think you're with us. As a matter of fact, I'd like your promise."

In the days and weeks following the barn-burning incident, young Augie Jorgensen had tried to figure out where he'd gone wrong. Had he declined to assure the older boys that he could be trusted with their secret, they simply would have gone ahead and set the fire without ever telling him. On the other hand, once he'd promised not to tell, wasn't he bound by his oath? The dilemma had bothered him so much that finally he'd disguised the story as best as he could, removing himself from it, and presented it to his father as a theoretical problem.

"What would you do, Papa? Keep your promise, or break it?"

Nils Jorgensen was a master shipbuilder, a no-nonsense man to whom there was black and white, but precious room for gray. For once, however, he was given pause. "A promise is a very solemn thing," said Nils. "But sometimes there are worse things than lying, or breaking one's word." Then he'd put Augie over his knee, told him to watch whom he was hanging out with, and given his bottom a good tanning, just in case the story hadn't been quite so theoretical, after all.

Years later, when Marge's doctors had confided to Jorgensen that the cancer had come back and spread throughout her body, he'd looked her in the eye and assured her that the latest round of tests had come back negative, and that she was going to be just fine. And at the very end, when the sores and blisters had covered her face and he'd had to hide her mirror, he told her she looked more beautiful than ever.

"You're lying," she'd said to that.

"No, I'm not," he'd insisted.

"Promise?"

And he'd promised. And in doing so, he'd lied to Marge—to him the single most important person on the face of the earth—deliberately promised her that something was true, when he knew full well it wasn't. Now he was being asked to make a promise he knew he wasn't going to keep. Only this time the person doing the asking wasn't Marge, it was Brandon Davidson. Brandon Davidson was nobody to Jorgensen, absolutely nobody.

Even so, he felt compelled to take a deep breath. Then he looked Brandon Davidson squarely in the eye and said, "I'm with you. I promise."

The meeting had broken up for good at that point, and Jorgensen, still without a hotel room, had decided his business in New York was done.

"Is there by any chance a phone I might use, to call a taxi?" he asked. "To take me to the airport?"

Davidson smiled. "We don't *call* taxis here," he explained. "We step into traffic and dare them to run us over. But don't worry. I'll have one of our drivers meet you downstairs, right in front of the building."

"That's hardly necessary."

"It'll be my pleasure," said Davidson, and they shook hands.

But the moment Jorgensen was out of earshot, Davidson pulled Jessica aside. "Better get hold of the Duke," he told her.

It remained for Jorgensen to use the rest room (an activity his seniority required him to repeat at regular intervals, and occasionally at irregular ones, as well), and to retrace his steps to the room he'd first entered when the elevator had deposited him on the fiftieth floor. The room where he'd left his bag.

The large black man who'd been manning the desk earlier

was no longer there. He'd been relieved by a white woman, younger but equally large, and wearing an identical military-type uniform. The thought occurred to Jorgensen that there might in fact be only one such uniform, which got passed on with the changing of the guard. Trial TV's version of equal-opportunity employment, perhaps.

HELP WANTED

SECURITY GUARD—Applicants may be male or female, white or black, young or old, but must be able to fit into a size 52 uniform.

He dismissed the thought, wondering again if his recent fall might have affected his thinking. "Excuse me," he said, "but I left a bag with the gentleman who was here earlier. That looks like it, right over there."

The woman rose from her chair and ambled over to a table, where Jorgensen's overnight bag shared space with several other items. But instead of picking up his bag, she reached for a clear plastic one, containing several boxes marked SONY.

"This one here?" she asked.

In the days to follow, August Jorgensen would wonder about fate, and marvel at fortune. He would also congratulate himself more than once on what was for him, at least, an exercise of extremely quick thinking.

"That's the one," he replied. "Oh, and that larger brown one next to it, as well."

The *car* that drove Jorgensen to the airport turned out to be a shiny black limousine, about a block and half long. He leaned back against—no, *into*—soft padded leather, watched the city go by through tinted windows, and had to use a telephone just to talk with the driver. But they seemed to make pretty good time, arriving at LaGuardia at quarter of five, in plenty of time for Jorgensen to catch the 5:31 flight to Charleston.

Or so he would have thought.

"If you hurry," said a ticket agent, handing him a boarding pass, "you can still catch it. Gate Nineteen. Run!"

So he ran, his bag tucked under one arm like a football, his lanky frame racing down the corridor, dodging people, golf carts, and other obstacles. Sweating and out of breath, he made it to Gate 19 just in time to notice an overhead sign indicating that departure time wasn't 5:31 at all, but actually 5:01. The attendant smiled tolerantly at his tardiness, took his boarding pass, tore off the end of it and handed it back to him, and—as soon as Jorgensen had stepped into the tunnel leading to the plane—swung the door closed behind him.

He located his assigned seat, shoved his bag under the one in front of it, collapsed in a heap, and buckled himself in. Less than a minute later, the plane was being pushed back from the gate, and Jorgensen was listening to instructions on what to do in the unlikely event of a sudden loss in cabin pressure. By the time the pilot's voice came on over the intercom a few minutes later, to wish him and his fellow passengers a pleasant flight to Charlotte, August Jorgensen was fast asleep.

TWENTY-ONE

There was something about the airport that looked decidedly unfamiliar. He'd been there that very morning; there was no way they could have remodeled the whole damn thing in his absence. Yet everything about it seemed different.

Not only that, but his truck was nowhere to be found. It wasn't simply a matter of its not being in the section of the parking lot where he'd left it, either; the whole parking lot wasn't where it was supposed to be. They'd moved it clear over to the far end of the building, and even changed the way it was laid out.

Again the thought came back to him that he must have hurt himself back in New York far more seriously than he'd realized at the time. He could have sustained a concussion, maybe even a fractured skull. He could be bleeding inside his brain right now, for all he knew. That could account for his confusion.

Wandering back into the terminal for assistance, he happened to look up. Large block letters on the outside of the building welcomed him to the CHARLOTTE-DOUGLAS INTERNATIONAL AIRPORT.

Charlotte?

He was supposed to be in *Charleston*. Had the pilot been forced to divert the plane because of bad weather? Jorgensen looked up again, this time at a clear blue sky. The last clouds he'd seen, in fact, had been over New York City. He remembered his rush through the airport, and the surprising departure time posted at the gate. He reached into his pocket, found the stub of his boarding pass, and looked at it.

FLIGHT: 856
DEP: NEW YORK (LGA)   5:01 P.M.
ARR: CHARLOTTE, NC   6:56 P.M.

Marge and he had once come across an item in the newspaper about an old man found sitting in a wheelchair at a dog track in Florida. It seemed the poor fellow had been in the advanced stages of Alzheimer's disease, and couldn't remember his name or explain where he was from. A nationwide search revealed that his sister, unable to care for him any longer, had abandoned him there. It became one of Marge's standing jokes: Every time Jorgensen suffered a lapse of memory (a "senior moment," Marge liked to call them), she'd threaten to pack up his things and ship him off to Florida.

"*Jesus*," Jorgensen said now. "I think I'm finally ready for the dog track."

Jessica Woodruff picked up the phone on the first ring, and said, "Hello?"

"My guy sez he didden get off the plane."

She recognized the Duke's voice.

"What do you mean, he didn't get off the plane?"

"He sez he waited till they took off all the bags, started takin' off the fuckin' *gawbage,* for Chrissakes. I'm tellin' ya, he wasn't on it."

"*Shit.*"

"Whaddawe do now?"

"Are there any later arrivals?"

"Only from Kennedy an' Newak."

"No," said Jessica. "We know he was dropped off at LaGuardia. *Shit,*" she said again. "How about the other thing?"

"Took care of that myself," said the Duke.

"All right," she told him. "Stay in touch, will you?"

"You goddit."

The agent at the Hertz counter insisted on knowing both Jorgensen's age and date of birth, looking him up and down and examining his driver's license for what seemed like a very long time. He was obviously having some misgivings about trusting such a disheveled-looking octogenarian with one of the company's rental cars.

He should only know, thought Jorgensen, *about my thinking they remodeled the entire airport in six hours. Not to mention my searching for my truck in the wrong state.*

In the end, he got his car, a little blue thing called a Ford Focus. *Focus?* Whatever happened to animal names, like Mustang, Thunderbird, or Pinto? Since when did they name cars after functions performed by eyeballs?

The Focus turned out to be long on special features, but seriously short on legroom. It came equipped with air conditioning, power steering, antilock brakes, power windows and door-locks, and a strange odor reminiscent of bubble gum. In the glove compartment were an ice scraper, a blank form to describe any motor vehicle accidents encountered, and several road maps. The maps were what caught Jorgensen's attention.

It was getting dark, and he needed a place to stay. If he turned right, he could see, he'd soon pick up Interstate 77 south, which would start him off in the direction of Charleston, South Carolina, and—hopefully—his truck. On the other hand, he could turn left, toward 77 north. To the north was Virginia. In fact, as he studied the map, it occurred to him that were he to continue on 77 north for a couple of hours, he'd cross the Virginia border, and an hour later he'd run smack into two places he'd visited not too long ago.

The first was Brushy Mountain.

The second was Roanoke.

Back home, Jake was in good hands. Jorgensen had told his

neighbor not to expect him back from New York for several days. It seemed like a long time that he'd been gone, but the fact was, he'd only left that very morning.

He turned left.

That night, as he tried to find a comfortable position for his 6'4" body on a 6' motel mattress, August Jorgensen recapped the day's events. He'd been up by five o'clock, in order to catch the first flight from Charleston to New York; he'd slipped into that viewing room just in time to watch the videotape of Kurt Meisner, and see how the folks at Trial TV were able to manipulate the date on it; he'd nearly killed himself tripping over his own two feet; he'd listened politely as a bunch of *true believers* explained how they were willing to sacrifice Boyd Davies in order to put an end to the death penalty; he'd committed larceny; he'd ridden in a limousine the size of Tennessee; he'd raced through an airport like a madman, just so he could get onto the wrong plane; he'd landed in the wrong city in the wrong state; he'd lost his truck; he'd convinced a rental agent to give him the keys to a car he couldn't fit into; and he'd ended up driving away from home instead of toward it, only this time on purpose.

"You never do anything," Marge used to complain to him. *Well, baby, look at me now!*

Still, sleep wouldn't come easily to Jorgensen. Thoughts spun wildly in his head. Was Kurt Meisner's confession among the videotapes he'd stolen? Or were they going to turn out to be nothing but beer commercials or promotionals of some sort, or Johnnie Cochran's life story? Did it make sense to go back to Brushy Mountain, to see how Boyd Davies was holding up? Or to Roanoke, on the chance that Kurt Meisner might be ready to talk to again?

But what kept Jorgensen awake the most, the thing that kept coming back to him over and over again, was the grand scheme that Brandon Davidson, Jessica Woodruff, and the others sitting around the table in Conference Room One had shared with him. His knee-jerk reaction had been that they were all crazy, that the notion of permitting an innocent man to die—particularly a man they'd taken on as a client, under the guise of saving his life—was so misguided as to be truly insane. Even as he'd promised them he'd go along with them, he'd mentally crossed his fingers, knowing that as soon as he got out of there, he was going to do everything in his power to stop them.

But now, lying in the darkness of his room, listening to the trucks roar by outside on the interstate, he forced himself to think about it. Suppose they were right? Suppose the nation *was* increasingly uncomfortable about the death penalty, and all it would take to tip the balance of public opinion was the execution of a single man who later turned out to be demonstrably innocent? Jorgensen hadn't kept up on the debate in the last few years, but he'd read enough to know that, Timothy McVeigh notwithstanding, there was indeed a growing trend against capital punishment. If it wasn't yet a sea change, it was certainly a groundswell. The Supreme Court wasn't part of it, of course, and with a Republican back in the White House to appoint right-wing judges, that wasn't likely to change in a hurry. Nor could politicians be expected to jump on the bandwagon; every one of them positively cringed at the thought of being labeled "soft on crime."

But could the execution of one man make the difference? It hadn't seemed to in the past. Oh, there'd been periodic outcries each time they put a retarded man to death, or someone whom the pope spoke out for, or on the rare occasion when the defendant was a woman, instead of a man. But in each of those cases, innocence had never been an issue; the proponents of capital punishment had always been able to say, "Yes, but look at the horrible crime he (or she) committed. Think of the victim, who was shown no mercy. Think of the victim's family. Aren't they entitled to some closure?"

Death, the Great Healer.

And when the people sitting around the table said the pro-death forces would spin a last-minute reprieve for Boyd Davies to their advantage, they were right. If Trial TV were to run the story now, Boyd would be freed; but the opposition would sit back smugly and cite the case as proof that the system had worked once again, weeding out any injustices.

Yet even if Davidson and Woodruff and the rest of them were right, who'd bestowed upon them the power to decide whether Boyd Davies lived or died? Even if their motives were pure—and Jorgensen was willing to believe that they were— didn't it still come down to playing God?

And suppose they were wrong. Suppose they did nothing, and let Boyd die. And then they went public with Kurt Meisner and his videotape, and people realized that a mistake had been made. What made them so sure anyone would care? Maybe the rest of the country would react precisely the same way they had—figuring that Boyd Davies had no life to begin with, that he was no better off than some dumb animal in a cage, and that when it came right down to it, he was no worse off dead than alive? Then they'd have stood by and let him die, and for what?

For nothing, that's what.

Boyd Davies might die a martyr, going down in history as the man who ended the death penalty. Then again, he might go down as nothing more than an obscure footnote to one more year's execution statistics. How could the *true believers* know which it would be?

But even as Jorgensen framed the question, he knew the answer: They would *make* it work. Not that he knew exactly how, or precisely when, or with the aid of what additional sacrifices. But somehow, they'd pull it off. They were television, after all; they could do anything. They'd make Boyd Davies a household name. They'd run his face in prime time. Kurt Meisner's videotape would become more watched than Zapruder's assassination film or O.J. Simpson's low-speed car chase. States would fall over each other, rushing to declare moratoriums on executions, lest they run the risk of being the next to "pull a Virginia." By the time the dust had finally settled, the death penalty would be a memory, a thing of the past. And that, August Jorgensen knew in his heart, would be a truly wonderful thing.

So why was it, then, that he now found himself draped over an undersized mattress in some overpriced motel, listening to an endless convoy of eighteen-wheelers roaring by? Why would he climb out of bed at the crack of dawn, contort his aching body into a goddamned circus car, and drive for three hours, all the time heading precisely 180 degrees from the place he wanted to end up?

Why? He wasn't sure. Maybe it had something to do with the fact that Boyd Davies *wasn't* just a dumb animal in a cage (though had he been, it is highly likely Jorgensen would have still thought he deserved the best). Whatever his limitations, Boyd was a living, breathing being. He had a disorder—an affliction, if you wanted to call it that—but he wasn't some sort of imbecile. And who knew enough to say that he didn't have the same kind of feelings other people do, and that he didn't dream at night of a better place? In a way he was special, Boyd was. He had a talent, remember, a true artistic gift that, were he ever given the right kind of opportunity, might even enable him to flourish, to be happy.

Was that such a crazy notion? Probably. He could imagine Jessica Woodruff and Brandon Davidson listening to his thoughts, and what their reactions might be. "Boyd Davies— flourishing, happy. *Right!*"

Well, maybe they had a point there. When you stopped and really thought about it, it was hard to predict that Boyd would ever have much of a life, even under the very best of circumstances. Maybe they were right. Maybe it would be a good trade, Boyd Davies for the end of the death penalty. One miserable life in exchange for hundreds. Thousands, as they'd pointed out.

If you chose to look at it that way.

The way Jessica Woodruff chose to look at it, it was the drawings that would sell the story. Without them, Wesley Boyd Davies was nothing but a name, a nobody—a black man with no family, no celebrity, no constituency, no marketability.

But as she sat on the floor of her living room, with half a dozen of Boyd's drawings spread out on the carpet in front of her, she was able to imagine the full range of possibilities.

With the Supreme Court argument now only weeks away, Trial TV had begun running spots about the case. The first two had featured August Jorgensen, and how he'd been lured out of retirement to argue the case. After that, there'd been a ninety-second autism tie-in. Autism wasn't exactly a hot-button issue yet, but Dustin Hoffman's *Rain Man* portrayal had at least put it on the map, and raised the level of public awareness just a bit. Now they were ready for the next step, the added angle of Boyd's artistic talent. They'd talk about how the police had seized upon it to extract a confession of sorts from him, leading first to the discovery of Ilsa Meisner's body, and eventually to Boyd's conviction. There was even a touch of irony to it.

Irony was always a good sell.

She looked at the three drawings Boyd had made sixteen years ago for Detective Wyatt. They were copies, of course, made from the originals, which had been introduced as exhibits at the trial and were therefore still part of the official record. Maybe after the execution, they could substitute the copies for the originals, which would someday be worth a lot of money.

Of the three, the drawing of the grave site was the obvious choice. It showed a patch of ground in front of a big tree, some ferns, and a stream in the background. And even as Boyd had made the drawing, beneath the ground lay the body of an eleven-year-old girl.

The other two—of the shovel and the place it was recovered from—Jessica would save for later, for the book. She looked around for another one she could use, simply to illustrate Boyd's talent. The trick, of course, was going to be tweaking the public's imagination, without going too far. If they over-did it—if they ended up making a cause célèbre out of him, it could backfire on them. After they lost the appeal, they'd have to go through the motions of filing a clemency petition with the governor. Virginia politics being what they were, that shouldn't prove to be much of a hurdle. But just to make sure nothing went wrong, they'd tracked down Ilsa Meisner's sur-viving brother and sister, and prepared letters for them, in which they stated their strong opposition to any commutation of Davies' death sentence.

She rejected several drawings Boyd had made of his mother and sisters. Those, she feared, might humanize him too much, might prompt people to regard him as someone who had con-nections to family, to loved ones. Better to save those for afterward.

So, too, did she reject Boyd's most recent effort, the drawing he'd made for Jorgensen of the mysterious three-fingered man—who, of course, had turned out to be none other than Kurt Meisner. Quick thinking by the Duke had enabled them to pry it away from Jorgensen, and although it was of poor quality (from Jorgensen's having shown it to half the state of Virginia), some day it would be an important piece of the puzzle, the link explaining how, months after Boyd's execution, his final draw-ing had led Trial TV to Meisner and the discovery of the truth.

In the end, she settled on an innocuous drawing of a tobacco field in summer, with tall trees at the edge of it, and wispy clouds just above them. It was pretty, and like the rest of Boyd Davies' drawings, it was strikingly photographic. That said, there seemed to be nothing about it likely to mobilize public opinion, or bring about some sort of movement to try to spare the artist's life.

There was no room for anything like that in the plan.

TWENTY-TWO

Boyd Davies looked a bit thinner than he had before, and his gaze wandered around the room nervously, but with no discernable pattern. He never once made eye contact with Jorgensen, and gave no indication that he remembered him from their previous visits.

"How are you, Boyd?" Jorgensen tried. But there was no way to know if Boyd could even hear him. Once, back when he'd been a trial lawyer, before he'd become a judge, Jorgensen had represented a defendant accused of robbing a bank. The fellow had been fortunate enough to make bail (perhaps it hadn't been the first bank he'd robbed), and on the eve of jury selection, he'd suddenly disappeared. The judge had ordered the trial to go forward without him, and Jorgensen had been left to represent the empty chair sitting beside him. He'd won the case, too, proving only that sometimes you could do better without a client to distract you.

There were times when visiting Boyd Davies was like representing that empty chair. Like the absent bank robber, Boyd didn't question your motives, second-guess your tactics, complain about his lot, or give you a hard time in any of the dozens of ways men who are locked up and unhappy about it are prone to do. Boyd simply walked into the visit room, sat down at the table, expected nothing, and asked for nothing. As soon as the visit was over, he'd be ready to stand up and leave, or do whatever else the guard might tell him to do.

He was easy, easy to a fault.

Jorgensen had brought paper and pencil with him, and now he took them and slid them across the table. Boyd picked up the pencil, but made no move to start drawing. It was almost as if he were some sort of a curiosity show, like a trained seal waiting patiently for someone to toss him a ball, or a circus bear taught to sit still until his bicycle was brought out.

Like an animal in a cage.

Maybe the folks at Trial TV were right. They'd said he had nothing to live for, that he'd be better off dead. Looking at him now, it was pretty hard to argue with them.

"Draw me something," said Jorgensen. "Draw me anything you'd like to."

There was no reaction from Boyd. Figuring out what he'd like to draw involved conceptualizing, self-examination. Things Boyd Davies wasn't capable of.

"Can you draw me your favorite thing?" Jorgensen asked.

Nothing.

"Can you draw me the place where you'd like to be right now?"

Still nothing.

"The best place you ever were?"

Slowly, Boyd reached for the paper. There was a moment of hesitation, and then he began drawing. Jorgensen realized the difference, and his own failure to distinguish between what Boyd could and couldn't do. Earlier, he'd asked Boyd to imagine something; this time he'd instead asked him to *remember* something. That, Boyd could do.

It happened as it had before—and *it happened* precisely the way in which Jorgensen thought of it. He remembered an old dog food commercial from years ago, back when Marge and he had owned a television set and used to watch the evening news together. "Just add water," the announcer would say, "and *gravy happens.*"

Beginning at the right edge of the paper (or the left, if you were sitting on Boyd's side of the table), a drawing was happening now, materializing from the point of the pencil and gradually spreading out across the page. Looking at it upside down, it took Jorgensen a moment or two to see what the subject matter was, but soon enough he could tell it was water of some sort, water in a pond, surrounded by rocks and wildflowers, or maybe just weeds that had blossomed. He was doing something to the surface of the water now, stippling it in a way that prompted Jorgensen to wonder if Boyd wasn't drawing bugs on it, or bubbles.

When the drawing was finished—and it was finished as soon as Boyd reached the other edge of the page, something that took in the neighborhood of ten or fifteen minutes—Jorgensen reached for it and turned it around, so that it faced him. It was raining, he could see then, and the raindrops, themselves all but invisible, were dimpling the pond's surface. The whole thing was so breathtakingly real that looking at it, Jorgensen could all but feel the rain, all but reach down and scoop the water up into his hands. So taken by it, so moved by it was he, that—quite involuntarily—he clasped his chest with his hand.

And to his astonishment, Boyd Davies mirrored his response, clasping his own chest with his own hand.

"It's wonderful," said Jorgensen, smiling at Boyd to further demonstrate his approval.

Boyd said nothing. Nor did he return the smile. Instead, his concentration seemed elsewhere. And as Jorgensen studied him, he noticed that even as Boyd kept his right hand pressed tightly against his T-shirt, he began keeping time with his left hand, moving it up and down, if ever so slightly, every second or so.

"That," said Jorgensen, "is your heart. It's pumping. It means you're alive."

And although an hour later he'd be unable to convince himself that it had been anything more than his own imagination, coupled with a good dose of wishful thinking, at the time August Jorgensen would have bet his life that he saw Boyd

Davies' lips part, and his tongue—without ever making a sound—touch his upper palate and form a single word.

Alive.

It was late afternoon by the time he reached Roanoke. He found it impossible to make good time in the Ford; it had about as much power as Jorgensen's truck—which meant barely enough to get it up and over the smallest of hills—and on top of that, it had an automatic transmission. Jorgensen kept forgetting, pressing his left foot down on the floorboard, and using his right hand to turn on the windshield wipers when accelerating. But it did get good mileage. They'd given him a full tank back in Charlotte, and for the first hour or so, he'd thought the needle on the gas gauge was stuck on F. He was accustomed to the one on his truck, which he could actually watch move to E.

The drive from Brushy Mountain to Roanoke had been a short one, not much more than an hour. He'd spent the first half of it reflecting on why it was he needed to see Kurt Meisner again, and the remainder composing the pitch he intended to make, once he'd gotten in to see him. It went something like this: *You're helping the wrong people, Mr. Meisner. The people you're helping don't care about Boyd Davies. They're willing to let him die. In fact, they* want *him to die; they* need *him to die—it's part of their plan. I want to save Boyd. I'm* the one you should be helping.

And if Meisner refused to see him again, and they wouldn't let him past the receptionist at the front desk, then he'd write it all out, and insist on waiting while they took it up to Meisner's room and waited for his answer.

But, hell, he'd get in. He'd gotten past that uniformed guard at Trial TV, and into Screening Room One, hadn't he? One way or another, he was going to get to Kurt Meisner, too. If need be, he'd play the age card. Sometimes it didn't hurt to be an old man in his eighties. Folks never seemed to take much notice when you wandered off, acted lost or bewildered, or started poking your head into this door or that. It was kind of expected of you.

"I'm here to see Kurt Meisner," he told the woman at the desk.

The woman looked up at him through thick glasses, and pursed her lips. Jorgensen thought back to Boyd Davies, mouthing the word *alive*. It had only been an hour ago, an hour and half at most, yet already he couldn't be sure it had really happened.

"I'm afraid that won't be possible," she said.

"My name is Brandon Davidson," Jorgensen told her. "I'm the president of Trial TV."

"I'm sorry, Mr. Davidson. But it still won't be possible."

"Why not?"

"Mr. Meisner," she said, "is no longer with us."

"He died?"

"No, no, hardly. But just last night, his cousin called for him, and picked him up. He explained that the family had decided to care for him at home. It happens."

Jorgensen felt suddenly lightheaded, had to reach out for the desk to steady himself. "Are you certain?" he asked.

The woman smiled sweetly. "I'm quite certain," she said. "I said goodbye to him myself."

"Did he leave a forwarding address, somewhere I can get in touch with him?"

"I'm just a receptionist. But," she added, lowering her voice conspiratorially, "I happen to know he didn't. His cousin was quite insistent about that, even when I explained to him that we might need to reach them to settle up any outstanding charges. But he said he preferred to have us total things up right then and there, so he could take care of it. And that's exactly what we did. It came to just over six hundred dollars, and he paid every penny of it. In cash, too. What do you think of that?"

Jorgensen didn't know what to think. He thanked the woman and walked outside. As certain as he was that something truly sinister was going on, he could think of nothing to do about it. He wandered over to the Ford and gave the front left tire a good kick, serving only to hurt his foot badly enough to cry out. He opened the door, began the delicate process of squeezing himself in, and was halfway there, trying to find room for his left leg, when something stopped him.

The day after Jorgensen unexpectedly walks in on the videotape of Kurt Meisner in New York, some cousin of Meisner's just happens to show up in Roanoke. That very evening, he whisks him out of there, and when they ask for a forwarding address to send any charges, he avoids having to give them one by paying Meisner's bill. In cash.

August Jorgensen was a great believer in coincidence. To him, things that seemed to be connected, like prayers being answered by miracles, uncanny premonitions of disasters, and primordial life evolving over the ages into humanity—even when such things occurred under circumstances so otherwise confounding as to all but prove a cause-and-effect relationship—were more often than not attributable to simple, random happenstance. There was always bound to be an inexplicable quirk or two in the data; otherwise there'd have been no need for the word *quirk* in the first place.

But as hard as he tried now, and as much as he would have liked to succeed, there was no way Jorgensen could look at the timing of the events, and convince himself that the confluence of his trip to New York and Meisner's sudden departure was a mere coincidence, a simple statistical aberration. And if it wasn't, there was something he needed to know.

He backed his body out of the Ford, unfolded himself, and walked back into the building, limping painfully.

"Excuse me," he said.

The woman looked up.

"Mr. Meisner's cousin," he said, "the one who came to pick him up. Do you remember his name?"

"Oh, I'm sure I wouldn't."

"Or what he looked like?"

She smiled. "He was a round little man," she said, "kind of funny looking. With a big mustache, if I remember correctly."

"And was there anything unusual," Jorgensen asked, "about the way he talked?"

"You've met him, too, I see. I tell you, I could barely understand half of the things he said. He certainly did talk funny."

"Funny how?"

"Oh, you know, funny like a Yankee. And as if that weren't bad enough," and here she dropped her voice to a whisper, "I think he may have been *Jewish*. Either that, or from the *Mafia*."

Under any other circumstances, Jorgensen might have laughed, might even have good-naturedly chided the woman for stereotyping the man because he spoke a dialect different from her own. But he didn't laugh, nor did he chide her. Her description, as it turned out, had been so on-the-money that it not only failed to strike him as funny, it literally ran a shiver up his back.

She had to be talking about Duke Schneider. The Duke, as they called him, had passed himself off as Meisner's cousin, in order to spirit him out of the seniors' residence. Buy why? What did that mean?

He didn't even want to think about the implications.

At that very moment, Jessica Woodruff was thinking hard about the implications of having been forced to bring August Jorgensen into the inner circle, the small group of people entrusted with the knowledge that the goal wasn't to save Boyd Davies' life at all, but to sacrifice it for a greater good. She was angry at herself for having given in, months ago, to those who thought Jorgensen would be the right man to bring on board. She hadn't trusted him from day one; everything about him had suggested he wasn't a company man, a team player. The guy was a hermit, for Chrissakes, a recluse. He lived in a goddamned lighthouse.

"But that's the beauty of it," they'd told her. "He's totally out of touch. We'll be in complete control. We'll wind him up and tell him what to do. He'll be perfect. You'll see."

Well, maybe now they could see what Jessica had seen all along—that August Jorgensen was nothing but a troublemaker. Worse yet, he was a snoop. He'd snooped in to see Davies, he'd snooped around till he found Meisner, and then he'd snooped himself right into the screening session where they'd been watching a demonstration on how easy it would be to re-date Meisner's statement.

And that promise of his, that he was *one of them*. Who was that supposed to fool? And what if he was prepared to break his promise, as Jessica was convinced he was? What were the implications of that? That was what occupied Jessica's thoughts now, sitting at her desk, as the city darkened outside her window.

For unlike August Jorgensen, Jessica Woodruff wasn't afraid to think about implications. Thinking about implications was what Jessica did best.

Swiveling her chair away from her desk, she propped her feet against the windowsill and looked out over the city. It was an unladylike position, she knew, one she would have avoided during normal business hours, when someone might have popped into her office unannounced. But the forty-ninth floor was all but empty now, except for one or two stragglers down the hall, and the cleaning personnel beginning to make the rounds.

The forty-ninth floor. It was quite a view she had. To the south was the Empire State Building, beyond it all of lower Manhattan, with the Battery in the distance and the Statue of Liberty out in the bay beyond it. Off to the west, across the river and just above the lights of New Jersey, was the last visible glow of sunset.

There were people who worked their whole lives in underground mines, or basements, or tiny cubicles that never saw the light of day. Jessica knew they would have given anything for a view of *any* sort, let alone the magnificent one spread out before her now. But as much as Jessica appreciated it, it never fully satisfied her. Because as spectacular as it was, when you came right down to it, it was still the forty-ninth floor.

It wasn't the fiftieth.

But that was going to change. That was going to change after the discovery that an innocent man had been executed. It wouldn't hurt, either, that the man happened to have been African-American, poor, and unable to speak, or that he'd been an extraordinarily gifted artist in his life. His death would cause the nation to rethink—and ultimately reject—the death penalty. And the credit for the discovery would belong to Trial TV, whose investigation had been spearheaded by none other than Jessica Woodruff.

The book would follow, Jessica's words coupled with the actual drawings of Wesley Boyd Davies. There'd be a small number of limited-edition copies, large and handsomely bound in real leather. An exhibit of the originals, nicely framed, might be in order, perhaps followed up by an auction, preferably at Christie's or Sotheby's. Then the movie, with— and this was the best part—Jessica playing herself. Denzel Washington might be good for the Boyd Davies' role, at least the adult Boyd. Best supporting actor in a nonspeaking part? That was an interesting thought. But hell, they could get anyone to play Boyd; after all, the movie was going to be about Jessica, about her never-ending crusade to see justice done. And by the time the dust had settled, she wouldn't just have an office on the fiftieth floor, she'd own the damn floor.

Unless something went wrong.

The way Jessica looked at it, there were only two things that could go wrong, two weak links in the chain. The first was Kurt Meisner, and if she'd understood the Duke correctly when he'd said that he'd taken care of the *other thing* himself, Meisner wasn't going to be a problem.

That left only one remaining weak link.

From Roanoke, August Jorgensen had driven straight through to Charleston, his heightened adrenaline level compensating for his usual aversion to being out on the highway after dark. At the airport, he'd had to wait three hours for the Hertz counter to open, so that he could turn in the keys to the Ford Focus, reclaim his truck from the parking lot, and drive the rest of the way home. By that time running on fumes, he'd barely been able to keep his eyes open, but somehow he'd managed to make it across the bridge and onto the barrier island. On the final stretch, he simply held onto the wheel and let some combination of instinct, memory, and sheer luck guide him to the lighthouse. Turning off the ignition, he knew full well that he had to have driven the width of the island, but he had absolutely no recollection of having done so.

Was that a case of autopilot, he wondered, or more accurately auto-autopilot? Or was that redundant? Jorgensen pondered it far longer than any normal person might have been expected to. He'd been noticing lately that whenever he was overtaken by exhaustion, he tended to lose his mind.

Once inside, he returned Jake's hugs and kisses, apologized for having been gone, and poured him fresh water and a bowl of food. Then he pulled off the clothes he'd been wearing for the past thirty hours, climbed into bed, and collapsed.

It was nighttime, and he was driving down a two-lane highway, much faster than he should have been. The headlights of oncoming cars blinded him, and he fought the steering wheel to stay in his lane. He took his foot off the gas, but there was no reaction. If any-

thing, the car just went faster. He reached for the clutch with his left foot, in order to gear down, but there was no pedal there, only flat floor. Then he remembered: He was driving the Ford Focus. Only it was even smaller now, so small that the steering wheel was touching his chest, and each time he turned it to the left or right, the bottom of it rubbed against his knees.

Faster and faster he went, reflectors whizzing by every second, the dots of the broken white line disappearing beneath him. A long down-stretch was coming up ahead of him, and he pressed hard on the brake, but the car continued to accelerate. He looked at the speedometer, saw the needle dancing between 90 and 95, thought about flinging open the door and jumping out, when—from nowhere—Kurt Meisner's face was suddenly in front of the windshield, screaming at him.

"THEY'LL KILL ME!" he shouted, "THEY'LL KILL ME!"

There was a loud thud, followed by a second and a third, and Meisner's head, ripped free from his body, bounced off the wind-shield like a soccer ball, disappearing into the night sky. Jorgensen felt something wet on his forehead, reached up with his hand, fully expecting to come away with blood, only to find instead that

Jake was licking his face, trying to wake him. A pounding noise was coming from somewhere. It took him a long moment to get his bearings, and to realize that he wasn't out on the high-way at all, but in his own bed, and that the pounding noise was someone knocking on the lighthouse door.

"Just a minute!" Jorgensen called out, but his voice was raspy and wouldn't carry, and he had to repeat himself twice to get the knocking to stop. He found a pair of jeans and a shirt, pulled them on, and followed Jake down the stairs. He swung the front door open—it wasn't locked; he never locked it—to find someone big standing there. But he couldn't see who it was: The sunlight behind the silhouette blinded Jorgensen, forcing him to shield his eyes and retreat back inside.

"Who is it?" Jorgensen asked, cocking his head and squinting, but still seeing nothing but an orange fireball. "And what happened to the night?"

"The night ended right around the time the sun came up," said a vaguely familiar voice. "And it's Chet Santee, here to help you put your boat in the water. Just like always, first day of April."

"What time is it?" Jorgensen asked.

"Almost three in the afternoon," said Santee, who was finally becoming visible.

Almost three in the afternoon. *Well,* thought Jorgensen, *at least that explained what the sun was doing in the West.* He'd *heard* about people sleeping half the day away; he'd just never actually done it himself.

"Want to get to work?" Santee was asking.

"Huh?" Jorgensen had been momentarily distracted. Something about being behind the wheel of a speeding car, heading down a highway at night.

"The boat," said Santee. "You want to put her in the water, or not?"

"Yes, sure. Why not?" Although Jorgensen was able to winch the boat up out of the water each fall, he had no way of getting her back in by himself.

"I mean, if you're not feeling up to it—"

"Not to worry," said Jorgensen. "I'm fine." A face, suddenly appearing in the windshield . . .

It took them less than an hour. Chet Santee had a mobile boat lift, a huge contraption that looked like a giant table he'd built from an Erector Set, and then gone and attached rubber tires to the bottoms of the legs. He fired up the engine, a noisy diesel that belched black smoke, and maneuvered the thing over the catboat, before shutting it off. Next, he unrolled a couple of big canvas slings from one side of the lift, ran them under the boat, and hooked them to the opposite side of the lift. Then he started up the diesel again. Using a panel full of levers that looked complicated enough to fly a jet plane, he raised the slings, gently lifting the boat clear of the wooden cradle that had served as her winter home. Finally, he drove the lift, the catboat now suspended between its legs like a toy, down the beach and right into the water, just deep enough to where the boat floated up off the sling, and Jorgensen was able to pull her free with a bowline.

Jorgensen wrote out a check for thirty dollars, the same rate as always, though he suspected the lift used more than thirty dollars worth of fuel just to get from the marina to the lighthouse and back again. Before Santee left, they sat and shared a pot of tea.

"So," said Santee, "I see you'll be going up to Washington in a couple of weeks, to give a big speech before the *Sue*-preme Court."

Jorgensen nodded. Used to be a time when people heard news. Now, with all the TV-watching going on, news was no longer something you heard; it was something you *saw*.

"Think you got a chance?"

"I don't know," said Jorgensen. "I've got a feeling they may decide at the last minute to send someone else, instead of me."

"How come?"

"Well," said Jorgensen, "I'm not entirely sure. But it seems the folks who asked me to do it are having second thoughts. They're starting to think it might be better all around if the guy got executed. It's complicated."

"What's so complicated about it?" Santee asked. "Man can't talk, can't read, can't write. We got no business killin' him. No two ways about it."

"You might think so," said Jorgensen, "you might think so."

Ten minutes later, Santee was gone. And it occurred to Jorgensen that in spite of having shared his insider's knowledge of Trial TV's grand design, he himself was still among the living. The sky hadn't clouded over, the heavens hadn't parted, and no thunderbolt had struck him dead.

So much for breaking promises.

———

"He's home," said the voice on the phone.

"It's about time."

"Ya gotta unnastand—the fuckin' guy lives at the edge of the fuckin' woild. It's not like I can be drivin' by mindin' my own bizness. A car goes out there, he's goin' to see it, you know what I mean?"

"So can't you go on foot?"

"Ya gotta be kiddin'." The Duke never went anywhere on foot. He'd drive to the toilet if it was more than two rooms away. "Butcha know what? Ya jes' gave me a very innerestin' idear."

"Wonderful. Do me a favor, will you? Just do whatever you have to do."

"Ten-four, sweetheart. An' don'tcha worry that pretty little face ayours."

She hated when he lapsed into that police jargon of his, and started *sweethearting* her, and *pretty-little-facing* her. But for once, in spite of herself, she found herself taking some measure of comfort from his reassurances. Which, as Martha Stewart might say, was a good thing.

Because they were rapidly running out of time.

She listened for a dial tone, and touched "1" on her memory panel. She waited through three rings, and was about to hang up, when she heard a click.

"Davidson."

"Hi," she said.

"Hi."

"Can you talk?"

"Yeah. I'm stuck in traffic on the Merritt. What's up?"

"Well," she said, "I was just thinking. Suppose the old geezer doesn't do the argument."

"He'll do it," said Davidson. "He gave us his word. That means a lot to someone like him. He'll be all right."

"Well, what if —"

"Don't worry so much, Jess."

"But don't you think we ought to have a backup, somebody who could step in at the last moment, just in case?"

"The thing's nine days away," he said. "Who are you going to get at this point?"

"I don't know."

"He'll be fine. If he changes his mind, I'm sure he'll let us know. Worse comes to worst, *you* can always do it. You know the case as well as anybody."

"It's the last thing in the world I want to do."

"And you won't have to. He'll be all right. You'll see."

They blew kisses from New York to Connecticut and back, and hung up. She loved him, she really did, but sometimes he could be so *dense*. Well, he might not be able to see Jorgensen's true colors, but she certainly could, and she was taking no chances. So, like a good soldier, she was sticking her own neck out to protect her superior, thereby keeping him out of the loop and providing him with—what was the term for it?—*plausible deniability*.

Wasn't that how they were always doing it in the White House?

TWENTY-THREE

Edna Coombs seemed more than usually glad to see Jorgensen when he dropped by the post office Monday morning. She had a biscuit for Jake (she still kept a generous supply of lollipops for children and biscuits for dogs behind her window; all others were on their own) and an envelope for Jorgensen, all red-white-and-blue and official-looking.

"Came in Saturday," said Edna. "Priority Mail, from New York City. I'd a driven it out to you myself, if I'd a known you were back from, from your *trip*."

Jorgensen briefly wondered how Edna knew he'd been gone, then dismissed the thought. Edna was the local Information Center. If there was something she didn't know about, chances were it hadn't happened.

Now she smiled and said, "That's the one your were waiting on, right?"

"Right," said Jorgensen, not wanting to disappoint her. Actually, the return address was that of Tulane University, and typed in above the printing was the name "Reynaldo Gilbert." That would be Ray, the law professor. He'd been at the screening of the Meisner tape, or at least he'd been in the conference room when they laid out their little plan for Jorgensen.

Ordinarily, Jorgensen took his mail home before opening it, as much to frustrate Edna as to read it when he was good and ready to. But on this occasion he decided to open the envelope right then and there—well, off to the side a bit—just in case it called for an immediate reply or a phone call. He had no desire to drive back in the afternoon, Edna's cheerfulness notwithstanding.

He'd torn open the envelope, extracted a one-page typed letter, and gotten as far as "Dear Judge Jorgensen," when Edna whispered from her window (and an Edna Coombs whisper could be heard halfway across the Atlantic, when she wanted it to be), "Good news, I hope?"

"Seems so," said Jorgensen, as he read on. "They're coming out here Wednesday—three of them, it sounds like—to teach me the Constitution."

"Teach it to you?" said Edna, with more than enough indignation for both of them. "I always thought you *wrote* the damn thing."

It was only on the drive back home that Jorgensen thought to look at the date on the letter (the envelope itself he'd discarded before leaving the post office, having no need of extra trash). "March 29," it said. Meaning it had been written, and no doubt mailed, the day before his New York adventure.

He wondered if they were still planning on coming. It would serve as a good barometer of things, he decided. If they showed up, it meant they trusted him, and were going to let him argue the case next Tuesday. If they didn't show, it meant he was out of the picture.

He crossed the bridge that separated the mainland from the island, slowing down as he drove through the dune grasses. It was nesting season, both for birds and turtles, and he didn't want the truck to disturb them more than necessary.

Still, as he rounded a bend, a woodcock (or it might have been a plover of some sort) suddenly took flight in front of them, rising perilously close to their windshield. Jake barked, Jorgensen braked, and the bird somehow escaped untouched. But Jorgensen's heart kept pounding and his hands wouldn't stop shaking the entire way home. The rest of the dream had come back to him in a rush. Now all he could see was Kurt Meisner's head, bouncing horribly off the glass and careening into space. And all he could hear was, *"THEY'LL KILL ME! THEY'LL KILL ME!"*

It was a crisp, clear morning, with a steady offshore breeze, and although the lighthouse barometer indicated the pressure was beginning to fall ever so slightly, Jorgensen figured whatever weak low front was causing the drop wouldn't reach the coast till evening. Ray Gilbert and his fellow tutors weren't scheduled to arrive until tomorrow. In fact, if a storm did come through, they'd be delayed or, worse yet, forced to stay over. By the time the weather had cleared up (and they'd cleared out), it would be the weekend, and Jorgensen would be busy getting ready for the trip up to Washington. If there was still going to be a Washington trip, that was.

What all of that meant was that if he was going to get any sailing in this week, now was the time to do it. Jake seemed to agree, jumping into the dinghy as soon as Jorgensen had turned it over, even before he'd dragged it down to the water's edge.

There was always something about the first sail of spring. You learned to become a landlubber over winter, and the sea was reduced to a picture, something to watch. A beautiful picture, to be sure, constantly changing in color, texture, and disposition. The winter ocean was a schizophrenic creature, wildly bipolar in her dramatic mood swings. She could be almost catatonically calm one moment, only to suddenly cloud up and darken into blackest depression the next. Gentle swells that promised to continue for days could suddenly crest and erupt without warning into ferociously violent storms.

But come the spring, almost as if medicated, she became a gentler, more predictable being. With cold weather gales having departed for the more northern reaches of the Atlantic, and tropical depressions still months away from brewing down in the Caribbean and forming the hurricanes of late summer and early fall, the sea turned manageable, dependable. You could count on her, trust her, without having to worry too much that she'd turn on you.

And yet, the first sail of spring was always an adventure, always something special, the way the first ski run of winter had been in Jorgensen's childhood, or the first day of bonefishing, or the first time back on a horse or bike after a long layoff. There was the initial uncertainty, the wondering if you still could do it, gradually giving way to the tentative rediscovery of an old love, and finally maturing into the comfortable sense that you'd never been away from it.

He caught the breeze on the starboard side and took up the slack in the sheet, signaling Jake to drop the mooring line, and they were off. The old catboat, her hull newly scraped, sanded and painted, heeled sharply and began picking up speed. The big sail filled smartly, without luffing. The smooth, worn wood of the tiller felt good in Jorgensen's right hand, the coils of the nylon sheet wrapped securely around his left. Jake took up a spot high on the port rail, where—whether by instinct or design—his weight helped trim the boat and decrease her angle of heel, permitting her to show more canvas to the wind. Jorgensen closed his eyes and listened, heard only wind and water. God, it was good to be alive!

"ALIVE."

The word Boyd Davies had mouthed, had come tantalizingly close to saying out loud. He could still talk—he would talk again, Jorgensen knew—if only they didn't kill him first.

"They'll kill me," Kurt Meisner had told Jorgensen the last time he'd seen him, words so ominous they'd come back and haunted Jorgensen in his dream. And now Meisner had conveniently disappeared.

"Coming about!" Jorgensen called, pushing the tiller hard away from him, and ducking low an instant later, as the boom swung overhead. As her bow crossed the wind, the catboat slowed only momentarily, as if to catch her breath before continuing on. Then, as captain and mate shifted their weight over to the port side, she picked up speed, pulling away from the shore, away from Kurt Meisner, away from Boyd Davies, too.

It was a weekday, which meant a workday for the rest of the world, and there was little in the way of traffic on the water. A couple of fishing trawlers worked the outer banks, and in the distance a container carrier, riding low in the water, steamed north, just beyond where the blue-greens of the continental shelf fell off and gave way to the deeper blue of the ocean. South of them, a cabin cruiser of some sort idled in the water, its pilot checking them out with binoculars. Well, they probably were a sight, a white-haired man and a seafaring dog, looking as though they had every intention of crossing the Atlantic in an old wooden bathtub.

The sun was high, but still slightly to the southeast, telling Jorgensen that it wasn't yet noon. They could continue tacking out for another two hours or more, safe in the knowledge that the same breeze they were fighting now would carry them back on a single, effortless broad reach, in half the time.

"You okay, mate?" he asked.

The mate responded with a quick glance and a wag of the tail. Then he returned his gaze to the horizon ahead of them, his mouth open, his nostrils flared, his tongue drinking in the wind.

On a day like this, it was easy for a man to leave his troubles back on the mainland, easy to forget Boyd Davies and Kurt Meisner and Jessica Woodruff for a few hours. It was easy, too, to fail to detect a decided warming of the air, and a somewhat more subtle drop in the breeze.

The intercom buzzer startled Jessica. She'd been daydreaming, daydreaming at her desk about arguing before the Supreme Court.

"Yes?" she said.

"Professor Gilbert on line one."

"Thanks," she said, "I'll take it."

A moment later, Ray Gilbert was saying hello. "So," he wanted to know, "do you still want me to go ahead and get together with Judge Jorgensen?"

Interesting question, thought Jessica. "When's that supposed to be?" she asked, buying time.

"Day after tomorrow."

She thought a moment. She couldn't very well call the tutoring session off, could she? Not without tipping her hand. And the fewer people there were that knew, the better for everyone. "Sure," she said. "Meet with him, get him ready for prime time."

"You trust him?" Gilbert wanted to know.

"Brandon does."

"I asked about *you*."

"And the last I checked," said Jessica, "I work for Brandon Davidson, and he calls the shots around here. In case you hadn't noticed."

"A little touchy today, aren't we?"

"I guess so," said Jessica. "Sorry, this whole thing's getting me nervous."

"Tell you what. I'll be seeing the old guy Wednesday. Why don't you let me feel him out, see which side of the street he's standing on. I'll give you a call Wednesday night, Thursday at the latest."

"That'd be good, Ray. Take care."

"You, too."

She hung up the phone and returned to her daydream. Maybe Brandon was right. He certainly was right about her knowing the case as well as anybody. In a way, it would be a blast, getting up and arguing in front of the Supremes. There was still time for Trial TV to run three or four days of promotions on how one of their own was willing to step up at the last moment, to try to save a condemned man's life. And so what if she lost the case, as she surely would. That might momentarily lower her star in the eyes of some, but think of the bounce she'd get later on, when she discovered the tape, the smoking gun that would force the nation to admit an innocent man had been executed. That would be more than enough to redeem her, to catapult her right to the top.

It was too bad she couldn't have it both ways. Wouldn't it be something if she could slip something into her argument suggesting she had doubts about her client's guilt. You know, just an aside, a footnote of sorts. That way, in hindsight, she'd come to be seen as an absolute visionary, the only one who'd ever believed in Boyd Davies' innocence.

The problem was, you didn't want to play up this doubt angle too much. If you weren't careful, *The New York Times* might pick it up, others would jump on the bandwagon, and before you knew it, the governor would be under pressure to commute the sentence or declare some sort of a moratorium on executions. All the studies showed that a majority of the public still endorsed capital punishment, but tended to get uncomfortable at the prospect of an innocent man's being put to death. It was that very discomfort, of course, that Jessica would ultimately exploit in order to bring down the whole system. So maybe it was better to keep her personal doubts to herself at this point, or at least confine them to a segment they'd tape, but not air until afterward.

The last thing she needed, after all, was a *premature exoneration*.

They'd tacked a dozen times, and put a good five nautical miles between themselves and the shoreline, before Jorgensen realized that the wind was dropping. The first thing he noticed was that they weren't pointing as well, were having increasing difficulty sailing close to the direction the breeze was coming from. At first, he attributed it to the catboat's single-sail design: Boats rigged with foresails to complement their mains were generally better at sailing upwind (upwind being a relative term, of course, since no boat could sail directly into the wind). But soon enough, there was a significant drop-off in their speed, as well as the course they could maintain. That was followed by a gradual flattening of the waves, accompanied by a rise in the air temperature.

Not that any of these developments—or even all of them, combined—were cause for alarm. August Jorgensen was an experienced sailor, and Jake was, if anything, more comfortable at sea than he was on land. Jorgensen simply swung the boat around and set a course for home. When home was a lighthouse, that was a pretty easy thing to do. The only thing they needed now was enough of a breeze to push them home.

Downwind sailing will never inspire an amusement park ride. Without lateral forces being exerted against the sail, there's none of the excitement that comes from heeling over. Instead of the bow knifing through oncoming waves (or at times even planing over them), the craft feels as though it's plowing ahead, pushed by the swells behind it. And because the boat is moving in the same direction as the surface water, even though the actual speed may increase, the perceived speed diminishes greatly. You may get there twice as fast, but you're only going to have half the fun.

Except that it didn't take too long before the catboat not only wasn't getting there twice as fast, it wasn't getting there at all. Within an hour—less, within forty-five minutes—the breeze had all but disappeared. The big sail luffed, and the boom swung lazily from side to side. Overhead, the early afternoon sun beat down through a thin haze, prompting Jorgensen to reach for the bailing can, and use it to pour water over Jake. It wasn't a good time to be thick-coated and black.

But it wasn't Jake's body temperature that concerned Jorgensen; the same coat that insulated the dog against cold would serve him against heat. Nor was it the fact of their being becalmed: Sooner or later, the breeze would pick up, and one way or another, they'd be able to ride it in.

No, what concerned Jorgensen was that haze. If you shielded your eyes and looked up at the sun—for that was the way to tell, early on—you could see that the haze was actually a cloud, made up of thinner and thicker layers. And the cloud appeared to be moving, though slowly, to be sure; in the calm, nothing moved fast. But the appearance of movement was bad. It meant the cloud was nearby, close overhead. And if it was overhead, it was all around them. Which meant it wasn't really a cloud at all. It was a closely related weather phenomenon, but one that went by another name altogether.

Fog.

In fall, dry, cooler air hovering above water still warm from summer produced condensation. Now, in spring, Jorgensen knew he was witnessing the opposite effect: moist, warmer air drawing up water still cold from winter. While the phenomena were the mirror image of each other, the results were the same.

One moment you were sailing under clear skies, into a fresh breeze. The next you were dead in the water, watching helplessly as first the horizon blurred, then nearby boats vanished, the sun disappeared from view, until you found yourself the center of a clearing around you, a perfect circle maybe fifty feet across, beyond which you could see absolutely nothing.

A hole in the fog.

This was the situation Jorgensen knew he was heading for in short order. And still he didn't panic, felt no need for alarm. With the sail now catching no breeze at all, he lowered it, letting its wooden hoops pile up at the base, and tying it loosely to the boom. Then, rummaging through one of the catboat's storage compartments, he found the pieces to his radar reflector. It consisted of four aluminum semicircles, which he interlocked to produce a three-dimensional object, not very different from one of those decorative snowflakes you see in department stores at Christmas time. He snapped a halyard onto its ring and ran it up the mast, where—no matter what direction it was approached from—it would present a target sufficient to translate into a visible image on another vessel's radar screen.

To a small wooden boat like Jorgensen's—powerless to move or maneuver, reduced to the status of a bobbing piece of cork, and all but invisible to other craft—the most dangerous thing about fog was being run into. Pilots of powerboats, from the smallest outboard dinghies to giant supertankers the size of mountains, continue moving ahead in fog, albeit more slowly. Unable to see Jorgensen in the fog, or hear him over the noise of their own engines, they'd literally be on top of him before they could do anything about it. The radar reflector was therefore the catboat's first and only line of defense, its one chance of being seen. To Jorgensen's way of thinking, that was a quality that made it nothing but a blessing.

Jake knew the drill, and with the boat sitting still he was permitted to jump over the side and into the water, so long as he stayed close by. Jorgensen tossed him a stick (it was actually an old sail batten), and the dog's retriever instincts took over from there. They'd repeated the game twice, and Jorgensen was about to throw the stick a third time, when he thought he heard something.

Now *thinking you're hearing something* is about as precise as it gets in fog. Fog distorts sound, either by muffling it, varying its pitch and intensity, or causing it to echo dramatically. But by far the most unsettling thing about fog is its ability to play the ventriloquist: A thick fog can take a sound that's dead ahead of you and bounce it off some unseen wall of mist behind you, so that you'd swear what you're hearing is astern of you.

Pulling Jake back into the boat, Jorgensen moved to the

bow, where he grasped the rail with both hands and cocked his head, trying not to be fooled, trying to identify both the nature of the sound and its origin. It was an engine, of that he was quite certain, but where it was coming from, he had no way of telling. It had to be either a boat or a plane. *Let it be a plane,* he thought. But a plane would come and go, he knew, and this didn't seem to be going. He moved to the stern, cocked his head and listened again, trying to get coordinates by triangulation. But the fog was too thick, the distortion too great. And still the sound kept coming.

"Speak!" he told Jake, and the dog barked once, twice, a third time. "Speak!" Jorgensen repeated, and Jake complied. There was a fog bell somewhere in one of the storage compartments, but no time to run it up the mast. Besides, the bark of a dog was just as good—better, in fact—because it couldn't be mistaken for a buoy.

He quieted Jake, to better hear the engine, but he needn't have. It was louder than ever, and no matter where it was, it was now dangerously close.

"Speak!" he shouted a third time, knowing it was more important for them to be heard than to hear. And Jake did his best, but it wasn't good enough: By now the noise of the engine was drowning out the dog's barks. It was so close he ought to be able to place it. It seemed to be off to their—

And suddenly it was right there, to starboard, a big cabin cruiser bearing down on them, heading directly for their beam. Jorgensen waved frantically, but it kept coming. It was twenty feet away, fifteen, its sharply pointed bow now looming overhead. There was a man at the wheel, with a pair of binoculars hanging from his neck, and a—

"JUMP!" Jorgensen yelled, but as he himself leapt clear from the stern, he had no way of knowing if Jake had heard him or responded. He hit the water hard, face first, and went under, the sudden cold of it forcing him to hold his breath. He thought he heard an explosion, decided his eardrums had blown. He felt himself tumbling, had no idea which way up was, tried exhaling to see the direction the bubbles would rise, saw only greens and blues and whites, all churning and colliding and mixing together, as though in some giant blender. Then blackness.

Nothing but blackness.

TWENTY-FOUR

Jessica Woodruff sat at her desk on the forty-ninth floor, reading the article for the fourth time.

AUGUST JORGENSEN, FORMER JUDGE, FEARED LOST IN SAILING MISHAP

———

CHARLESTON, S. C., April 3 - August Lars Jorgensen, a highly-regarded former federal judge who sat on the United States Court of Appeals for the Fourth Circuit, was missing and presumed dead today after his 17-foot wooden sailboat was struck by a larger vessel in dense fog off the coast of South Carolina.

Judge Jorgensen, 82, was known was an experienced sailor, and had made the barrier islands his home since his retirement in 1990. He was known as a lifelong opponent of the death penalty, who stated at the time he stepped down from the bench that he could no longer abide the increased number of executions being carried out by the various states, or the fact that poverty, race and retardation often determined who lived and who died.

Only last month, it was reported that Judge Jorgensen had been lured out of seclusion to argue an appeal before the United States Supreme Court, on behalf of a prisoner afflicted with autism. The case, *Davies v. Virginia,* raises the issue of whether executing an individual who cannot make the connection between his crime and the death sentence imposed for it, constitutes a violation of the Eighth Amendment's prohibition against cruel and unusual punishment.

In Judge Jorgensen's absence, the case for the prisoner, Wesley Boyd Davies (whom legal scholars give little chance of success), is expected to be argued by Jessica Woodruff of New York. Ms. Woodruff is a former prosecutor who currently serves as a director and occasional anchorwoman for the Trial TV network.

No charges were filed against the operator of the powerboat, Ekud Redneisch. According to a Coast Guard spokesman, Redneisch, a Lithuanian national who is visiting family in Charleston and had chartered the boat out of Hilton Head Island, never saw the sailboat because of severely limited visibility. "It's a tragedy," said Major Harper Griswold, "but the old guy should never have been out there in those conditions. He was a sitting duck."

Judge Jorgensen leaves no known family. His wife, Marjorie Redding, died in 1992. Plans for a memorial service honoring Judge Jorgensen have not been disclosed at this time.

Jesus, she thought. She hoped it had been an accident; it *had* to have been an accident. All she'd told the Duke was to go pay the judge a visit, make sure he was under control. But *this* . . .

Her eyes scanned the article for a fifth time. A director and occasional anchorwoman? How about *senior* director and *prime-time anchorwoman,* if you don't mind? God, how she hated print journalists. But, she was forced to admit, she did like the bit about legal scholars giving the appeal little chance of success. That was good; it lowered expectations. When she'd been back in the D.A.'s office, trying cases for Bob Morgenthau, she'd hated it whenever they gave her a strong case to try. "I want long-shots," she used to tell her bureau chief, "cases that no one expects me to win." And Jim Burke would always give her some lame answer, like, "We try not to indict those cases, Jessica." Which was why she was out of there, the day after her four-year commitment was up.

She hadn't heard from the Duke yet, but everyone else had checked in. Brandon Davidson had reached her at home, likening Jorgensen's death to a *deus ex machina,* some modern-day god suddenly reaching down and plucking the troublemaker out of their hair. Ray Gilbert had heard the news down in New Orleans. He'd promptly canceled his trip, and was instead flying up to New York, to help prepare Jessica for the argument. Someone from the Virginia Attorney General's Office had left a message, offering to consent to a postponement if Jessica felt she needed one. She'd phoned back immediately to say thanks, but no thanks. She wanted to do this, and do it quickly, before her presence in the case blew it up into something they couldn't control.

She swung around in her swivel chair so that she faced the window. Standing up, she leaned forward and peered out over the building tops at the city beneath her. She had to squint a bit, in order to block out the afternoon sun. On the fiftieth floor, she'd noticed some time ago, the offices had special glass, designed to filter out the heat and glare.

TWENTY-FIVE

Hiroshi Matsumoto stood at the port rail of his fishing trawler, squinting into the distance. After several hours of limping through fog so thick it had eventually brought him to a complete standstill, he and his crew were finally moving again. Which was a good thing, because to Matsumoto, time meant fish, and fish meant money.

In the fishing industry, Matsumoto's boat, the *Katie II,* was known as a long-liner, taking its name from the mile-long line it dragged up and down the outer banks. All along the line were hooks, baited at this time of year to attract the spring run of swordfish heading north for colder waters. The line was so heavy, even when empty, that it had to be fed out and hauled in by giant power winches. It took a crew of twelve, often working eighteen-hour shifts, to bait the hooks, man the winches, boat the catch, and ice it down. It was grueling, back-breaking work, almost as dangerous to the men as it was to the fish. But there was big money to be made in long-line fishing, with a full catch often bringing upwards of two hundred thousand dollars. Even after the owners had taken their share and expenses had been deducted, a deckhand could pocket ten thousand dollars for two weeks of work, if he was lucky enough to survive it.

Matsumoto and his crew had been at sea for eleven days now. Still, they were coming in early, with their ice chests only three-quarters full, something they hated to do. But Felippe

Garcia, the cook, was sick, running a fever and complaining of pain in the lower-right side of his abdomen. Appendicitis was suspected, and it was felt that Garcia needed urgent medical attention. Even more to the point, there was no one else on board who could cook a decent meal.

When you're doing backbreaking work eighteen hours a day, food tends to take on something of an added importance.

Matsumoto had radioed the Coast Guard, to see if they could send a helicopter to lift Garcia off. But they told him it would be impossible: The entire coast, from Savannah on up to Myrtle Beach, was fogged in so thickly they couldn't get off the ground, much less attempt a rescue. Matsumoto tried raising other boats in the area, but the few that responded were either too far away to help, or having their own difficulties with the fog. Out of options, he'd made the decision to pull the line and head for shore.

The *Katie II* was equipped with state-of-the-art radar, a G.P.S. navigational system, and a highly calibrated electronic compass. Even when Matsumoto couldn't see the tip of his own bow, his control panel told him where he was, what direction he was heading, and what—if anything—lay in front of him. As he inched eastward, his five-knot speed no more than a jogger's pace, his eyes darted from one instrument to the next. At the moment, he was watching a big vessel south-southeast of him. From the size of the image she made on the radar screen, she had to be a tanker, a freighter, or a cruise ship. She was moving north, but was going fast enough that she would cross safely in front of the *Katie II*'s path. There was another, smaller image in front of them, suggesting a boat in the thirty- to forty-five-foot range, heading east at what seemed to Matsumoto to be an unsafe speed, considering the conditions. But since it was on pretty much the same course as they were, it posed no problem.

What had caught Matsumoto's attention was an even smaller blip, showing up so small that it could be a buoy, or something floating in the water. The only thing was, according to his charts, there wasn't supposed to be a buoy there. And anything floating would have to be good-sized or metal in order to show up on the screen at all.

Just in case it was a small boat, Matsumoto tried raising it on his radio, identifying it by its position, but he got no response. That left him two choices: He could give it a wide berth, in order to avoid hitting it, whatever it was; or he could head toward it, to investigate.

Men who earn their keep on the ocean are, by all accounts, a breed apart. Not all of them are misfits, unable to adapt to shore life and hard-drinking when forced to abide it; but those credentials seem to apply to a good number of them. They work unimaginably hard, under conditions most humans wouldn't, couldn't put up with for an hour. Yet they go back to sea, over and over again. And each day out, they quite literally place themselves at the mercy of Nature, and in the hands of Providence. It is little wonder, then, that they form bonds that stretch from boat to boat, season to season, year to year, generation to generation—bonds seldom understood by nonseafarers, save perhaps those whose lot it is to share foxholes, police cruisers, or fire trucks. The rule is that when one of them gets into trouble, the rest respond, no questions asked.

Hiroshi Matsumoto turned the wheel slightly to port, straightening it as soon as the tiny blip on his screen lined up dead ahead of them.

In the seconds after August Jorgensen had leaped clear of his boat to avoid the impact of the oncoming cabin cruiser, he'd come about as close to dying as a living thing can, without quite getting there. As he hit the water and went under, only some combination of icy temperature and pure reflex had prevented him from gulping in huge quantities of sea water. Disoriented and unable to fight his way to the surface, he'd blacked out and—with little body fat and no life jacket to provide buoyancy—had already begun slipping toward the bottom. With nearly three hundred feet of ocean beneath him, it would have been a long slip, indeed.

But Jorgensen's number must not have been up that day. Some force—unseen, unfelt, and entirely unbeckoned by him—took hold of him, somehow arrested his descent, and brought him to the surface. Nor did it loosen its grip on him there, at least not until the old man had coughed and sputtered and flailed and gasped, and finally discovered how to breathe again. Only then did the force open its mouth—a long, streamlined contraption, insulated with cold- and water-repellent materials and controlled by powerful jaw muscles—the end product of thousands of years devoted to breeding the perfect amphibious retrieving machine.

"Good boy," Jorgensen told Jake, though he had no idea just how good he'd actually been. Jorgensen looked around now, trying to assess the situation. Jake paddled nearby; except for him, there was nothing in sight. The water was flat, so they were in no danger of being swamped by waves. And ocean water has enough salt in it to allow a body (whether human or canine) to stay afloat with a minimum of effort. Their immediate problem, he knew, was the cold. He guessed the water temperature had to be 60 degrees, 65 at most. Maybe that didn't sound cold, but since the exterior of the human body was somewhere in the neighborhood of 93 degrees, it wouldn't take long for them to begin losing heat. From there, hypothermia would become a problem, leading to fatigue, disorientation, and loss of will. He figured they had an hour or two, maybe three if they were lucky.

"Good boy," he said again. His thought was to calm Jake down, to keep him from panicking. But the truth was, the dog seemed to be having a pretty good time, swimming around in circles, far less bothered by the cold than Jorgensen himself was, and far less apt to panic.

Just as they had been in the boat, they were in a hole in the fog, a small clearing bordered by a circle of opaque white. Somewhere beyond that border, Jorgensen knew, was their boat—or what remained of it. The catboat was wood; if it had been splintered, there had to be debris, flotsam they could hold onto, maybe even pull themselves up on, and get at least partially out of the water.

On the other hand, there was the possibility the boat had been swamped, completely filled with water, without breaking up. He didn't know whether she'd continue to float under those circumstances. She had a leaded keel, after all, and some metal fittings. But even then, in salt water, he doubted she'd go under.

The problem was, he had absolutely no idea which direction she lay off to. There were as many possibilities as there were degrees on a compass. So unless she turned out to be just out of sight, their chances of finding her would soon climb to one in 360. Talk about sucker odds! Furthermore, if they started swimming, they'd be losing energy, and body warmth, at an accelerated rate.

Jorgensen slowed his arm movements, using his legs to tread water and keep afloat. Without the splashing, it was quieter. He cocked his head, listening for engine sounds. The boat that had hit them—or maybe veered away at the last instant—should be looking for them, crisscrossing the area, knowing they had to be there. But there was no sound to be heard, not through the fog and over the sounds of their own breathing.

The hardest thing was doing nothing. Once, years ago, Jorgensen had been walking in the woods with Marge, and they'd come within a foot of a good-sized rattlesnake. Jorgensen's impulse had been to jump back, but Marge had put a hand on his forearm, holding him still. Next he'd looked around for a rock or a branch, but again she'd stopped him. And afterward, once the rattler had retreated, she'd told him that sometimes the best advice you could give a person in a crisis was, "Don't just *do* something; stand there!"

But how were you supposed to stand there when *there* was the middle of the ocean? Or might just as well have been. That was the question Jorgensen was pondering when suddenly, out of nowhere, Jake barked.

Jorgensen's first thought was that a fish might have gotten the dog's attention. His second thought was more specific, and far more ominous.

Sharks.

They were certainly out far enough, and he knew from first-hand experience that the water was cold enough. And although sharks were said not to care much for the taste of human flesh (they tended to swim off after the first bite or two), who could say what they thought of dog meat?

Jake barked again, and now it was clear that he was barking *at* something, something Jorgensen couldn't see, but had to be off to their right.

"What is it?" he asked, as though the dog were fully capable of answering. Jake responded by looking at Jorgensen, then back to whatever it was he was reacting to, and barked a third time.

Well, Jorgensen decided, there had to be worse ways to die than at the mercy of a Great White, though none came to mind at the moment. Whatever it was, they were going to find out, one way or another. "Go get it, boy!" he said. And as though suddenly released from a leash, Jake stopped circling and began paddling purposefully in one of those 360 directions, Jorgensen following closely in his wake.

They continued for five minutes like that, maybe ten, and it occurred to Jorgensen that his dog may have been hallucinating. But then, just when he'd been ready to call a halt to their efforts, there, right at the edge of the fog bank, something came into view. All he could see at first was that it was long and thin and slightly tapered, and rising out of the water at a low angle. Its body looked brownish, but its head was round and shiny and irregular, suggesting hollow eyes and a jagged mouth. A giant sea snake? He'd heard tell of such things, but had always thought of them as up there with UFOs and the Loch Ness Monster.

"Easy, boy," he whispered to Jake, but there was no stopping the retriever's instincts now. Whatever terrible sea serpent lurked ahead of them, whatever strange denizen of the deep lay salivating for its next meal, they were about to do battle with it.

Hiroshi Matsumoto was having difficulty homing in on the blip on his radar screen. The thing was, it kept appearing and disappearing, making it hard for him to keep track of. To Matsumoto, that suggested it was something riding so low in the water that each wave or swell obscured it from the radar's eye. But there *were* no waves, and no swells to speak of, at least not where Matsumoto was.

He figured he was maybe a quarter of a mile from it, and as far as he could tell, it wasn't moving. That meant he could continue at his present speed until he was almost on top of it, then throttle back to avoid running into it, or over it, or whatever. Craig Lanahan, the first mate, had joined Matsumoto at the controls, and they were taking bets on what it was.

"A buoy of some sort," guessed Lanahan, "even if it's not marked on the charts."

"Probably some kind of flotsam," suggested Matsumoto. "Like the tip of a cargo container, with a hundred Chinese stowaways trapped inside."

The Duke reached Jessica at home that night, as she was looking over her wardrobe, trying to figure out what might be most appropriate for a Supreme Court appearance.

"Didja hear what happened?" he asked.

"Hear? It made *The New York Times*. Was that you?"

"Naaahhh," he said. "That was some commie mowed him down. Still, it woiks out for us, don't it?"

"I guess so," said Jennifer. "How about the other guy?"

"Safe and sound," said the Duke, "safe and sound."

"Good," she said. "Make sure he stays that way, okay?"

"You got it, Babe."

She hung up, not knowing what to think. As hard as it was to believe that Jorgensen's death had been an accident, she was eager to accept the notion. People died every day in accidents, didn't they? They built a bridge or put up a skyscraper, somebody always died in the process. They made one of those big-budget movies, somebody was bound to die, falling off a horse or trying to pull off some stupid stunt. It happened all the time. Even the insurance companies accepted it, chalked it up to the price of doing business.

Besides which, he'd been an old man. How long had he had to live, under the best of circumstances? Five years? Ten, tops. Still, she found herself feeling bad. The truth was, she'd rather liked the old geezer. Sure, he could be a royal pain in the ass at times. But that didn't mean he deserved to get run over by a boat. She was glad it hadn't been the Duke's doing; she didn't need to be part of something like that.

She took a deep breath, tried hard to get past it, to put it out of her mind. She wondered if a pants suit might be a bit too informal.

It was only as they drew close to the sea serpent, Jake paddling in the lead and Jorgensen struggling to keep up, that the true nature of the beast revealed itself. It was the catboat's mast, snapped clean but still tied fast to the hull, which now lay just beneath the waterline. And the creature's head—the shiny, circular thing at the tip, that from a distance had seemed to have hollow eyes and a jagged mouth—turned out to be the aluminum radar reflector, which Jorgensen had hoisted in an effort to save them, but which instead had made them the perfect target.

The exertion of the swim had warmed Jorgensen, but he knew the sensation was only an illusion: As soon as his heart rate returned to normal, he'd feel the loss of heat. He needed to get more of his body up out of the cold water and into the warmer air. At the same time, he needed to provide Jake with some added buoyancy, before paddling became too tiring for the dog. The problem was that as soon as Jorgensen leaned against the mast, it started going under, and he was afraid his added weight might be enough to cause the whole boat to sink. He needed to somehow free the mast from the hull, from the leaded keel that was dragging it down. But the only knife he had was on the boat—or more likely, by this time, on the bottom of the ocean. Without it, his only chance was to untie the halyards that still connected the mast to the hull.

Scissoring his legs around the mast to grasp it, he set to work at the tip. His fingers were by this time numb, his hands badly cramped, and his whole body had begun to shiver involuntarily—the early onset, he knew, of hypothermia.

There were three halyards connected to the mast tip, a heavy one that lifted the sail, a lighter one that raised the peak, and a third that served as a spare. The heavy one came free rather easily, simply by Jorgensen's drawing it through the pulley. Luckily—if that could be considered the appropriate word—the cleat that held the bitter end had broken loose from the base of the mast. But the remaining two lines were still fastened at the base, and it took Jorgensen three trips underwater just to loosen and untie the first of them. On his third attempt he inadvertently took in a mouthful of water, and he spent the next few minutes coughing and choking. But he knew he had to get back to work: Jake seemed to be paddling with ever-increasing effort, and his eyes had begun to take on a frightened, slightly wild look.

Jorgensen threaded the second halyard through its pulley and freed it, and went back under to begin untying the third. By this time he could barely get his fingers to work, so cold and fatigued were they. At one point, he tried using his mouth, but his teeth were chattering too much to be of use. Finally, on the sixth trip down, he managed to loosen the last coil. Suddenly, the base of the mast came free from the hull, lifting Jorgensen with it as it rose to the surface. At the same time, the hull dropped away

beneath him, and slid out of sight. As it did, it released the cover
to one of the storage compartments, a flat piece of wood the
size of a small tabletop. It knifed its way upward, striking Jorgensen painfully in the back of his right leg.

On the surface now, Jorgensen managed to pull his body up
and onto the thickest part of the mast, which—now that it was
free of the hull—was buoyant enough to support his weight.
He knew he had to somehow get Jake up there with him.

"C'mere, boy!" he called, and Jake obediently paddled to
him, with whatever strength he had left. Grabbing the dog by
his neck, Jorgensen hauled him up, only to have him get tan-
gled with the one halyard that remained attached to the far end
of the mast. Holding onto Jake's collar with one cramped
hand, Jorgensen used his other to snap the line like a whip, in
an attempt to free it. Whatever he did worked, and the bitter
end snaked away from him and traveled the length of the mast,
slipping through its pulley at the tip. He watched as it began to
sink, realizing too late that as it went down, it took with it the
creature's head.

The radar reflector.

The blip had disappeared altogether.

Hiroshi Matsumoto had grown accustomed to its vanishing
for a few seconds at a time and then reappearing. Now it was
simply gone. He throttled back his engine, slowing to almost
idling speed.

"What are you doing?" Craig Lanahan asked.

"If I'm right," said Matsumoto, "and it is a container, it
could be just underwater now, not high enough to present a
target for our radar. We could be on top of the damned thing
before we ever see it."

"At *this* speed?"

"At any speed. Fucker'd be like an invisible iceberg, just
waiting to rip us apart."

"So what are you going to do?"

Matsumoto thought a minute. The blip still hadn't reappeared. For all he knew, it could have been a whale or a big fish or a sea turtle that had heard them approaching and sounded. Even though they weren't metal, things like that showed up on the screen from time to time, if they were dense enough. Or the blip might have been nothing more than an electronic glitch of some sort. *Artifacts,* the radar manufacturers called them.

Matsumoto had a very sick man on board, a load of fish that wasn't getting any fresher in the heat, and a crew anxious to make shore. Whatever had been making the blip on his radar screen was gone now. There was no disabled boat in the area, no one needing assistance. Matsumoto spun the wheel to the right and eased the throttle forward, determined to give a wide berth to anything that might still be lying in wait, just beneath the surface.

Lying on the mast with one arm wrapped underneath it and the other steadying Jake as he bobbed alongside him on the storage compartment cover, August Jorgensen thought he detected the sound of an engine, but he couldn't be sure. The fog did that to you. He knew that without a radar reflector, they were completely invisible, knew that he should try waving or shouting or getting Jake to bark. But he was simply too exhausted to do anything. All he could do was lie there, and hold on to the mast and his dog.

After a while, he could no longer make out the sound, if indeed it had been a sound in the first place. All he could hear now was Jake's breathing and his own, and the faint lapping of the water around them. Every muscle in his body ached, every cut and bruise stung. His eyes burned from salt and fatigue, and even though he knew he couldn't risk falling asleep, he allowed them the luxury of closing, just to rest them for a minute or two.

He was young again, twelve or thirteen maybe, skiing down a mountain slope. It was fresh powder, dry and ungroomed, and he felt almost weightless in it. At each turn, he'd plant a pole and pump his knees like twin pistons, causing him to unweight. His entire body would rise up out of the snow, allowing him to turn his skis without resistance and change direction in midair. He was all alone on the slope, skiing faster and better than he ever had, faster than he could have dreamed, faster than he imagined anyone had ever skied before. All he could hear was the sound of his own breathing. At each turn, his skis created huge plumes of snow, leaving clouds of powder that hung in the air and drifted, a visible, white fog all around him . . .

TWENTY-SIX

O yay! Oyay! Oyay! All those having business before the Supreme Court of the United States of America, draw nigh, give your attention, and you shall be heard. God save this honorable Court and these United States. The Chief Justice, and the eight associate justices of the Court, presiding. Be seated please."

There was a rustle as spectators resumed their seats, and a hush fell over the room. "Good morning," said Chief Justice Rehnquist, and a muffled "Good morning" rose in return from the audience.

"Case Number Oh-one-three-three-seven," intoned the clerk, "Wesley Boyd Davies versus the Commonwealth of Virginia. For the petitioner, Jessica Leigh Woodruff. For the Commonwealth, J. Taylor Bradford."

In spite of her years of experience appearing before judges, juries and cameras, Jessica felt the sudden rush of adrenaline. *Relax,* she told herself, *you can do this; it's nothing but an interview.* She rose from the front row, reserved for the litigants, smoothed her skirt, and began making her way to the lectern. She'd decided against the pantsuit; Brandon Davidson had told her to go out and buy something special for the occasion, that Trial TV would pick up the tab. She hadn't found anything at Bloomingdale's, but a navy ensemble at Saks, on sale at $695, had struck her as both flattering and appropriate. The top had a V-neck, and she'd spent twenty minutes in front of her mirror this morning, trying to decide how many buttons to leave open at the top. Two seemed a trifle much, but one made her look positively priggish. In the end, she'd gone for the two, over a lacy black bra, just in case anything showed. They knew she was a TV personality, after all; they could hardly expect her to show up looking like some kind of nun.

She took a moment to arrange her notes on the lectern, as well as a pad and pen to take notes, if the need arose. Then she looked up and smiled—one part nervousness, one part practiced professionalism.

"Ms. Woodruff," said the Chief Justice, "as much as we mourn the death of our friend and colleague Justice Jorgensen, it is our pleasure to welcome you. You may proceed."

"Thank you," said Jessica. "If it please the Court—"

Always start out by saying, "If it please the Court," Ray Gilbert had told her. No one knew exactly why, or who had first uttered the words. But it had become tradition, and tradition was what the Court was all about.

"—this case brings before you the issue of whether a state may lawfully take the life of a man who, though admittedly not retarded and found competent to stand trial, possesses absolutely no understanding of why he is to die."

"Well," said Justice Scalia, "there's never been an actual finding to that effect. Am I correct?"

"That's right," Jessica agreed, surprised to have been interrupted after only a single sentence. "The district court conducted an evidentiary hearing, but never made findings of facts. Instead, the judge ruled that it made no difference, one way or the—"

"And the Fourth Circuit affirmed," said Justice O'Connor.

"Yes."

"So," said Justice Scalia, "you're coming here today to tell us we should expand the Eighth Amendment to read that any time a state satisfies the myriad of other due process requirements and decides to execute a murderer who has been found both sane and competent, the prosecution must first bear the additional burden of demonstrating that the murderer understands precisely why the state is executing him. And that if it can't meet that burden, the execution *a fortiori* becomes cruel and unusual."

"No, and no," said Jessica. "I don't believe we're asking you to expand the Eighth Amendment at all. And I haven't for a moment suggested that the state should bear the burden of proof on the issue, just that there should be findings—"

"Wouldn't you be the first to argue," suggested Justice Ginsberg, "that it would be an impermissible burden to place upon a *defendant?*"

"I'm not certain I—"

"Let me see if I understand this," said Justice Kennedy. "We're concerned here only with the penalty phase of the trial, right?"

Jessica nodded, then quickly remembered to say, "Yes, your honor." She felt like she was being ganged up on. Ray Gilbert had told her to expect questions and interruptions, but this was ridiculous.

"The petitioner concededly was sane at the time of the crime," continued Justice Kennedy. "He was found competent then, and continues to be competent now. There's no indication from the record that he didn't receive a fair trial below—in both the guilt phase and the penalty phase—and there's no claim of actual innocence, is there?"

"OH, YES, THERE IS!"

Although her mouth was open, the voice was decidedly not Jessica Woodruff's. It was far deeper, identifiably male, considerably older, and appeared to be coming not from the lectern at all, but from the rear of the courtroom, where one of the huge doors had just swung open. Every head in the room turned in that direction now, every eye focused on the apparition that had just entered their presence.

And *apparition* is about as close as one could come to

describing him. He was tall and thin, thin to the point of being gaunt. White hair fell across a sunburned and blistered forehead. He was unshaven, with white whiskers sprouting from hollow cheeks. He wore a suit, but it was a faded, purplish thing that looked as though it had been slept in, perhaps for a week or more. And as he ambled forward, he limped badly, as though trying to favor first one leg, then the other.

"Who is this man?" shouted the clerk, as uniformed U.S. marshals quickly moved in and restrained him. "And what's he doing here?"

"My name is Jorgensen," said the man, "August Jorgensen. And I'm here to argue my case."

A murmur rose from the spectator section.

"We thought you were dead," said Justice Rehnquist.

Jorgensen managed a crooked smile. "Me, too," he said, "at least for a while there."

The marshals still had a firm hold of the man, and were now looking to the chief justice for guidance. "Let him go," said Justice Rehnquist.

"Thank you," said Jorgensen, staggering slightly and wondering if maybe he hadn't been better off in their grip.

"Well," said Justice Rehnquist, never much a master of the *ad lib*.

Justice Scalia, however, was more than up to the task. "Just when it was beginning to look as though there was nothing to say on behalf of Mr. Davies," he noted, "all of a sudden he has not one, but two lawyers to say it."

"Well," said Justice Rehnquist again, clearing his throat. "We welcome you back to the living, Justice Jorgensen. But Mr. Justice Scalia does have a point. Which of you will speak on behalf of the petitioner?"

Jessica Woodruff did her best, but never got past, "I will." She was simply no match for August Jorgensen. Not this day.

"I speak for the petitioner!" he boomed, making his way to the lectern and all but pushing Jessica away from it. "And I have an answer for Justice Kennedy's question. Wesley Boyd Davies is *absolutely* innocent, and I can prove it."

As far as anyone could remember, it was only the second time in over two hundred years that the Supreme Court had been compelled to take a recess in the middle of an oral argument (the first having been occasioned by a particularly nervous young attorney from Ohio who, when unexpectedly interrupted by a probing question from the bench, had suffered the misfortune of vomiting upon his shoes).

The justices retired (single-file, and in order of seniority) to the conference room, along with the litigants—a bewildered assistant attorney general from Virginia, and both Jessica Woodruff and August Jorgensen. The conference room, Jorgensen noted, was nothing like the one at Trial TV: It was a large room with a long table and a bunch of chairs around it, but it was uncarpeted and seemed built for business, not for show. The walls were lined with casebooks, and at the far end of the room was a second table, far smaller than the first, with a computer, several telephones, a television set, and some other electronic gadgetry.

The chief justice took his seat at the head of the table, the other justices assumed what seemed to Jorgensen to be assigned seats, and the lawyers took what was left. "Now," said Justice Rehnquist, turning to Jorgensen, "as irregular as all of this is, some of my colleagues here are leaning toward indulging you, and entertaining your, uh, *offer of proof.*"

Jorgensen couldn't be certain, but he thought he detected a wink from Justice Souter. "Thank you," he said. Then, pointing toward the table with the gadgets, he said, "By any chance, is one of those things an RV?"

"I'm afraid not," said Justice Scalia. "Have you misplaced your Winnebago or something?"

"What is you want?" asked Justice Souter.

"One of those things," said Jorgensen, "that can play movies on a television set."

"That we have," said Souter. "You're sworn to absolute secrecy, but we have a hidden camera that videotapes the oral arguments. You know, just in case any of us should fall asleep and end up missing something." This time, he seemed to wink in Justice Thomas's direction. Or maybe he just had some sort of facial tic, Jorgensen decided. It was hard to tell.

Jessica, meanwhile, was busy trying to imagine what the secret videotapes might be worth, say the ones of arguments in high-profile cases, like *Brown v. Board of Education*, *Sirica v. Nixon*, or *Bush v. Gore*. "Do you save them?" she asked.

Nobody answered her.

"What is it we can we do for you?" Justice Rehnquist asked Jorgensen.

"I need my assistant."

"Your assistant. And where might he be? Or she?"

"He," said Jorgensen, "is presently being detained at the security desk. They weren't certain he was old enough to be permitted in the chamber. Apparently they had no such reservations about me."

Justice Rehnquist rose, walked over to the gadget table, picked up one of the telephones, and punched a couple of buttons. Glancing over at Jorgensen, he asked, "What's his name?"

"Who?"

"Your assistant."

"Crawford."

"Cindy?" asked Justice Thomas.

"Crawford," Jorgensen repeated. These guys were almost as deaf as he was.

Justice Rehnquist asked the person on the other end of the phone to escort Mr. Crawford to the conference room. Then he rejoined the rest of them at the table. "So," he said, evidently feeling responsible for the silence that had settled over the room, "what happened out there on the water?"

"Nothing much," said Jorgensen. "Fog came up, boat rammed us, spent a day or two hanging onto the mast, Coast Guard picked us up, hospital patched us up and pumped some fluids into us, dropped off my dog, rounded up my assistant, caught a plane, took a cab. The usual."

They were all staring at him as though he was certifiably insane, when there was a loud knock on the door.

"Come in," said Justice Rehnquist.

The door opened, a uniformed deputy marshal poked his head in, and said, "I have a Mr. Crawford with me."

"Yes," said the Chief Justice. "Show him in, please."

The marshal stepped aside, and Zachary Crawford, all ten years, four feet, and sixty pounds of him, strolled in. He was wearing sneakers, shorts and a Carolina Panthers T-shirt, and—as something of an afterthought—one of Jorgensen's old neckties. The tie had been so long that Jorgensen had been forced to tuck the ends into the waistband of Zachary's shorts; what he hadn't counted on was their protruding from the bottom of the shorts.

Clutched in both of Zachary's hands was a box, maybe 4" × 8" × 1". Printed on the outside of it was the name SONY.

Jessica Woodruff, who until that moment had seemed distracted to the point of total preoccupation, suddenly sat up in her chair, the color draining from her face. "You stole that," she said.

"Did not," said Zachary.

"Not you, *you!*"

"*Mea culpa,*" said Jorgensen. "But, I'm afraid, not nearly so *culpa* as you."

"You can't use that," Jessica told the judges. "It was taken illegally; he just admitted it. It has to be suppressed."

"Correct me if I'm wrong," said Justice Breyer. "Although we continue to honor your colleague by referring to him as *Judge* Jorgensen, it's my understanding that he's in the private sector now, and no longer affiliated with the government. No illegal governmental action, no basis to suppress

anything. Pretty fundamental stuff, no? Are we all in agreement?"

Eight heads nodded. Nine, if one were to include Zachary's.

Jessica felt as though the room were shrinking, the walls literally closing in on her. She opened her mouth to speak, but
no sound would come out. For perhaps the first time in her
life, she was at a total loss for words.

But Justice Souter wasn't. A sometimes sports fan, he seized
the opportunity and said, "Let's go to the videotape."

TWENTY-SEVEN

When, later that same day, the media assembled in the court's press room, they were treated to their own viewing of Kurt Meisner's videotaped statement, complete with a superimposed date that wouldn't occur for another eighteen months. As soon as the viewing, and the briefing that followed it, were over, reporters rushed to the phone banks (the few who didn't have cellular phones of their own) or to camera crews waiting in front of the courthouse steps. In the multitude of televised specials, radio announcements, and front-page stories that followed, the revelations made public by August Jorgensen were most often likened to the dropping of a bombshell.

It turned out to be an overstatement of sorts.

In the weeks and months that followed, a more apt metaphor suggested itself. It was as though, suggested one commentator, Jorgensen had simply tossed a pebble onto the surface of a pond, and the resulting ripples had gradually spread out in all directions, until they left no shore untouched.

Jessica Woodruff was summarily fired by Trial TV. Two months later she was indicted by the United States Attorney for the Southern District of New York, on obstruction of justice charges. In order to avoid the possibility of a prison sentence, Jessica voluntarily surrendered her law license and cooperated against her superiors at Trial TV, including Brandon Davidson. Although Davidson himself was never formally charged (given Jessica's own culpability and her relationship with Davidson, she was considered an unreliable witness who might not be believed by a jury), he was eventually forced to resign both his presidency of the network and his seat on its board of directors. Today, Jessica works as a paralegal in Cleveland, while Davidson is employed by a title insurance company in Sacramento. Their romance, once it had been exposed to the light of day, wilted and died.

Reynaldo Gilbert also lost his job, and was permanently barred from practicing law in the state of Louisiana. Timothy Harkin fared somewhat better. Having received no response to the note he'd left on the door of Judge Jorgensen's lighthouse, Harkin had soon after left the defense team. But for failing to blow the whistle on those who remained, he was suspended from practice for three years.

Michael Schneider, whose known aliases included "Mickey," "Willie," and "the Duke," was indicted for the attempted murder of August Jorgensen, as well as the kidnapping of Kurt Meisner. Schneider's insistence that he had no connection with the Lithuanian national who'd run down Jorgensen's boat was seriously undercut by the discovery that the letters in the name "Ekud Redneisch," when rearranged, spelled out "Duke Schneider." Ultimately, Schneider pleaded guilty to attempted assault, and is currently serving ten years in a maximum-security federal prison in scenic Otisville, New York.

Kurt Meisner surfaced when he was expelled from an old age home in Miami Beach—not because he was fourteen years shy of the minimum age for admission, or because his German ancestry was discovered by the Jewish director. While those minor flaws might have been overlooked, Meisner's inability to continue paying for his stay (once Trial TV stopped footing the bill) could not be. He currently lives in a men's shelter in downtown Miami.

Zachary Crawford returned to school from spring break. When his turn came to describe what he'd done over vacation, Zachary entertained his classmates with a story about how he flew to Washington, D.C., met all the justices of the United States Supreme Court, and played a movie for them. Zachary's teacher, who for some time had been concerned about the boy's propensity to confuse fact and fantasy, sent him straightaway to the principal. But the truth was eventually discovered, and the teacher was required to write, "I shall never again doubt Zachary's word," twenty times on the blackboard.

August Lars Jorgensen returned to his lighthouse, on his barrier island. He bought himself a new boat—if, that is, something thirty-two years old can be considered new. On breezy days, he can often be seen sailing in and around the coves; he no longer ventures out into the open ocean quite so far as once he did. And these days, Jake's weight is no longer needed to trim the boat; in semi-retirement the old Lab is permitted to ride full-time as a spotter at the bow, his ears pinned back by the wind, his open mouth drinking in the salt spray. His former job as first mate has been handed down to another who, it turns out, loves the rhythmic rise and fall of the boat, the steady beating of wind against canvas, the constant thrumming of taut lines, and the comforting slap of water against wood as much as anyone. Not only that, but he speaks these days, albeit a little. He never did get around to saying "alive" out loud. Before he'd had the chance, he'd succeeded instead in uttering a different, albeit related, word.

Free.

Currently, they're working on *home.*

Boyd has resumed his drawing, and Jorgensen recently introduced him to watercolors. Boyd took to them instantly. As of late, his work seems to be undergoing a transformation of sorts, from pure photographic re-creation to something more akin to realistic impressionism. The quality, though, remains every bit as high as before.

That said, the ripples ended at the shore, as ripples have a tendency to do. Capital punishment supporters did indeed seize upon Boyd Davies' exoneration as proof that the system works to protect the innocent. The Commonwealth of Virginia continues to put people to death, as do most of her sister states.

August Jorgensen feels bad about that, and there are even times when he's forced to acknowledge that Jessica Woodruff and her friends had a rather noble idea. But then he looks across the boat (or the room, or the front seat of the truck) and sees the human being they were ready to sacrifice, and he knows that the end could never have justified the means.

Late fall has come to the barrier island. Leaves are turning, and hordes of raucous migrating birds are stopping over on their long journey southward. On cool mornings, dry breezes drift over an ocean still warmed by the Gulf Stream, magically drawing water up into air and turning it to visible cloud. August Jorgensen is teaching Boyd Davies the word to say when that happens.

Interestingly enough, although no one seems to understand quite why, ample anecdotal evidence tells us that individuals who suffer from autism tend to draw great comfort from the sensation of having physical pressure exerted against their bodies. This phenomenon may explain why, when the offshore breezes die down and the ocean swells flatten out, the worry lines vanish from Boyd Davies' face, and are replaced by an expression of quiet calm. Jorgensen says nothing then, but he senses it is at such times that the young man has somehow managed to escape the bonds of his affliction and found peace, nestled safely in the enveloping arms of the fog.

Jorgensen worries some about what will happen after he dies, but he also believes that, for the most part, things have a way of working out. Besides which, Edna Coombs has taken quite a liking to Boyd, and Edna's only seventy-three. And if it should turn out that Edna's not around, someone else will be. Barrier islands are strange places, their inhabitants few and far apart. But there must be something about being constantly battered and humbled by the sea that teaches folks to look after one another. Perhaps it's simply a matter of knowing that if they don't, there's likely to be no one else around who's going to.

So Boyd will be okay.

Or as August Lars Jorgensen might put it, "Not to worry."

ACKNOWLEDGMENTS

I'm deeply indebted once again to my editor, Ruth Cavin, her assistant, Dan Kotler, and the rest of the good folks at St. Martin's Press who continue to put up with me. I thank that agent of mine in Connecticut, Bob Diforio, and John Ufland out in faraway L.A.

My wife Sandy never seems to tire of serving as my first reader, harshest critic, and most ardent supporter. I'm grateful to her on all three counts. I thank my children Wendy, Ron, and Tracy; my sister Tillie, her husband, David; and my sister-in-law Carol for their early comments and input. I thank Sterling and Terrence Kenny for helping out with stuff about South Carolina.

Finally, to the extent that I've taken the liberty of borrowing actual people and using their names and personas in my story, I beg their forgiveness and trust that anything that has sounded even remotely negative about any of them will be ascribed not to any character flaws they may or may not possess, but purely to my own imagination.